CAPTAIN *Z Z Y Z X*

Michael Petracca

~/~

CAPTAIN

ZZYZX

JOSHUA ODELL EDITIONS   CAPRA PRESS 1992

Published by Joshua Odell Editions/Capra Press
Box 2158 Santa Barbara, CA 93120

Grateful acknowledgement is made to Sheridan Blau, Christopher Buckley, Cynthia Cornett, Carl Herzig, Richard Helgerson, John M. Landsberg, Francess Lin Lantz, Otto "Baba" Laula, Annie Lorimer, Frank McConnell, Joshua Odell, Katie O'Neill, Irene Papoulis, Betsy Uhrig, Stephen Williamson, Noel Young, Muriel Zimmerman, and Craig Spirka, who suffered a two-inch gash on his face in pursuit of an old photo of Zzyzx Road that never got used. Special thanks to John D. Spalding, who labored tirelessly over this manuscript and kept his sarcastic comments to a minimum.

AUTHOR'S NOTE:
This is a work of fiction. I made it all up. I am somewhat more highly evolved than Harmon Nails, as anyone who knows me will confirm. I was never addicted to Altione, nor does any such drug exist in the "real" world. I wish I could play guitar as well as Harmon claims to, but I can't. The names of people in this novel, characters, settings, and occurrences are likewise the product of my imagination or are used fictitiously. Any resemblance to actual living or dead human beings, parakeets, small fish, incidents, parades, bars or other localities is entirely coincidental. Really.
— M.P.

LIBRARY OF CONGRESS CATALOGING–IN–PUBLICATION DATA
Petracca, Michael, 1947–
Captain Zzyzx/ Michael Petracca. —1st ed.
p. cm.
ISBN 1-877741-06-X
1. Title
PS3566.E779C36 1992
813' .54—dc20

Book designed by Albert Chiang
Cover designed by George Delmerico
Cover photo color–tinted by Deja Hsu
Printed in the United States of America

FIRST EDITION
10 9 8 7 6 5 4 3 2 1

CONTENTS

~♪~

For Janny, for all the big ideas

PART ONE

GIN

PEOPLE
EVERYWHERE JUST
GOT TO BE FREE

⌁

righteous rebirth: By pursuing a tiny fragment of dead turtle, I've saved myself from a life of isolation and depravity.

My last book told how I received a Ph.D. despite my dissertation, which was filled with improbable narrative and bogus footnotes.[1] True to form, I missed the commencement ceremony because there were waves that day: five foot, low tide, south swell, warm afternoon offshore breezes at the first jetty, and Ma couldn't complain since I was a doctor at last. Soon thereafter I took a teaching job at the state university in Fiesta City. In my new position everyone expected absurdly lofty accomplishments of me. Critical articles, desks arranged in the classroom just so, self-sacrificing committee involvement, attendance at literature conferences nationwide, tenure and eventual full professorship, more articles: ridiculous — no, impossible — for a young man of extensive recreations like myself.

So I became a drug addict instead.

---

[1] *Doctor Syntax*. Capra Press, 1991. $9.95 (bargain).

1

It started innocently enough. I had volunteered to deliver a talk on John Stuart Mill to the assembled Anguish Department, and I had to prepare for it. OK, maybe not volunteered, exactly. The truth is that every member on the Committee on Victorian Belles Lettres (or CVBL), to which I was assigned upon my arrival at the U, had to select a Victorian writer and bung together an hour-long talk on this person's contribution to literary tradition. Naturally I waited until the last moment, hoping they'd run out of eminent Victorians and that I could escape the ordeal.

No such luck. There on the sign-up sheet, unsullied by attendant signature, was the pallid J.S. Mill. He was no doubt feeling slighted at being unchosen, as I used to feel when they were choosing up sides for flag football and, being littlest, I always got picked near last. Nevertheless, though I could empathize with J.S.' humiliation, I still wouldn't have picked him. I would have picked Bobby Browning, on whom I can wax eloquent *ad aspergum*. All I remembered about Mill from my master's orals was that his initials look like a shorthand way of expressing "Jism," and that the cove was big on freedom . . . but then who isn't? And how much can you say about it, anyway? People everywhere just got to be free.

Being thus uninformed, it followed that I had to do some extensive research on John Stuart Mill. Even relatively interesting study makes my 'roids flare, and this effort uncovered a colorless, self-effacing, windy literato who had produced an abysmally abstract body of work—prose which compares to good writing as a kid's sandhill, eroded by waves, compares to a Rodin. Worst of all, I had to *read* the essays, since not even the most determined Cliff Notes scribe had managed to get through J.S.' tortured wordiness sufficiently to produce crib sheets on it.

As the days grew closer to the presentation, I went from my usual fitful sleep to a condition of total REM deprivation. At the same time my immune system was compromised to such a degree that I developed a urinary condition which caused me unutterable agony every time I had to run a bit of water. In such a state of mind and physical deterioration I betook me at length to the office of one Dr. Moss, a physician whom I picked out of the yellow pages. Any doctor whose ad read, "E. *Thomas Moss, M.D., Dipl. Ac., C.A. O.M.D. Holistic Medicine — Shiatzu — Disorders of Sleep and Concentration — Diet & Nutrition — Genetic Reassessment — Guemecke Patterning — Satisfactory Elimination — Whole Life Support — Problem Solving — Nontoxic / Noninvasive Alternative Procedures,"* sounded worth visiting, I figured, if only for the comic relief.

The squat, bearded E. Tom tried a vast number of naturopathic remedies — hypnosis, acupuncture, biofeedback, acupressure, kundalini breath of fire, megavitamins and glandular extracts — before resorting to the tranks, as all doctors sooner or later will. "Ah me, Harmon," he sighed, slumping in his chair, his puffy red face tortured with remorse at not having been able to find a holistic cure for my puzzling constellation of symptoms.

I tried to reassure him. "It's not your fault, really, Dr. Moss. In fact, I think the extract of bull testicle did give me a few hours of relief when I first took it, but then the symptoms returned, along with an urge to charge down cobblestone streets and gore fleeing townsfolk."

"Ah me," he sighed.

"So what now, shall we channel a dead urologist?" I made sort of a joke.

"Ha, ha, *hc.*" Dr. Moss had a clipped laugh, like the valve of a commode interrupting the influx of water when the bowl is filled. "As you know, I believe in exploring every alternative to traditional medicine, but we may have arrived at an impasse. Have you ever tried Altione?"

"No. Drugs don't agree with me. Taking an aspirin makes me swoon," I hyperbolized.

"Most likely that is a manifestation of anxiety. In small doses, drugs of the chlorodiazepone group are known to be of great benefit in reducing anxiety, bringing on sleep and even relaxing muscle spasms, which I believe are at the root of your urological complaints."

"Isn't there any other way besides drugs?" I imagined myself ten minutes after ingesting the pill, tumbling helplessly into dream-fugue, my eyes fixed wide at a pandaemon of searing flashes in colors all inflamed, my limbs caught up in a whorl of torsions whose abrupt violence would cause me to slam my car into an innocent bicyclist pedaling home from school . . . which is exactly how my friend Richard Bindhover died several months later. A van hit him.

"I'm afraid I've run out of ideas, Harmon." He called me Harmon. "And I believe that Altione might really help."

There remaining but a few pale droplets in the crystal decanter of my lifeforce, the prospect of any symptomatic reversal looked damn good. I therefore overrode my qualms. "All right, Dr. Moss," I said querulously, "if you're sure it's OK."

"One is never sure of anything in medicine." I could envisage the slavering spectre of a malpractice suit prompting the good doctor to cover his fiscal bum. "As long as you don't exceed the recommended dosage and discontinue treatment once your symptoms are cleared up, I think you'll have no trouble."

Read the warning on the label, you who dare enter here.

THE
ANCIENT BUZZING
SEWERPIPE

~

Ah me, Harmon! After I overcame my initial timorousness, Altione gave me two of the most unperplexed, delightful months of my life. My John Stuart Mill presentation was a success. I dilated resonantly on Old Jism's theories concerning poetics and history. So moving was my speech that Dr. Vindt, eminent and doddering Chair of the CVBL, approached me afterwards, grasped my wrist in a crusty palp and spurted, "Congratulations, Dr. Nails, on a presentation well done. Too many of our young scholars overlook the numerous contributions which Mill has made to the Victorian *zeitgeist*."

I beamed broadly, flush with success, loose and confident from the effect of the bad little A's plugging their bad little benzene rings into my neural receptors. "I agree," I said, winding up the bird. "Too many young people today have no conviction, and those who do possess a measure of conviction fail to convert it to conduct."

"Precisely!" he exclaimed, o'erbrimming with raptures. "You must come have dinner with myself and Mrs. Vindt, to fur. her explore the importance of the individual in a world threatened by overpopulation, declining morality and drugs."

"Righty-ho!" I said.

Unfortunately, the first warm glow of Altione chilled out in a hurry. This should have come as no surprise to a poker player like myself, one accustomed to the vagaries of fortune. A motto among frequenters of California Lowball parlors is "No Rush Lasts" — meaning if you hit a winning streak, ride it and then cash in your checks, because your luck will inevitably turn like Boethius' wheel — and the same thing applies to downers. After less than a month the drug ceased to have its miraculous effect as my body built up tolerance. I woke up from restless sleep barely able to haul myself from bed, my wits frayed, limbs enfeebled, my humor petted and homicidal, eyes barely able to tolerate even a shadow of the sun's magnitude without sharp pain.

I soon discovered that if I washed the prescribed dose down with a swallow or two of red wine, I could once again steal quietly through the wreathed doorway of paradise. Sadly, paradise again lasted barely a month, and to maintain the drug-induced state I had to keep increasing the dosages and ingesting an arcane combination of sedatives, hypnotics, depressants and painkillers. By this point I was not only using pills for sleep and study but for all activities requiring the transient glories of narcosis: teaching, watching TV, walking to the corner market, walking home from the corner market, digesting, breathing.

I was also amassing a library of Alexandrine dimensions on the subject of central nervous system depressants. I kept a *Physician's Desk Reference* by my bed, along with a bottle of Asti Spumante, and I could name each lovely colored tablet in the publication, its brand name, its generic name, its effects and side effects and contraindications. I had an extensive listing of physicians across the city, hell's own roll call of venal shrinks and neurologists and orthopedists who were only too willing to write a scrip for the price of an office visit. The waiting rooms of these pestilential vermin looked like the morning lineup at the methadone clinic, with every serious doper in Fiesta City chain-smoking, legs crossed and twitching nervously, waiting for that blessed scrap of paper that would score another thirty Ludes, TID, use only as directed.

In the deepest Mariana Trench of my poly-substance addiction, I possessed three sweat socks full of controlled substances I had obtained legally from disreputable doctors, or scored at no small expense from musician connections, or pilfered by rummaging through my friends' medicine cabinets every time I'd drop over for a visit. I secreted the pills within my underwear drawer, reasoning that a suspicious narc would look there last, he being too manly to paw through another man's panties. My hosiery contained Tylenol with Codeine, APC with Codeine, Darvon, Seconal, Sequestral, Tuinal, Amytal, Dilaudid, Talwin, Elixir Terpin Hydrate, Chloral Hydrate, Placidyl, Benadryl, Dalmane, Restoril, Halcion, Meprobamate, Quaalude, Chlor-Trimeton, and all of these I ingested by the handful, pledging all the mortals of the world with the full draught of an hour's quietude, until the shit wore off again.

Strangely, no one knew I was an addict, least of all myself. After all, I was holding down a job of responsibility and prestige, I was watching TV, walking to the corner market, walking home from the corner market, digesting, walking, breathing. Being a naïf in matters pharmaceutical, I thought all junkies had tracks on their arms. Even my mother didn't suspect, although she did comment on certain aberrations in my behavior, like the day I visited her in L.A. and cheated at Scrabble, giggling stupidly while I stole all the best tiles and went out time after time. Upon discovering my subterfuge, my mother became enraged as a swatted mud dauber and accused me in her Georgia patois, *"Hahhmin, ah belieieve you've been smokin' merriwhauauna."* I assured her with a high degree of truth that I most certainly had not altered my consciousness by inhaling toxic fumes—omitting, of course, three crucial details, *viz.* the two Dilaudid caps and the beaker of Cinzano dark vermouth with which I had washed them down an hour earlier.

It wasn't until I nodded out at the wheel and mushed my

car into a parked truck that a pale, clear ray of self-awareness penetrated the darkling wood of denial. Having come close to killing myself — the thick steel bed of the truck missed my right cheekbone by *this* much — I realized I had to stop taking drugs or next time I wouldn't be so lucky. And so I did stop — many times, in fact, sometimes for as long as two days.

I will skip lightly over the paramilitary rigors of Casa Seca, the clinic I eventually had to enter. Such worthy enterprises have already been portrayed in best-sellers by the wives of many of our nation's leaders. Suffice it to say that dire wolves howled outside the window of my cell while demiurges tromboned from gothic spires; that I became an adept in the subtle art of pacing small circles in carpet; that I cleaned up and haven't slipped since. Perhaps more important than my unseating the dark forces of appetite, though, was the healing that took place in the chronically irritated tissue of my own little family dyad.

As rough jewels will occasionally surface through the earth's stubborn mantle, so my mother was unexpectedly supportive during my detox. Although Fay must have been deathly concerned for the well-being of her onlyborn, she somehow managed to inceive a Zenlike detachment, the wordless message of which penetrated the wounded galaxy of my withdrawal as: "I did my best with you, Harmon. I love you and now I release you. Do what you have to do."

Having been perpetually chastised by Ma for offenses as petty as scuffing the kitchen linoleum with the heels of my cycle boots, I had expected a world of ragging. Instead I got kindly offerings: a tin of her homemade *mandel broit*, a battery-operated calculator, my father's old portable chess set — the one with the pegs and holes and the missing pawn replaced with a segment of toothpick dipped in white shoe polish. I was touched by these gentle, nostalgic expressions of concern, and I even wept on the maternal shoulder a couple of times, washing clean the dark blot caused by thirty-some years of mutual annoyance and mistrust. Thus, while it would be capricious for me to recommend that you try to improve your lot with your own mother by becoming a dope fiend, this most trying of circumstances worked some wonderful alchemy on our affiliation.

Timely, too. My mother died the following year.

She fell victim to cancer. In the hospital, before she lapsed into coma, my mother said, "Harmon, I'm as proud of you as a mother can be of a son," and smiled weakly despite her great pain. I had always thought of my mother as an anxious woman, one in whom heelmarks or cobwebs inspired bouts of melancholia, but now she was heroically finishing off a life that had seemed to me singularly unheroic. I was reminded of Samson in that monostrophy — by Keats I think it was — who became heroic late in life, just like my mother. Or perhaps she had been heroic all along, and I was just too much of a punk to see it.

"My parents brought me up," she continued, "to believe study was the highest achievement. They meant well, but what's right for some people is not right for everybody. I've been thinking about it, and I realize the university might not be the place for you. It's been all downhill for you since you spelled 'brazier' wrong."

A bit of subtle humor on her deathbed, a joke: My mother, of all people, was cracking wise as she surrendered her ticket to the nevermind! She was alluding to my fifth-grade spelling bee where, after several rounds of elimination, the competition had been whittled down to the two best spellers in the class, me and Lisa Vandegrift. I had been the odds-on favorite, since Lisa was notoriously weak with Anglo-Saxon morphologues, but she got an easy hanging pitch, a Latinate floater: *preponderating*. Mine was also easy, but the dude pronounced it wrong, I swear. My word was *brazier*, but the principal, a masonic blot on the playground named Mr. Raleigh, was reading in his usual soupy tone of voice and said *brassiere*. I swear. I went through my routine — "Brassiere, b-r-a-s-s-i-e-r-e, brassiere" — and the school auditorium erupted in gales of laughter like waves without dimension breaking on illimitable shores.

I had all but erased this incident from memory, and my mother's dredging it up now, on the brink of her own extinction, was as inspired a bit of wackiness as you're apt to find in any intensive care ward. She was right, too. After the brassiere incident, academics never did hold the same charm for me that they had when I was the graphemic golden boy of Canyon Elementary. I felt unsurpassed admiration for my mother, not only for having plumbed my aversion to academic life, but also for attempting to mitigate the gravity of the blackwatch, for my sake. How she arrived at the means to face her end with such selflessness and acceptance and humor I have no clue, but maybe I'll find out when the time comes.

My mother concluded, "You're smart, Harmon, and not because you have a Ph.D. or you're a professor. You don't have to prove anything. You're young, you've got time; find something that brings you great joy, and go after it with your heart." She reached out, the full extension of her arm restricted by her weakness and by the transparent tubing in her arm. I leaned over and kissed her forehead, searching her eyes for a final look of understanding and connection, but she was already somewhere else, her eyes focused on a vanishing point beyond the farthest coast of darkness. *"Mommity mommity mommity,"* she said in a girlish singsong. Having made peace with her kid, she seemed to be conferring now with her own departed mother, which is right in such circumstances, I suppose. While I've gotten pretty close to the ancient buzzing sewerpipe myself a few times, I've never gotten *that* close, so I'm only guessing. I sat by my mother for many hours, but I was asleep when she breathed her last.

Thus it was, with Fay's blessing, that I tendered my resignation from the Anguish Department last year. No one mourned, save Dr. Vindt, who was still surcharged with affection for me because of my Mill report. I promised I'd stay in touch with him, and I have. I had dinner recently with him and his wife, and they turn out to be real nice folks. Dr. Vindt has a pool table in his basement and, surprisingly, shoots a decent game of seven-ball. We play once or twice a week now. You'd like the Vindts, especially if you've come up dry in the parental department as I have.

Meanwhile, since my mother bequeathed me enough money to buy this modest estate in the hills, with enough left over to keep the monthly dividend check coming in, I can pursue my joy and enchantment, which consists of nothing harmful to the general weal, I hope: penning my modest lyrics, shredding tubes at the local beachbreak, volunteering to bundle newspapers eight hours a week at the local recycling center, practicing my poker, pool and backgammon, and playing lead guitar for two local bands — my only paying gig at thirty bucks a night.

And so it was, after replacing the ailing lead guitarist in a local band called The Corporeals — they were playing weekends at Cafe Bla — that I made a late-night, post-gig visit to my girlfriend, Gin Stabler, on whose property I had lost my rare tortoiseshell flatpick: a sequence of events that propelled me inexorably, as though hoist upon the shaft of a meticulously feathered and carefully aimed Fate, to visit Gin's pond the next day in search of my pick.

There at the water's side, I encountered the mysterious red-headed stranger.

LIVE FISH ON LAND

～

In hazy, late morning sunlight I searched fruitlessly for my flatpick[2] on Gin's blighted property, ending up in her garden: a square, chickenwire-enclosed area where the sun reached only early in the morning, and where some stunted horsetails were growing. These plants, with their hollow, grayish stalks and their scaly leaves like waxed paper peeled halfway down a fudgeroll, weren't doing so well in the cool, swampy garden. But then it was remarkable that the horsetails were doing any living at all. A lot of former things in Gin's garden weren't.

Gin enjoyed having life around but also had what she termed a Darwinian attitude toward plants and animals. If they could survive her benign neglect, then they deserved to live. If not, then, "Fuck 'em and let 'em die." She said she treated her ferns no worse than God treats us, and I couldn't argue. Some other plant would come along and take the place of one that died, and so on, and a hundred million years of prehistory are hard to refute.

---

[2] It's *real* tortoiseshell, almost impossible to come by anymore, since tortoises are protected species and rightly so. That's why I was going to so much trouble to find it.

That was Gin's worldview: cold, practical, coarsely home-spun horse-sense.

Gin had dug a pond for raising fish in her backyard, because she was doing doctoral research on fish ears. Something about the way fish metabolize certain inert compounds, and if you cut thin cross-sections of their tympanies and look at them under a microscope, then you can see differences that mean something to scientists in the galvanic world of fish ear research. Gin had tried to explain it to me several times, but I always got C's in bio. Besides, I was much more interested in watching her clumsy carp swim around, bored sexually and utterly graceless but shimmering with the iridescence of offshore seaspray and watermelon ice, annealed siding and wet quarry clay. I liked the way the fish would crawl out of the pond with feisty determination to fetch a pellet of food from the plate Gin placed at the water's edge.

Until I fell in love with Gin Stabler, I never knew fish could hold their breath—which for fish means holding their water, I suppose. But there they were: Live Fish on Land. If her fish didn't learn to hold their water and crawl, then they'd go the way of Gin's horsetail population—that is, they'd starve, eventually die, and fuck 'em.

I gave up on finding my lost flatpick in the fern garden and walked around the shed, and there was the strange woman. She slept by the pond with one arm in the water. Pale light played on the white stillness of her arm and fat, grainfed carp swam by it, no more concerned than if the woman's arm were a peculiar doughy waterplant. Her hair, the same bright copper-blush red of Gin's fat goldfish, was pulled to the side so that it resembled a rusty waterspout, whose sweep accented the sharp outlines of cheekbone and jaw, over which stretched luminous pale flesh mottled lightly with a wash of freckles.

I stared at the woman. She seemed insubstantial, like a cloud of particles given unity, or at least visibility, by a sheet of light, and in this she was certainly different from Gin, who resembled nothing so closely as a potato in her nurturing density and in the width and contour of her hips. The stranger,

who was more like one of those smooth-skinned, pearly cocktail onions than a potato, lolled on her back and opened her
eyes.

With pupils the pale blue-gray of the ocean churned by
windswell, she fixed me with a regard that suggested both sexual welcome and fig rinds decomposing. The tension between
the two made me uncomfortable, as though H. Nails, Ph.D.,
one of the most dangerous lead guitar players in town, had
gone to a job wearing thrift store breechers several sizes too
large and of a houndstooth pattern not absurd enough to be
cute.

In our met glance it seemed we shared a moment of sympathy, not merely personal and realtime but reaching across the
scattered tribes and back through millennia . . . and at this
Awakening I felt hungry. Actually, I felt empty, felt a deep
sense of loss for something I wanted to create but couldn't: a
sound, maybe, that would break the silence of this untilled
dirt, or some really ancient collective muzak that would fill the
spaces between the celestial marbles and stars, but all I heard
was the sound of doggish yapping, likely my own, and the
betrayal in it.

So I called it hungry because I couldn't deal with it.

~✌︎~

Gin had been at a job interview in South Carolina while I was goggling at the semi-immersed woman. Now, two days later, Gin had returned and was laying out dinner. She had baked and placed on the rich planking a chicken pie with a steaming, yeasty crust and a filling of seasonal greens picked from her garden: dandelion leaves, thistlehearts, calliope root.

Gin's chicken pies in no way resembled the chicken pies of my youth, tame assemblages sanitarily prepared by an apron-girded Ma and laid out on gaily glazed Aviva!® dinnerware. When Gin cooks a chicken pie she gets real dirt under her nails from uprooting her organically grown produce, real warm blood on her big hands from slaughtering the animal herself. The only time I observed this primal carnage, Gin went out back to her coop and selected one of the oldest layers, Corinne, a scrawny hen with candy-apple feathers. Gin talked sweet nonsense to Corinne while she wrung her neck. Then she chopped off Corinne's head, plucked her, picked the pinfeather stumps carefully from her skin and threw her, rather unceremoniously I thought, in an aluminum pot of boiling water. When Corinne's flesh came apart, Gin tossed out the bones, took strips of the long, tough muscle, chopped it into inch-long chunks and cooked the flesh into the pie, along with the vegetation which she picked from her garden.

I was revolted by this spectacle in the same way that watching a bowel resection on public access TV revolts me. It's not so much the gore itself but the absolute verification in blood-crimson and gristle-white that you and I are nothing more than meat . . . and cheap cuts at that. Gin has no difficulty with this idea since it's consistent with her fuck 'em determinism, but it sullies my romantic conviction that beauty and imaginative pleasure make us immensely richer than our mere physical components — a view which is shared by John Stuart Mill, by the way.

Shaken to the very footings after watching the summary execution of Corinne, I vowed never again to eat flesh. But as often happens, the shock soon wore off and my craving for the robust satisfactions of animal protein forced a rethink. This time I vowed never to observe the untimely dispatch of a family pet. Therefore, while Gin was preparing tonight's pie by killing another of her chickens — a saintly little hen named Mary who had a sweet disposition, as I recall — I was sitting out by the Air Shower, practicing scales on Gin's old gutstrung Aïda acoustic guitar.

We ate Mary. After dinner Gin made us some hibiscus tea. I was feeling sort of chirpy, but I couldn't figure why until I remembered the strange redheaded woman, whose milky, vaporous image engendered in me a species of elation I can only describe as tonic. Desiring information about this watery apparition, I raised the subject discreetly as Gin cleared the table and I washed the dishes. "Good dinner," I said.

While Gin was a phantom of delight in certain tuberous ways, her voice was not what one would call euphonic, tending to resemble more closely the fulminations of a territorial gander startled by intruders. "I'm glad," she honked.

"Capital chow."

"Hmn." Gin was the strong, silent type when it came to common pleasantries. Say something once, why fuckin' drag it out? was her motto.

"Topping, a taste-tempting rhapsody," I insisted.

She handed me the last of the dirty dishes.

"I stopped by your place while you were gone," I said, leaping into it.

"Hnn."

"I thought I dropped my tortoiseshell flatpick when I was leaving last time."

"D'jew find it?"

"Nope."

"Hmn," she said, stoically accepting my loss, "bummer."

"Yes," I said, nudging the conversation toward the sticking point while I dumped soapy water out of a glass salad bowl, "and there was someone else there."

"There's always people there."

This was true. Gin lived on a rented tract of land in the Santa Ynez foothills, a weedy, scrubby few acres which she shared with several other squatters. I don't know who gave it the name originally, but everyone who lived there fondly called the place Squalor Holler, or just The Farm. Gin's house, which sat on the northern corner of The Farm in the shade of two large sycamore trees, had been a milking shed back in the days when cows were allowed within city limits, so not much energy had been spent on equipping the structure with comforts that most people take for granted, like walls. There were cracks between the rough-hewn whitewashed boards that were alleged to be walls, and when the wind blew I had to huddle by Gin's small Franklin woodstove to stay warm, in spite of the gritty tarpaper she put up on the outside of the structure as weatherproofing. There were fist-sized gaps between roof and siding, and these allowed easy ingress to several platoons of small brown wood rats, mice, spiders and roaches who were welcomed by the unswept scraps of food and the relative warmth of the shed. Gin appreciated that life could bloom in so many charming forms, and she took a measure of pride in the fact that she wasn't deranged by the intrusion of these critters into her home.

Another rustic, Katie O'Gordon, lived with her two young

daughters at the other end of Squalor Holler, next to a stream
fed by mountain runoff. Katie was a hardy, stoical, single
mom and a fine Irish musician who played fiddle and pen-
nywhistle in several local acoustic stringbands, and when the
stream wasn't thundering with boulders being carried down-
stream by the runoff from a winter storm, you could catch thin
wisps of ethnic music on the breeze and imagine yourself
camped luxuriously on heather or mired in a peat bog.

On the bluff above Gin were the many mobile homes of
Tom Morris, an eccentric photographer who collected things.
He would lade one trailer with knickknacks and gewgaws, art
treasures and antiques, mannequin legs and doorknobs,
Christmas ornaments, Santa Fe pottery, dogfood cans, rusted
marine fittings, refrigerator motors and scrap redwood, until
there was no longer room for him and his army cot. Then he
would haul another trailer into The Farm and start the process
all over again. He was on his fourth trailer, this one already
about a third full of neat stuff. Tom had a girlfriend, a librari-
an, who stayed with him in the other army cot when there was
room, and he had two boys by a marriage that dissolved when
his ex realized she could no more stem the influx of junk into
her living quarters than she might stop the ocean tides. Tom's
boys stayed at The Farm every other weekend.

So I had to agree with Gin. It was no surprise that someone
was at The Farm. "I know," I said, and then appended cryptically, "but this was someone who's not usually there."

Gin didn't seem particularly interested in this disclosure
and began wiping the counter with a dishtowel. I continued,
"It was a woman. She was sleeping by your fish pond."

More wiping. I could see I was going to have to do this all
myself. "She had red hair."

"Oh, that must be Ondine," she said in an offhand way.

"Ondine," I said. *Ondine!* The name curvetted about the
palate and gums, gamboled breezily over the tongue, finally
to spread a silken kirtle of melodie among blossoms blown.
"Who's Ondine?" I said, disciplining my flights of lyrical
fancy.

"Someone Katie met. She's a jeweler but plays a little folky guitar. Katie said Ondine could stay in her spare room for a while," said Gin and looked at me piercingly. "Am I way off, or do you want to fuck Ondine?"

Gin sometimes had a, well, *direct* way of approaching delicate issues involving the human heart, rendering them brutish and sordid. She also had keen insight, as evidenced by the above query. Took me aback, as one might well imagine. "Not a bit," I protested, manufacturing and marketing a laugh like tiny waves lapping a gently sloped beach. "I was just surprised to see someone sleeping by your fishpond." I threw up an unsubtle diversion, the best I could muster. "Do you want to shoot some pinochle?" I asked.

Gin and I were in the habit of playing rummy after dinner, not pinochle, but I liked the phrase "shoot some pinochle," which I heard delivered by a character in a play once. The cool gambling term stuck with me, and I like to use it even though I don't know how to play pinochle. Gin and I used to shoot rummy to five hundred points, nickel a point. Being as Gin was a listless player, without the killer instinct when it came to cards—she confined herself to barnyard fowl when it came to bloodletting—she owed me about two hundred bucks in markers.

"Deal," she said.

To hear me drift into reverie at the mention of Ondine's name, you might think me an unprincipled poltroon, since I was with Gin at the time — *with*, as in committed, monogamous, on ice, the door's closed, the light's out, the butter's getting hard. Were you to embrace a fundamentalist view of monogamy, you might even be outraged at my base impulses in the direction of Ondine. In my defense, however, let me say this about that. Our relationship had been cooling. Gin was already casting the roving eye a bit herself, as I found out later on. Furthermore, while I admit to having thought about it from time to time, I never cheated on Gin . . . not once, from the moment I first saw her squatting over a roasted pig.

I met Virginia Stabler during a barbecue at Squalor Holler, at which bucolic event I was playing Irish tunes. This was right after my detox, which left me tender as a Thompson seedless with all its skin off. In this condition I quite understandably took pains to protect myself from the lashings of disequilibrium. The first decision I made toward this end was to swear off playing amplified music, because lead guitar, replete with distortion and cranked to the max as all good blues should be, flashed me right back to the beastly excesses of my doperhood.

In the two years before my detox I was always stoned when
I played—so stoned that I attained the status of local rock legend when I fell off stage at Rimbaud's Basement during an extended rave-up on Freddie King's "Hideaway." I was at the
time obliterated by three different brands of synthetic opiate,
and I was leaning into the double-time solo with my eyes
closed. I just kept leaning, I guess, because reliable accounts
had me doing a reverse triple-gainer, seven-point-two degree
of difficulty, into the dinner seats. With the exception of the
couple onto whose *souvlaki* and red wine I fell, everyone in
the audience cheered and thought it was the coolest thing they
had ever seen. Cooler still was the ensuing: I never missed a
chop. I continued playing while lying on my back on the floor,
my black curly cord stretched out straight, blood staining my
shirtings and my guitar hopelessly out of tune, until some
good folk hauled me backstage. It was less cool, though, when
I had to come up with the eight hundred bucks to rewire the
pickups on my rare mid-fifties Fender Strat, reset the action
and reinforce the cracked peghead. Not to mention the twelve
stitches to reset a Nails chin abraded by the business edge of
a wineglass and debrided by a fruity Bordeaux.

Given a similar history, most people would avoid reliving
such scenes of dissolution. They might even stop playing electric music entirely, as I did. Still, I judge my consequent behavior to be extreme, since I sold a lot of irreplaceable musical
stuff. During my first month of sobriety I rashly unloaded my
Marshall stack, my classic Leslie rotating speaker cabinet
that makes everything you play on the guitar sound just like
Jimmy Smith on the Hammond organ, my original wah-wah
pedal and all the rest of my effects boxes: chorus, phase-
shifter, flanger, signal compressor, noise gate, tube overdrive—all for ridiculously low prices to musicians who didn't
suffer pang one at taking advantage of me. Having sworn off
amplified music, I let it be known around town that I was interested in playing acoustic guitar, and shortly thereafter
Katie O'Gordon recruited me to do some fingerpicking in a
newly-formed stringband called Sheebeg and Sheemore, after

a couple of famous hills in Ireland, I think. We made a sweet
little group of plinkers, soulful in a harmless Celtic way, which
was just what I needed at the time. No edge, no harm, no
foul.

The barbecue at which I met Gin was a celebration of no
particular holiday but an annual gathering of local amateur
old-timey musicians to play tunes — pronounce it *'tyoons'* for
maximum biscuits-and-gravy articulation. Sheebeg and Sheemore, with H. Nails on Martin dreadnought hollowbody,
played two sets until the sun went down, and then the partiers
started jamming. Playing three-chord Appalachian and Irish
tunes requires no particular concentration for a guitarist who's
as comfortable circle-picking thirty-second notes in mixolydi-
an mode as he is brushing his teeth. Therefore, while we were
plinking harmlessly at "Saint Swithen's Lament" and "The
Maid Behind the Berm," I had plenty of time to observe in
amazement the Squalor Holler scene.

Of all the amazing sights of that amazing place, Virginia
Stabler caught and held my eye in flight. She had taken
charge of cooking the buried pig, and I was charmed by the
way she squatted over the wood fire to turn the glowing logs,
by the way she swayed her hips unselfconsciously to the music.
To one whose childhood was too long in L.A. pent, the world
of Squalor Holler was refreshing in its simplicity, enchanting
in the wildness of its unmown grassy barrows and its steaming
compost piles, intriguing in its chaos of dogs, chickens, geese,
stray cats, its tall weeds, boulders, fallen fences, woodpiles,
hayricks. A living refutation of my family's fearsome struggle
against the forces of entropy, Squalor Holler waved a dirt-
encrusted finger at waxed floors and Scotchgarded furniture,
upturned a mocking nose to mouthwashes, deodorants and
pine-scented air fresheners. The Farm hinted at a world that
could get along just fine, thank you, without our therapeutic
interventions. Gin, in her faded paisley parachute skirts and
bare feet, her tangle of coarse hair in armpit and crotch, her
overpowering odors of the sulfur-bog, her vocal timbre *de
foie*, became for me a dark emblem of this trackless vale, and

a summons. I wanted to know Gin, and through her the wisdom and spirit of nature untamed. Call me romantic if you will, a pencil-necked geek if you must, but never forget Set and Setting. Ma had just died, and I was still an emotional husk from my detox.

Besides: What clod alive hasn't pursued some species of myth and looked a damn fool in the process?

LEAVES OF THREE

~

I courted Gin ardently for several months. She was with someone else at the time—*with*, as in committed, monogamous et cetera—and you know I ordinarily wouldn't move on another dude's woman. However, from the stories Gin told me about her boyfriend, Tennessee, this was one excrescent bofo who deserved the gate and a generous ration of deep burrowing splinters to go with it. For example, Tennessee wouldn't make love with Gin without first covering her head with a burlap grain sack so that he could fantasize about other women. This contemptible bagging hints at a serious breakdown of the imaginative faculty, not to mention just plain bad manners. Gin also told me in confidence that the churlish Tennessee used to insult her intelligence and looks, neither of which bears the tiniest shard of disparagement.

Nobody can call Gin a dummy. In fact she's probably better equipped intellectually, in a linear sort of way, than most people. Gin has a doctorate in vertebrate ecology and can reel off phylum, genus, class, kingdom and all the rest just as well as the bookish fellow who invented those classifications. Alton Lister, I think she said his name was. Furthermore, Gin is a lovely woman in face and figure, a fair colleen with wavy dark

hair and dewy inquisitive eyes the color of cornflowers on the
heather or cobalt-leaded glass in a wee kirk. You may hear me
from time to time call her a potato or a malapert, but in reality
I always lavished heartfelt praise on Gin because I admired her
mind, I lusted after her dusky loins, and I appreciated her din-
ners. I make the occasional disparaging remark about her only
because she hurt my feelings.

Ow!

As a kid, Gin had perceived herself as unattractive, because
she was squat and chunky. She was shunned by her classmates
because of her size, and because she engaged in activities that
were considered less than feminine, like playing full-contact
dodgeball, sitting on bullyboys and battering them with her
meaty fists. Sexually Gin flowered late — in her early twenties
— and there, eager to snip the unfolding bloom, was Jimmy
"Tennessee" Jahnker, an Aryan charmer in the soiled coveralls
of his joy and profession: repairing tractors behind the only
feed store in Fiesta City.

Tennessee didn't take to using the burlap sack immediately. His and Gin's conjoinment started out starry, as most do.
The sack came later, when the thrill of the chase was past and
one grows accustomed to the same face, even if it is a reasona-
bly attractive face. You may be dealing with this problem
right now in your own arrangement, maybe even secretly
wishing you could check out someone new. Take it from me:
Your current partner is nicer, safer, plenty good-looking in
subdued lighting, and most of all there. *There,* as in accessi-
ble, available, and presenting. If your sex is on the crouton
side of fresh, work on it is my advice. Pretend you and your
significant other are strangers; wear outlandish disguises and
assign one to pick up the other in an unsavory bar, then bring
the other home and boff him or her in exoteric ways. Experiment with corn flakes and badminton gear. Just be generous.

The only generosity Tennessee ever sent in Gin's direction
was to name her cat for her. From time to time she fed and
sheltered a yellow tom who would sojourn in her shed a few

days and then depart, presumably on an erotic turn of the surrounding neighborhoods. I'm not sure why Tennessee called
the tom Asterix. Certainly part of the reason was that Tennessee didn't know how to pronounce or to spell asterisk (a lot of
people don't, in my experience). Maybe also because the cat's
ears, torn to crusty ribbons in street fights, looked like halved
asterisks. Whatever: By the time I entered the picture and began pursuing Gin in earnest, the cat's name had already undergone several morphological shifts and become Ix.

Sporting among weeds and plumbing the depths of gopher
holes with a dirty yellow paw, Ix followed Gin and me as we
climbed the bluff next to Squalor Holler and watched the sun
go down over Fiesta City. The airport and university were far
in the distance, so far that we could hear neither the jumbo
jetliners rising into the sky, nor the ladder faculty with their
jumbo egos blowing supercharged wind in classrooms and
offices. Gin and I talked until the sky paled, then darkened,
the air cooled, and the mosquitoes began to light on our forearms and to fill our ears with resonances like tinnitic queries
from adenoidal angels. Ix dozed. I expanded at length, and
with a baroque profusion of variations, upon a central theme:
that Gin's conjoinment with Tennessee was keeping her from
being the best that she could be, her own true self, fully actualized and all that. I laid it on in painterly coats, and eventually she had to agree. She said she would dispatch Tennessee
and did so the next day, telephonically and without remorse.

We didn't consummate that evening on the bluff above
Squalor Holler, although I think we both wanted to. I know
I did, but I was less than assertive for a few reasons. Since my
detox I had consummated with nobody but myself. My good
right hand and I, always good friends, had become rather intimate of recent months—I stray from the crumbling path of
delicacy here—and I thought I might be, well, rusty with another person. Besides, there were biting mosquitoes in the air,
biting snakes and bugs on the ground, no blanket, neighbors
possibly with infrared binoculars, no Troika jimmy-hats with
the patented reservoir tip, not to mention my allergies and the

possibility of poison oak nearby. Leaves of three, let them be, is my motto. I never expose my genitalia where they have the remotest possibility of contact with a plant that exudes caustic toxins. No percentage in that.

Instead I fingered dead sycamore leaves nervously, ripping out the brittle, satiny webbing, and the only thing that got erected that night was a hummock of leaf-parts, petioles, sticks and stems.

The next day, Gin took an extended trip to the Phipps Pelagic Institution near Santa Gila, where, as part of her dissertation project, she had to implant transmitter chips in some sealife whose endangered status she was documenting. She was gone three weeks.

On her return she came directly to my house, under the pretext of wanting a warm shower. Although Gin and I hadn't been lovers or even Victorian-style hand-holders, we were already accustomed to seeing each other naked, since everyone at Squalor Holler rinses off from time to time in the Air Shower—that's what everyone calls it—next to Katie O'Gordon's house. The Air Shower is really a green garden hose attached to a wooden contrivance which looks something like a gallows: an inverted, L-shaped wooden apparatus with a clothes hook to hold the hose. This contraption is more than adequate for bathing when the weather is clement, which it is frequently in the Santa Ynez foothills. Fiesta City is close to the ocean and therefore susceptible to wannish, numbing fogs, but go fifteen miles inland and the sky is a cloudless blue, the heat often fierce, and in such temps I will compromise my modesty for a brief, chill dousing with the overhanging rubber hose. Such dousings are less welcome and can be downright pneumoniac on late fall evenings, though, when temperatures drop fast in the hills and a howling north wind funnels down the canyons . . . which was the ostensible reason for Gin's coming to my house that night.

From the moment she walked in the door, it was clear that Gin had designs beyond the mere removal of a week's accumulated grime. Logically, she could have taken a shower in La Jolla, since they do have running water there, I believe. Then, too, there was a certain lunar distraction about her, a sort of radiating agitation or tension, sweet but verging on urgent. This intuition was substantiated by Gin's subtle body language when she began to undress in front of me, chatting about the four-wheel-drive Jeep that kept breaking down in the middle of the beachy dunes near San Clemente or somewhere, while at the same time bending down to remove sweatsocks and swaying her substantial dark breasts this way and that like some kind of fleshly metronome.

Gin was looking damn good and she knew it. Her dark, almost purplish skin and body parts had an aspect of ripe plums, plum skin covering an amplitude of sweet plum-flesh, and her blatant body hair, those tire-black bat grottoes, were a darkly overhung tropical bower of enchanting fragrances. Gesturing at the shower, she honked, "Want to join me?"

Honks sound good sometimes, as when Miles bends the crisis at the end of an inspired balladic passage. They can even sound sexually appealing—I guess that's why geese thrive—and the honk in question stirred me to the compass of my bluejeans. Heartened by the apparent functionality of the Nails nail, I was soon out of trousers and shirtings. Decency forces me to vault stoutly over the subsequent few minutes, but one of my kitchen stools needed recovering afterward.

My budding connection with Gin seemed promising, because we discovered that we had nearly identical tastes and opinions in several key areas. With music our similarity was almost preternatural, considering how diverse our tastes were. Pick a tasty from this sampler of sounds we liked; you can't go wrong: pre-'67 small-combo jazz and bebop, especially Monk and 'Trane; New Orleans rhythm and blues, especially Fess, Nevilles, Meters, Doctor John; anything by the Grateful Dead but especially the Pigpen sides and "Hard to Handle" in particular; Segovia; Ella any year; Mendelssohn's octets; Sex Pistols; Otis Redding; The Zydeco Twisters; The Eroica; all live Marley; and even early Dolly Parton when we were of a mood. We detested contemporary producers' habit of in-studio overproduction, their laying track upon track of machine-generated drums, synthesized strings and horns, vocals with a Velveeta delivery like stones tumbled to an artificial luster in a drum of sand, the record companies' industrial fervor for making a pleasant and easily digestible product out of music, an art form that is at its best imperfect: bumpy, unpredictable, surprising, demanding, challenging, irritating.

Good recordings, Gin and I agreed, contain the funky clams produced in the most elevating of live performances, the odd dynamic wobblings, burps and bruits, the rhythmic halts like a sudden braking by a locomotive at full speed, the unexpected timbre shifts and modulations to farflung keys, the squalls of discordancy and charged quietnesses that sometimes follow. Since most people seem to prefer the eunuch-safeness and minipadded sanitarihood that characterizes modern pop, Gin and I saw ourselves and each other as alienated throwbacks to a time when music could saw your legs off and make your ears bleed, when pingponging meant bounding a plastic ball over a six-inch net, when drumkits came without microchips. Thus we found in our coupling a strong bond of artistic sensibility.

We also shared the basic assumption that—as much as it tries to get itself organized—the universe, like the compulsive gambler who knows better but always ends up back at the table, fights a losing battle against its own impulses toward disorganization, coldness and vacancy. In this the universe resembles, perhaps more than gambler or lover or any other addict, a motel off the interstate, one whose carpets are perpetually stiff with bodily exudations, whose commodes are recurrently stained and stuck with wiry depilations, and whose towels keep getting soiled . . . all despite the manager's daily efforts to keep the place straightened. However, even the tackiest backroad motel has someone in charge, and if Gin and I agreed on anything, we agreed on the issue of the Supreme Being, or the Supreme Lack thereof, without having to speak it. No desk clerk here, let alone a manager. No second chances, no UFOs helping to erect stone monoliths or landing strips among Mayan ruins, no happy reunions in the clouds. My own brand of agnosticism tends toward the eclectic, borrowing heavily from Sartre while drawing upon physics, cosmetology and even some organized religions — the Zen koan, the Passover seder read in Hebrew so you don't have to embarrass yourself by speaking to the King of the Universe directly, and lots of Christmas prizes. Gin's philosophy differed from mine in that it was more scientific and less humane to my way of thinking, yet despite our minor variations on the hypermodern theme, we both rejected as absurd the image of the big stickman calling shots as the spheres collide and ricochet and spin.

Beyond our shared antipathies to easy listening and easier metaphysics, I'd even go so far as to say that time and mutual proximity nurtured in us a sort of blood-kinship. Having lost with my mother's death the last direct line to and from my own childhood, I was ripe to the possibility of surrogation, and along came Virginia Stabler: fond, enfolding, and replete with enough relatives to fill my orphan's heart with that curiously reassuring admixture of support, embracement and aggravation that only family can impart.

Gin's father was a former Marine gunnery sergeant who had gone deaf in Korea as a result of one artillery volley too many and who had, since I'd known him, been on full disability. He communicated with Gin by means of a computer which allowed them to type messages to each other over the phone line and see the words displayed on a small, one-line liquid crystal display on the other end. This was no doubt a boon for

hearing-impaired persons round the world, and certainly the
best kind of use for microchips—much better than building
heat sensors for sidewinder missiles or circuitry for drum
machines—but it also spotlighted the desperate banality of
much human intercourse, like watching trite conversation being displayed on the moving lightstrip above Times square:
H..O..W   A..R..E   Y..O..U   P..O..P..S   F..I..N..E
H..O..N..E..Y   H..A..D   M..Y   H..A..I..R   T..R..I..M
T..O..D..A..Y, and so on.

Jack Stabler had an engaging grin, a nature even more plac-
id and unflappable than Gin's. He hadn't a brutal bone in his
whole frame—this led one to wonder how he ever survived the
Marines, let alone drilled young recruits in the manly art of
savaging other young recruits with sophisticated weaponry—
but he did have a mean sweet-tooth. During our visits to Gin's
parents' house, Jack would disappear into the kitchen after
dinner and return with two half-gallon drums of fudge ripple,
from which he'd fill the bowls of everyone at the table. Jack
derived his own brand of creative joy from this activity, and
he went at it with great flourishes of elbow and scoop.
Touched by his willingness to include me, a newcomer, in this
gay postprandial custom, I'd accept his hospitality each night
of our visit . . . with the result that during the course of
each visit to the Stabler household, I'd put on three or four
pounds and would, on coming home to Fiesta City, have to
double my daily Exercycle regimen to regain my usual athletic
leanness.

Sylvia Stabler presented a more complex case than that of
her husband. Gin's mother came from sturdy New England
stock, wealthy automobile dealers with small brown eyes and
small brown minds to match. These hardy provincials mis-
trusted anyone whose ancestors arrived on the western hemi-
sphere after the eighteenth century and from anywhere other
than Merrie England, and they plainly hated anyone whose
ancestors had the poor judgment to get themselves sold into
slavery in any century. Add to this blacklist anyone who spoke
a foreign language or had a last name that sounded foreign,

anyone who ate continental cuisine or who drove any foreign car but especially one made by the Japanese, who voted Democrat or advocated a social program that smacked of socialism, welfarism or New-Dealism, or who adhered to anything but the most restrictive form of Protestantism, and you get the full palette of their prejudice.

Sylvia had to grow up with these zweibacks for parents, and with their bigotry as a birthright she couldn't help her vocabulary, which was littered like El Segundo beach after a sewage spill with phrases like "played bridge like a Chinaman," "Jewed me out of twenty bucks," "niggertoes" for Brazil nuts, and much more. On the surface Sylvia seemed to be unaware of the hatred that shored up these slurs, but her soul must have sensed it. In her thirties, when Gin was still a child, Sylvia developed a bipolar manic-depressive illness—due, I'm guessing, to the unbearable tension between her parents' profound mistrust which she had internalized and her own basic sweet nature which was apparent to all who knew her. Sounds plausible; but remember, I'm guessing. This much, however, is certain: Medication left her incapable of performing any but the most rudimentary of activities—watching television and eating the same sweet, starchy and fatty foods to which her husband was so partial. Still, she never failed to extend a warm welcome to me when we came to visit, even though she frequently couldn't remember my name. I forgave Sylvia her lapses of memory, since I could empathize with her—in the depths of doperdom I often forgot my name—and because I was hungry for acceptance into the bosom of family.

Jack and Sylvia Stabler spawned a new generation of good eaters. Gin's brother, Lipscomb, four years her junior, was unfortunately named after his grandfather but had none of the patriarch's meanness. A huge man, Lipscomb could crush your hand with one firm clasp if he was of half a mind. Lipscomb often *was* of half a mind, come to think of it, due to his extensive thirst and taste for beer, but he was one of the gentlest men I've ever met, with the same evenness of temperament that characterized Gin and her father. In fact, he took their placidity a step further. Where Gin at least aspired to earning a degree that would allow her to study fish eardrums, and where Jack Stabler had somehow managed to get himself promoted to sergeant in spite of his genial disposition, Lipscomb the Younger had no such lofty plans for his life, preferring to perform what he called "twelve-ounce curls"—bending a seemingly endless series of Miller Hi-Life cans from table to mouth—playing Willie Nelson tunes on an untuned Mexican nylon-string guitar, and eating near-toxic quantities of fudge ripple. Still, in spite of his torpor and complacency, I have to grant Lipscomb this: He pursued his joys without having to be instructed to do so by a dying mother, and he seemed to have achieved a peace of mind usually attained only by Yogis and Lamas.

And while I'm in a mood to hand out concessions like party hats, let me concede an admiration for parents who managed never to plague their firstborn son with unrealistic expectations, pressures or judgments, as my parents did to me in my Wonder Years, with nearly deadly results.

For all their girth and wackiness and lack of professional enterprise, the Stabler family always seemed to me closely bonded, friendly, and—dare I say it?—happy.

THE TINY MICRO-
STOMICHETHIOBRIOUS-
BASHFORDDINI

~/~

Some of the sweetest times I spent with Gin, now that I think back on them, were those associated with families, like holidays. For instance, since purchasing My Own Place with my inheritance, I had never gotten around to putting up a Christmas tree. Passing by tree lots in my car gave me a bruised feeling, reminded me of simpler and more innocent times when I no more thought of mortality, mine or my parents', than I think of deconstruction or semiotics or any other literary theory today—in other words, not at all—and when it took nothing more than a burp gun or an electric train layout to fill my heart with boyish glee.

The first year I was with Gin, she refused to accept my blues as an excuse for passing up such a hallowed institution as the Christmas tree, steeped as it is in the rich foenugreek of family. She came home one afternoon in early December with a Star Pine in a large black plastic pot and plunked the tree cavalierly atop one of my stereo speakers. She gestured toward the tree and honked with ceremony and pride, "Yer not gettin' out of Christmas this year, if I have somethin' to say about it."

Gin had already fetched a couple of white towels that I had

borrowed from the health club and was arranging them about
the plastic pot in such a way as to suggest a deep mountain
snowdrift, or a work action at a commercial linen rental facility. "Where are your balls and shit?" she asked, not extinct to
the ambiguity of her phrasing, which moved me to seize a
handful of the Nails manhood roughly while grunting something Italo-American like, "You want balls, I gotcher balls
. . . " and so on.

We eventually did get the tree decorated, though, and a
handsome job it was. It's amazing what change a few glass
bulbs and painted wooden angels and strings of petrified pop-
corn can wreak, turning the humblest of natural creations into
an artifact of rare majesty. In my garage we found the old
cardboard banana crate which I, all teary-eyed from grief, had
used to pack away the accumulated Nails family Christmas
gear after my mother died. Many fragile bulbs and crystal
frammies had been shattered in transport (in my grief I had
neglected to pack the ornaments in newspaper) but enough
had survived intact to lade the tenacious little pine fully. At
the bottom of the crate I uncovered a singular treasure—a tin
Star of David which used to adorn the top of every Nails family Christmas tree for all the years of my youth.

My mother and father, raised orthodox Jewish and practicing Catholic respectively, both forsook their religious up-
bringings when their families disowned them for marrying
out of their faiths. My parents figured any religion that placed
strict obedience above love was not worthy of their continued
allegiance, and so they created their own, a kind of univer-
salist antifaith. The tin Christmas Star of David was a perfect
emblem for this atheological nonstruct, whose messages to me
as a child were: God is a myth; organized religion is an out-
moded set of pointless regulations; by heredity you're a Jew
because your mother is Jewish; by tradition you're a Catholic
descended from devout Roman Catholic stock; the icons and
rituals of both of these religions are beautiful so long as they
are stripped of all religious meaning; you have unlimited free

choice with regard to what you believe as long as you don't believe any one thing too much.

The Star of David qualified as one of those beautifully meaningless icons. My parents always saved the Star for last, as a kind of ceremony. After we had bent the limbs of that year's tree under the dead weight of real leadfoil tinsel, two packages worth, after we had eradicated a sizeable portion of the ozone layer by unloading two aerosol cans of artificial snow on those already-stressed branches, and after we had draped the multicolored electric lights and burblers with their twisty, haggard wires that would make a fire inspector cringe, my father would reach into a box and upraise the Star of David. "And now for the crowning glory," he announced every year, and my mother and I clapped our hands with unrestrained gratulation.

The Star was nothing special to look at. It had your six basic Jewish points but looked rather like a cheap and flimsy cookie cutter which had been bent, crumpled and reformed many times during years of service. Still, for me it held immense symbolic power, representing as it did the ecumenical spirit of my parents — and, by extension, my own aforementioned agnosticism in its larval stage — not to mention the magical hope that kids feel just before they receive lots of toys.

I was entrusted with the job of Scotch-taping the Star to the topmost tip of the tree. I've never been a laddie of the skies, but the annual Nails Christmas tree decoration ceremony, drenched as it was with festivity, moved me to overcome my fear of heights. My father would steady our steel-reinforced wooden stepladder, while I would shakily mount the apparatus until I reached the penultimate step, right below the apex of the ladder's two compass-arms. Climbing up, crinkly *Mogen David* resolutely in hand, filled my youthful heart with elation and gave me a vista of higher truths, along with my father's bald spot.

Somehow Gin must have intuited the well-being that I associated with the tin Star, because on our first Christmas together she dragged my aluminum ladder in from the garage and, bracing it for me with her ample hips and livestocky thighs, said, "This is your job, Duke." Duke was her one and only pet name for me. When Gin was a kid she had a pup, a beagle-cocker mix named Duke, and something about me must have reminded her of Duke—my loyalty, spunk and un-flagging good nature most likely, or maybe the way I howl and hump the air when I'm happy.

"I know," I said gratefully.

Still shunning the top step, with Gin steadying the ladder, I affixed the ancient Star to the uppermost, tender and still-growing green tip of our tree, and in so doing felt an almost unendurable luxury at the heart-connection with parents now long-deceased. I was so moved by this experience, and by Gin's having initiated it, that over the succeeding few weeks I spent literally hundreds of dollars on gifts for her, a gesture which was utterly new for me. I usually don't go in for expen-sive displays of sentiment, preferring to give or receive items with a more personal touch—a hand-braided lanyard, a poem hand-written on heavy gray stock and read aloud to the in-dividual who inspired it, a pinecone discovered at a deserted beach at sundown, a chunk of beach-shale with some cool wormholes in it, the bleached skull of a desert mammal. But on this Christmas I buzzed and flitted bumblebeelike from re-tail outlet to retail outlet, charging on my credit card a food processor here, a platter with a colorful painted cow there, a twisted copper bracelet which its maker guaranteed was effec-tive in warding off arthritis,[3] and many articles of clothing that befitted her taste for the loose-fitting, in paisley or gingham.

On Christmas morn Gin tore into each gift lustily, giving each the old east-to-west and expressing the requisite surprise before moving on. She was clearly touched and pleased by my purchases, though not necessarily in that order.

Meanwhile, I had presents to open, too. Gin, remembering

---

[3]Gin's family has a history of joint inflammation. She had had no symptoms as yet, and the bracelet would keep it that way.

that I had a fondness for handmade prizes, had painted a
water-colored copy of a Georgia O'Keeffe. Gin's reproduction
wasn't what you'd call thoroughly bad, but it was a bit murki-
er than the original. Gin's painting more closely resembled a
gross blowup of what the hard-core porno rags call "showing
pink" than a hibiscus in bloom. To one with a clinical eye, the
flower might well have been called vulviform. I didn't mention this to Gin of course, but I was dashed if I was going to
hang such a picture on any wall in my house, where it would
invite my poker buddies to make tasteless witticisms and sexual innuendoes. I felt sad, because Gin had plainly put much
time and effort into an artwork which would find its way posthaste to the ministorage area under my bed, but I smiled,
thanked her and moved on.

The next present I opened was another piece of art, this not
of Gin's own making but rather one which she had picked up
at an estate sale somewhere. It was nine postcards in an oaken
frame. The postcards were all old, hand-painted and lettered
in French, glued threesquare to a piece of brown construction
paper or cardboard under glass, and each had a very lifelike
underseascape featuring a fish captured in an attitude of de-
tached repose, like those ancestral portraits you see above
wood-paneled staircases in English greathouses, except these
paintings were of turbot and squid, not aristocrats. Furthermore, like chiropractic office charts of hypertrophic men and
their meridians, these postcards had not only representations
of sealife, but also arrows pointing to their organs, and labels
such as *l'oreille* and *l'estomac* to go with them. Each card introduced an unusual finny fact. One, for instance, was devoted to the tiny *microstomichethiobriousbashforddini*, about
which the text read, *"C'est le seul poisson dans le monde, le
nom duquel est plus grand que le poisson même."*

It took me a while and a *Petite Derailleur* French dictionary
to figure out that the tiny *microstomichethiobriousbashforddini*, an otherwise nondescript smelt-looking character,
seemed to have the distinction of being the only fish whose
name is longer than it is. An unlikely assertion, it seemed to

me. There must be lots of miniscule fish in the sea which could
have names like *niddliniddli* or even *nurmi* and still be shorter
than their own names. Besides, it would depend upon the
typestyle with which the fish's name was printed, not to mention the age of the fish in question, its nutritional habits, and
so on. These inaccuracies notwithstanding, the fish-portrait
series was an oddity which delighted me to the marrow the
moment I unwrapped it. I still have those fish pictures hung
in the dining room where I play poker, and they always get
the guys yawping about thirty pound monofilament, overhead casting, "hooking a hamburger," the potential edibility
of the tiny *microstomichethiobriousbashforddini* when fil-
leted and pan-fried, and other manly idiocies.

But of all the touching gifts on that touching Christmas
morning, the one I liked best was the simplest one, em-
blematic as it was of Gin's sweetness. I smelled it long before
I opened it. Wrapped in a a silvery kind of paper embossed
with flying mallards, it emanated a rustic sweetness, faint but
insistent, and when I removed the outer layers of wrapping
paper from the box, its contents suffused the room with a fragrance at once old-timey and musical, redolent of fiddle-bow
rosin and cotton candy and antique A-hole mandolins of curly
maple, rainy autumn evenings with the Franklin stove burning seasoned avocado wood while chips of cedar bark smoul-
der atop the stove's hot cast-iron belly. Removing the last wads
of packing tissue from inside the box revealed three miniature
pillows about four inches square and hand-stitched in faded
paisley cotton. On her last trip to the New Hampshire woods
to visit her grandparents and their summer cabin, Gin had
gathered several paper bagsful of aromatic balsam needles and
had returned to Fiesta City with them. She had sewed the balsam sachets in secret, by hand, in her shed.

Gin told me they were called "dream pillows," a venerable
tradition among New Hampshire backwoodspeople. Legend
had it that if you slept with a dream pillow under your normal
pillow during the night, their aroma would give you pleasant
dreams, and if you asked the dream pillow a perplexing life-

question before you went to bed, the answer would come to you during the night. If you've never gotten a whiff of a pouchful of balsam, you should; their presence in a room, whether dream-inducing or not, is undeniably soothing. I still have mine, and after all this time the dream-pillows have lost only a small fraction of their good smell. I keep them around the house, at certain key nodes where the greatest concentration of foot traffic occurs. Whenever I pass within olfactory range of one of those sachets I experience an order of balm unparalleled in many turns around life's banked track.

After opening the dream pillows, sniffing and admiring them at some length, I surprised Gin by dragging out two stockings lumpy with prizes, one stocking for each of us. Some time earlier Gin had confessed that she'd never received a stocking of her own at Christmas. While her father was supervising the shelling of peaceful Korean peasant villages and losing his audition in the process, her mother, in the manic phase of her bipolar illness, was busy calling realtors under the pretext of being interested in expensive income properties. It's hard to believe that anyone, especially a trained sales professional, could take Sylvia's real estate fancies seriously, especially when she would appear at the door in a chartreuse flannel nightie while jabbering about positive cash flow and termite inspections and macaroons and so on. I guess it just goes to illustrate the power of greed, the lure of the quick sale, which compelled agents and brokers alike to overlook Sylvia's peculiarities. Gin's mother never bought anything, of course — she just liked getting driven around in Jaguars whilst wearing her chartreuse nightie — but her obsessive interest in properties left Gin in charge, familywise.

During her formative years, until her mother got herself stabilized on medication, Gin had full responsibility for taking the Tater Tots and breaded fish sticks out of the freezer, heating them in the oven, setting the table, doing the laundry and the rest. Her father, if I remember Gin's narration correctly, did make it home for Christmas sometimes and on those occasions did buy a tree. The Maine grandparents always did manage to airmail some token gifts for the kids, but no one had the time or the soundness of mind to deal with comparatively unimportant frills like stockings and stuffers.

Deeply moved by this neo-Dickensian tale of madness and deprivation, I went out to the neighborhood five-and-dime and bought Gin a generic Christmas stocking, a pink felt one with a white cottony throat like the beard on a department store Santa. To the front of the stocking I glued a length of red yarn in such a way that it read *"VIRGINIA"* in an intentionally juvenile script, and I also affixed a Girl Scout patch which had somehow found its way into my mother's wicker sewing box (now mine; I inherited it, along with all the rest of her stuff). The Girl Scout patch was a seasonal green — in actuality closer to an Army Air-Cav "Death From Above" khaki than to a yuletide green, but close enough for a woman who never had a stocking before, and its incongruity added a touch of whimsy — a Nails trademark, by the way — to the otherwise solemn occasion.

To go with Gin's newly-created stocking I also reprised the Christmas stocking of my youth. In the late fifties they must have had stores and factories devoted to nothing but Christmas stockings, because mine was a professionally designed and engineered product, replete with carefully pinked edgings, neatly tucked and sewn seams, machine-stitched lettering that said, "Merry Christmas Harmon," in a vibrant red. Lamentably, the intervening years between its manufacture and my first Christmas with Gin had not been altogether kind to the stocking. Its hems were coming apart, the felt was pilling up, and it looked as though someone had dumped several cups of eggnog or maple syrup on it. No matter: The stocking portion of the morning was Gin's Special Time, and the presence of my stocking was necessary only insofar as it completed a pair. I'm sure she never noticed the stains, since Gin never was one to be offended by grease spots and collar grime anyway.

I had filled my stocking with bulk, just for looks — an or-

ange, a racquetball, some walnuts, jawbreakers and gum.
Gin's I filled with real valuables. In it I put the usual gag gifts:
the chunk of granite that's actually made of foam; the tube
of Mystic Smoke that makes your fingers stink and looks more
like nasal discharge than smoke when you rub it between your
fingers as directed; the windup bug that crawls crazily across
the floor; the balsa glider with the rubber-band propellor; and
some practical ones, like designer soap and rubbers. Gin
opened each of these with her usual gusto, ripping vigorously
at the wrapping paper and honking her gratitude at each token remembrance. By the time she reached the bottom, she
seemed perfectly satisfied with the stocking experience, and
even pleasantly expended from her exertions. She was thus
unprepared for the last gift, the best and biggest surprise of
all, which was crammed into the very tippytoe of the stocking,
in a wad of the previous week's sportspage. Inside the scrap of
newsprint was a ring.

I hadn't gone near a jewelry store since Brenny and I
shopped for her wedding band many years previous. As you
might imagine, the breakup of my first and only marriage engendered in me certain negative ring-associations. My poor
benighted subconscious probably saw buying a ring as a swelling prelude to the inevitable separation which would leave me
emotionally blasted, like a tree which has been hit by lightning and gone up in one great explosion of pitch and volatile
resins. That's why, in custom-ordering Gin's ring at the Sunday beachside crafts show which has been a Fiesta City tourist
draw for as long as I've lived here, I made sure there was nothing weddinglike about the ring. I told the jeweler, a tiny
bearded gentleman named Arthur Orbin, that I wanted a
broad, flattish band with a large dark-colored semiprecious
stone—a zircon perhaps, unquestionably *not* a diamond—
mounted on it.

Arthur was dubious. "It sounds kind of thick," he said.

"Thick is fine," I said, thinking of all the wedding bands I
had ever seen-sleek, aerodynamic aggregations of rolled gold
and channeled stones, never what one would call thick.

On unwrapping it Gin was touched by the ring, both literally and figuratively. Arthur Orbin had selected an aquamarine
the pale blue of heavily chlorinated pool water, had mounted
it in a nodule of gold alloy which he had pounded thin and
wrapped around the circumference of the ovoid jewel and then
soldered to the band in a tasteful way. Arthur clearly knew his
stuff and had put his heart into it. His creative enchantment
wasn't lost on Gin, who actually wept at his handiwork.

Tears were not characteristic of Gin, who was normally all
stoicism and practicality. Holding her hand at arm's length[4]
while admiring the ring, she said that no one had ever given
her anything so beautiful and she thought no one would ever
give her anything so beautiful and she had never seen anything
so beautiful and so on. I had never known Gin to be so gushy
before, and I was baffled until I realized there was a lesson
there, something beyond gifts and the appreciation thereof. I
realized that in buying a ring, I had inadvertently tapped into
an animistic realm, one in which certain images cannot be
separated from very specific meanings, like the cross from Jesus
or the Louisville Slugger from Joe DiMaggio. Rings, too, carry
an enormous burden of mythic suggestion. They can mean
only three things — marriage, marriage, and more marriage.

While I had no particular thought one way or the other
about what the future held in store for Gin and me, getting
hitched certainly wasn't in my plans, neither the immediate
nor the long-range. I had intended the ring to signify fondness, monogamy, admiration, respect and love but certainly
nothing so permanent and life-threatening as marriage. My
divorce from Brenny had eliminated *that* as a possibility.

Of course Gin had no way of knowing the boundaries I had
placed on the object as a signifier and may therefore have mis-
taken the ring for a token of husbandly intent. Thus the first
foul drippings of poisonous ambiguity may have been in-
stilled in the clear bouillon of love, long before either of us
became aware of it.

---

[4]Any further and she would have ripped her arm out of the socket.

A NICE GOUDA

～

Ine way in which I belie my Southern California
upbringing is that I'm not the kind of person
you'd call kicked-back. For some reason — bio-
chemical, most likely — I cannot abide good
times without a ration of bumps and potholes
and good old-fashioned friction along the way for their vita-
min content. I believe that was the problem with me and Gin.
As a unit we lacked the opposition necessary to sustain interest. I guess. In endeavoring to drink from the thick malted
that is Truth, I feel as though I'm sucking through a soggy and
inwardly collapsing flex-straw, because when I think back on
those three years and try to identify the exact point at which
our love's ascendent sun began to dip, I get lost and find myself fixating on some inane little melodic figure or advertising
jingle that keeps running through my head. Clearly as I can
figure it, though, our affinity was compromised by our
sameness.

I've already discussed Gin's and my sameness in religion
and music and so forth. What I haven't yet documented is our
unique method of communicating. In the comparatively short
time Gin and I were together, we evolved a unique — read
weird — way of communicating with each other. You may

have noticed that in describing my interactions with Gin, I have not included much conversation beyond brutish grunt-ings and monosyllables. This was not an oversight, nor does it indicate a lack of candor or mere laziness on my part. Fact is, conversation is the easiest thing in the world to write, after commercials, and helps fill up space between the covers. See all the extra white stuff at the end of this paragraph? That's the writer's goal, the more the better. Readers like it, too, be-cause they find small, airy textual helpings less formidable than big inky paragraphs, which appear as dark looming mass-es of basalt they must move singlehandedly with intellectual ropes and pulleys. So if there had been any lengthy conversa-tions worth reporting between Gin and me, I would have done so, faithfully.

I didn't have the chance to include much dialogue in the preceding chapters about us, because there wasn't much to re-port. This was not, as one might suspect, due to our having spent an inordinate amount of time apart from one another. Except for Gin's trips to Phipps, we saw each other every day. Rather, I had little conversation to report because much of the time Gin and I were together, we frequently spoke like a cou-ple of pre-verbal toddlers, the kind you sometimes see being pushed along side-by-side in one of those two-seater strollers on the sidewalks of Beverly Hills or Pacific Palisades — infants exchanging sentences which, if you aren't paying close atten-tion, seem fully formed and pregnant with meaning but are actually mere batches of nonsense syllables charged with in-tention but void of denotation. I guess it's because we had such similar views of things that we didn't have much to say about a given topic. One of us already knew what the other thought anyway. Thus relieved of the need to relate informa-tion or opinions to one another, all that remained in the ver-bal sphere were routine endearments and pet names.

If anyone, such as a diligent federal employee conducting a routine unconstitutional wiretap, had overheard us talking on the phone, he might have had the impression that Gin and I were talking in some highly sophisticated code, so cryptic was our dialogue. Here's what it sounded like, to the best of my recollection:

"Halloo?" says one of us. The speakers are interchangeable. Either of us could have placed the call, either of us could have uttered any or all of the subsequent inanities.

"Little sweet and friendly brisket of beef?" says the other.

"Hnn." Uttered with a inflection that rises first and then falls gently, like a dove cooing but with its beak closed and a bit of sinus congestion, this is intended as an expression of contentment and satisfaction.

"Hnn." Trolled in a slightly higher pitch than the previous, thus indicating reciprocal contentment and satisfaction.

"Hnn."

"What doin'?"

"Oh. You know. Nothing."

"Hnn."

"So?" With a rising inflection.

"So?"

"What's it gonna be, chili sauce?" An oblique sexual reference having to do with certain naturally pungent secretions.

"Chili sauce," with mock force and urgency.

"Good news."

"Good news for the economy."

"I thought so."

"Haaa." A slatting laugh, like that of a young child who's just discovered his toes, or a Cat-capped tractor-pulling contestant after a good run through mud.

"I know."

"I know you know."

"Haaa!"

"Hm-*hmmm.*" Placing heavy stress on the second syllable and uttered in a mock-transport of discovery, like Holmes himself running smack into a less-than-elementary deduction while in the depths of cocaine psychosis.

"Good news again."

"Woof."

"What a good dog."

"Good dog, Duke."

"Awww." Sympathy and nostalgia over the little puppy, Duke, who died.

"I know that."

"I'm gonna head on over now."

"K."

"Get dressed and come over."

"K.O."

"Time for dindin."

"K."

"*Cibo!*" Food in the native language of Neapolitans.

"K."

"And shave my face and."

"Do a little dance?"

"Um-hmm."

"All righty!"

"Righty-ho!"

"So." We're talking some serious white space here.

"So?"

"So there."

"O.K. now."

"O.K., love."

"O.K., Beeda-Bee."

"Beeda-Bee!" Another canine allusion. I used to work summers at Larchwood, a left-wing day camp for the progeny of Hollywood producers and linen rental service executives. The camp's mascot was named Beans, but Judith Creighton, a slim, straw-blondish counselor on whom I had a crush,[5] loved the dog and called him Beeda-Bee.

"Bee!"

"Bee." In a sultry, suggestive tone.

"Lumen." Changing the subject from apiculture to botany, Gin's area of expertise.

"Flumen!" There's a boarding stable on the land that ad-

---

[5] And with whom I had a brief, slippery affair that ended when she tired of awakening in the back of the VW bus I owned and lived in that summer.

joins Squalor Holler. Once, when we were following the foot-
path into the chaparral, one of the horses, a stallion or roan
or something, made a huohynyming noise and began foam-
ing at the mouth. Naturally, I thought the beast had gone
rabid and should be reported to county animal control, but
Gin reassured me, "That's just his flumen." I immediately fell
in love with the word, partially because it rhymed with lumen,
which was already one of my all-time favorites for repeating
inanely, and partially because it's wonderful that The Language actually contains a word for horse-spit.

"Phlogiston." Medieval scientists used to think light and
fire were made out of particles. Nowadays quantum physicists
and fans at Grateful Dead concerts are starting to realize the
medieval scientific community might not have been far off.

"Fleidermaus."

"Fieldmouse."

"Little sweet and frisky mouse."

"Frisket of beef."

"Frisket of Freeth." George Freeth was the first person ever
to surf on the west coast. Make that the first white person,
since generations of Chumash were probably getting tubed
and doing fully rad off-the-lips and floaters long before
George dragged his first redwood plank down to the sand at
Windansea and rode the soup thereon. Selective historicism
is a wonderful thing.

"Hnn."

"Good news for the economy."

"Good noodles for my embroidery." You get the picture:
variations on no theme.

"Bye now."

"Do you have to?"

"I've got a doody pressing."

"On your doody-bottom?"

"Precisely."

"Ohhh-Kaaay." With resignation but also with understanding of and support for the urgencies of peristalsis.

"Bye."

"Bye, noodley."
"Bye, numen."
"Bye."
"Ciao, baby."
"Don't ever change."
"Haaa."
"Bye."
"Bye."

Pretty shocking talk for well-educated and scholarly (at least in Gin's case) adults, I admit. Once, in a French seminar I took to satisfy the graduate school's Breadth and Breeding requirement, we read a piece by a playwright who got paid good money for dialogue that sounded remarkably like Gin's and mine. The play was about a family who all turn into hippos or bull terriers, and they eventually get hauled away by county animal control. The thematic intent of that bit of post-modern theatricality was to ridicule the way human beings interact, the implication being that we make a lot of noise while saying relatively little, all in the name of polite conversation. This certainly seemed to be the case in my conversation with Gin. Yet she didn't seem to mind it a bit, or if she did, she never complained about its Absurdity.

For my part, I confess I found the interchanges between Gin and myself comforting, in the same way that an infant, suffering flashbacks of incunabular horror at having been thrust bloody and gasping into this vale of alarums, is soothed by a close relative leaning over the Tailor-Tot and intoning googlies and dadas. Unfortunately, during these exchanges I also had—and in much denser concentration—the inverse feeling, which is to say I felt as though the once-green bays of my life had been sullied with vials of contaminated coagula, undissolved fecal matter and Clorox bottles. Glory, spontaneity, joy and freedom were behind me, and all that remained was to pass day after obtundent day in a state of stuporous comfort, marked by breakfasts of soft-boiled eggs and instant grits, kisses with slack lips, and the predigested pabulum of mindless love talk. With every cloying, honeyed endearment my stomach twisted itself into a tight bindle enwrapped with hempen twine, the sturdy, unyielding strands of which pulled tighter every time I heard myself hnning in bell-like singsong . . . which is why I began assaulting Gin with ambiguities.

My acts of sabotage started out innocently and unconsciously, which is to say I began poking little poleholes in the gondola of love without malicious design or forethought. Holes they were nevertheless and percolative, too. For instance, when Gin started hinting that she might enjoy cohabitation some day, I would respond by shrugging noncommittally and then changing the subject quickly to something safe.

"I just adore my ring," Gin might begin, and in a very un-Ginnish tone. The prospect of conglutinate bliss does weird things to certain people — often to people you would never in a googol of years expect to hear comporting themselves as was Gin: constricting the vocal cords to produce a repertoire of high pitched simpers, chirrups, croons, purrs and joyful Noises unto the Lord while making big wide eyes, like O-rings on a cylinder head.

"I'm glad." I was, truly. That's why I bought the ring for her. Her gladness made me glad. "I heard Scioscia got put on the disabled list," I might add, there being no topic safer than baseball, in my experience.

"Aren't you glad I'm not one of those girls who care about all that frilly shit, like diamonds?"

"Hnn," I responded, at a loss for a smooth out or even an intelligent response.

"I think a tasteful gold band is all you really need."

Wedding bells closing fast off the port bow, Captain. Dive, Dive! Desperately I broke into song. *"Dlee Noodledee Noodle, Dlee Noodledee Noodley Noodledee Noodle. Noodledee Noodledee Noodledee Noodledee Noodle,"* I sang to the tune of Freddie King's instrumental shuffle, "Hideaway." Noodling usually worked to divert attention from any subject by creating a silly, carefree mood in the midst of which nothing could be considered seriously.

Except marriage. "I know, Duke," said Gin. "You're still a little scared because of your last marriage. That's all right, these things take time."

A little scared. And the United States is a little in debt, and the ground near the San Andreas fault is a little unstable. Certainly there was no denying that my marriage and divorce left me feeling as though a layer of my skin—no, all the layers— had been pared away like the rind off a nice gouda, and I didn't want to expose my cheesy emotional quick that way again. Besides, I was used to living on my own, liked being able to fill the sink with dirty dishes, enjoyed playing cards until all hours without having to report to anyone, got off on leaving the cap off the toothpaste tube, didn't mind misplacing my specs once in a while and having to overturn the house and all its contents to find them, derived great pleasure from returning home at night, crawling all snuggly between my unrumpled percale sheets and watching old Star Trek reruns until Morpheus visited upon me a night of solitary rest.

Gin was right. I was a little scared of losing all that, and it showed.

YUGOSLAVIAN
HAIKU

~✿~

The tear[6] came when Gin got a letter offering her a postdoctoral position in South Carolina. Certain eminences in the Department of Ecology there had applied for and received a grant to determine whether blackthroat bass near the Savannah River nuke plant had ingested radioactive dilithium in levels toxic to the local human population. The research model involved the removal and dissection of bass ears and the subsequent study of said freeze-dried membranes using the latest in electron microscopy. Naturally Gin, who had by this time earned a reputation as being the nation's foremost published expert on piscal tympanies, was offered the position. She could move right into a vacant flat in married students' housing, the rent for which would be paid for by the university; she would have a generous monthly stipend while she pursued her research; and she'd command a team of graduate assistants who would do the laborious data entry, freeing her to put on her hip-high waders and chase bass around the shallows. An exciting opportunity for the eldest Stabler offspring,

---

[6]Rhymes with *unfair*.

if not for the fish, who probably had little interest in donating their scaly physiques to the study.

Gin was duly flattered. She audiblized same with great windy fulminations, but abruptly her mood changed—a rare event for Gin, whose temper, if charted longitudinally on graph paper, would resemble the EKG readout of a patient pronounced dead several minutes previous. Gin regarded me solemnly and asked in a voice pregnant with import and softened by timid hopefulness, "Do you think I should go?"

If one were to make a bas-relief topographical chart of the narrative at hand, this would be the summit. From the prospect of this rummy pinnacle one can see a cyclorama of choices, each with a cascading avalanche or slowly grinding glacier of consequences. To cite one particular, I could have responded to Gin's "What do you want me to do?" with a simple, practical wimpout, such as a curt "Hnn," or even an earnest "Noodley noodle," and thereby have evaded the whole issue. Then again, I could as easily have taken a starboard reach and said, "Please, dearest, don't do it," a protestation which would have cemented a life with Gin. But I didn't. With cohabitation bearing down on me like Hurricane Sid moving darkly and palm-uprootingly toward the Gulf coast, I fluted with mock-optimism and bonhommie, "I think you ought to give it a try, honey. If you don't like it, you can always come back."

Gin's countenance fell. She asked, in a tone spongy with pathos, "You *want* me to go?"

I was as reassuring as I could be, given that I did want her to go. "It's not that I want you to go," I said. "It just seems to me that it's the kind of opportunity you shouldn't pass up. For your career."

Her career. Pretty flimsy and transparent, I avow.

Looking squarely at my own behavior in the harsh heliarc glare of hindsight, I realize I was being manipulative and unforthcoming—OK, a shitheel—not out of any overt malice but rather a craven terror of moving forward with Gin into that dark place where the gorgon Intimacy resides: a terror born of ambiguity, all seven types at once, and deadly. The ambiguity in this case was, as most ambiguities are, a complex son of an ore, which is to say it contained all manner of facets and flaws, cracks and impurities. To get the whole picture we must therefore, like Vasco De Gama[7] make a thorough round of the isometric lozenge that was my personality in those days, charting all sides as we revolve.

For starters, there was one side of me that saw our separating as inevitable, due to the aforementioned sameness and childish babble and so on. A man can only engage in baby talk for so long without spitting up. Simultaneously there was another side that felt comfortable with Gin and liked her very much and was her best friend and didn't want to jeopardize that friendship. There was yet another side that clung to some vestigial ideal of marriage, a big double bed, joint checking, a mutually purchased dinette set, the works. With Gin came a ready-assembled family; we might even extend that nurturing circle with our own passel of good-eating younguns some day in the future . . . so far in the future that I could imagine it without being terrified by its reality. Then of course there was the infantile side we all have, the one that has a terror of being abandoned and left all alone.

All these sides were fighting it out on the soggy battlefield of my brainpan, and it was up to Me—the wise, parental, governing faculty they used to call superego before Freud came to be considered reductivist—to resolve the issue as best I could. As a compromise solution, Me proposed Gin's acceptance of the post-doc as a win-win situation. With Gin in South Carolina, I would have My Own Place while retaining my best friend and lover in Gin. Win-win, at least for me, if not for Gin, who probably wanted to hear that I couldn't live without her and that I had commissioned the creation of a tastefully filigreed gold band to prove the depth and breadth of my commitment to a life with her.

---

[7]Who circled the globe in quest of the Fountain of Youth, only to find Disney World.

To her credit, Gin didn't give voice to her disappointment by pleading pitifully, "But what about *us?*" as I did when Brenny told me she wanted to abort our marriage in its third trimester. All Gin did was look at me with those big sad pupilless browns — just like a moocow eying the rancher with tragic acceptance as he leads her up the ramp to the abattoir — to make me feel like the aforementioned heel. "It'll only be for a year or two," I reminded her.

"A year or two," she repeated dully, as though she were a stage hypnotist's shill.

"Yes," I chirped hopefully. "We'll see each other during quarter breaks and every summer. Couples do it all the time. It might even be good for us. Make us appreciate each other more, and all that."

I meant it, too. My friend, E. Ford Frazier, a post-brutalist poet with paid-for pieces in all the major literary rags, spent two years in Yugoslavia on a Bengaigh Fellowship, from which he returned with a small chapbook of haikus about New Mexican landscapes. While Ford was in Yugoslavia, his wife, Sally, stayed in Fiesta City, where she had a gratifying administrative position at a hospice facility. She liked her job and didn't want to leave. The Fraziers were apart two years and came out just fine. In fact, they conceived their second child, Ford Jr., while spending one of Ford's school breaks together. Junior is now four years old and shows no ill effects from having been conceived and born while his parents were doing their separate things.

When I told Gin the story of Ford Frazier and Yugoslavia, her aspect lightened somewhat, as though the rosy blush of dawn was breaking over a storm-tossed seascape. And when I further reassured her that I didn't see her trip to South Carolina as a necrotically swollen prelude to our breaking up, this seemed to buck and mollify her, because she started smiling. It was a remarkable change that took place on the bleak terrain of the Stabler face. Gin's beamish grin told me she saw sincerity behind my eyes.

However, I realize now that Gin's lightened aspect probably had nothing to do with her believing and being comforted by my assurances. More likely, she had at that moment looked squarely at my ambivalence of recent months and had recognized the utter futility of our situation, as embodied in the paradox I was presently delivering. By urging her to move away while assuring her that we would remain lovers, I was telling Gin something closely akin to *I love you*, but at the same time I seemed to be saying *go away*. Taken in sum, then, the message must have come across to her as something like, *I love you, so go away*, a minor variant of the old song title — Waylon and Willie and the boys, wasn't it? — which, if not unfunny on a record album, is certainly schizophrenogenic coming from your lover.

I was presenting Gin with a riddle, a kind of Yugoslavian haiku to which there could be no answer except insanity or enlightenment. Having had her fill of insanity in her bipolar bear of a mother, Gin chose enlightenment, and the smile I saw on her face at that moment was genuinely beatific, like that of Saint Anthony being released from this prison of arrow-mortified flesh into a realm of pure spirit and airy goodness.

She maintained that firm smile-on as she rang up her travel agent and made the necessaries, and, call done, she laughed.

"Hawhawhaw!" she said in that cute way she had.

A FISSHE
THAT IS WATERLEES

~~

A couple days after her relocation Gin called me up, honking excitedly about the possibilities for progressive research into the vertebrate metabolism of heavy isotopes and the friendliness of the Southern people in general, about grits and ham which make an unparalleled, serotonin-stimulating breakfast, about how she finally had found a culture that wasn't plastic and superficial and image-conscious to the point of narcissism like that of Southern California in general and Fiesta City in particular. She said that in visiting Greaven, South Carolina, she felt as though she had gone home, and that she could live there forever.

I hadn't expected her to be so happy. To the contrary, I'd assumed that she'd be regretting the day she accepted the job, pining tragically and yearning for the reassurance of my embrace. Her effervescence therefore concerned me, suggesting as it did the possibility that Gin might be all right—or even better than that—without me. This caused me no small degree of insecurity, and I responded by becoming clutchy—a quality which I detest when I see it in other people, even moreso when someone points it in my direction, and which I loathed in myself almost to the point of suicide.

But I couldn't help myself. "I miss you," I simpered.

"Aww, that's sweet," said Gin. I couldn't tell whether she thought my plaintive tone was a put-on and was playing along by responding in a parodically solicitous tone of her own, whether she was genuinely affected by my vulnerability, or whether she was going for the exposed Nails carotid with some real vicious sarcasm, now that she sensed she had the upper hand.

"No, but I mean it," I said, bringing a bit more mannish resonance to my expression this time. "I changed my mind. I really don't want you to stay there after all."

"But you're the one who told me to go," she reminded me.

"I didn't tell you to go," I protested. "I just suggested you check it out."

"You said the job would be good for my career, and you were right." She paused. "As usual."

Again with the tone. She was clearly toying with me, perhaps getting her getbacks for my having so carefully nurtured emotional distance like a bed of prized tea roses during the three years we were together. I conceded the scoring touch to her. "As usual," I agreed in a tone of exaggerated self-deprecating glumness.

She appeared indifferent to my mood. "I used to be away at Phipps half the time anyhow," she honked cheerily, a gosling flapping in clear water on a warm day. "So this won't be so different."

"It's completely different. I'll be depressed all year instead of once a month," I moaned.

"You never told me you were depressed when I was gone. Besides, you're the one who told me to go," she repeated with tone of cold logicality.

"I didn't think it through, all right?"

"Anyway, it's too late now. I already told them."

"You didn't sign a contract or anything, did you?"

"No, but—"

"So you can tell them you changed your mind," I said, applying pressure as best I could, given my tactical disadvantage.

"But I didn't change my mind," Gin said, infuriatingly immune to my games.

I persisted, "But you could."

"But I won't. I like him here."

A telling slip! I pounced as would an undernourished dingo on the carcass of a felled impala. "Him here?" I demanded.

"What?"

"You said you 'like him here.' "

"No, I said, 'I like it here.' "

"No you didn't. You said, 'I like him here.' Who's 'him?' "

"I don't know, because I didn't say 'him.' I said 'it.' "

"Did so say 'him.' "

Silence. A nonspecific gravity burdened the proceeding, in spite of the comical sonar beepings, distracting cellophane crackles and hydraulic hissings of the transcontinental trunk line. Leave it to that wacky, fun-filled ITT to lighten things up. After some moments, Gin leapt back into it with a surge of courage. "I met someone," she ventured.

An afflux of adrenalin jazzed all the organs in my abdominal cavity, making my joints ache suddenly and all at once, as though a traveling company of influenza virions had been invited in for free eats and had accepted without hesitation. The shock of the moment, like a Taekwando finger-stab to the solar plexus, caused me to aspirate some saliva, sending me into a rictus of coughing and wheezing.

"What was that noise?" Gin asked.

I replied, "Nothing, just some interference over the transcontinental trunk line." I cleared my throat and lungs as best I could. Confronted with the terrible bleak vista of impending solitariness, my mind reeled. The room seemed to be rotating. "It must be that wacky ITT," I added.

"Did you hear what I said?" Gin said in an insistent tone.

"You said you met someone," I said, gasping between syllables and feeling for all the world like a fisshe that is waterlees, as Chaucer used to say.

"Well, how do you feel about that?" she asked, as though she had been awarded and hand-delivered an emeritus degree in counseling psychology and so felt qualified to practice Rogerian promptings on me.

To forestall the inevitable I said, "It comes as no surprise to me that you met someone. You're a fun person. You've probably met quite a few people since you've been there."

"I mean I met someone I like," Gin said, thereby increasing the rotation and yaw of my mind.

"Like a friend you mean," I wheezed, still feigning stupidity as my vision dimmed.

She paused pregnantly. "Yes, but I think Steve is going to be more than a friend." She had a smug lilt to her voice that made me want to balkanize her face.

"Steve."

"Yes. That's his name."

"Steve's name."

"Yes."

Restating the obvious and making the explicit even more explicit to no end save bilious sarcasm, I said, "So what I hear you saying is that you're going to become more than friends with someone named Steve, whose name, coincidentally enough, is Steve."

"Yes."

"Who the fuck is Steve?" I blurted.

"Steve is a Forest Ranger here," she said, not quite to the point and in the same maddeningly pulpy voice. "He plays mandolin, too. I think I love him."

Generally I don't fancy myself one of those belletrists who feels it's his duty to take up twenty or thirty pages describing every scene and then gives you a dab of action before going on to the next evocation of set and setting, so that what you end up with is three pages of plot — young lad defies father, goes to sea — and three hundred pages depicting Newfoundland in all its seasonal aspects. In so many so-called classics I was supposed to read in college, you'll find whole chapters devoted to no action at all: just an airplane overhead, or a pair of glasses on a roadside billboard, or fog in the Salinas valley. All lovely and symbolic and rendered in gruesome detail I'm sure, but as a reader, I like to get on to the good parts, meaning the car chases and happy unions.

Here, however, I must make an exception. In order to understand what impelled Gin to settle in South Carolina, it's crucial that the reader experience what she experienced on her first trip there, even though I'm making it up from the little information Gin volunteered during subsequent phone calls. The story goes something like . . .

Upon Gin's arrival at the University of South Carolina's Department of Ecology and Vertebrate Studies, the staff—faculty, administrative assistants, lab techs, freeze-dried membrane-carving and -observation specialists—are predictably enchanted by Gin's unique combination of down-country unaffectedness and technical brilliancy, and when they find out she's a world-class fiddler to boot, they immediately organize a hoedown or hootenanny, inviting all the old-timey musicians in their acquaintance. Since most southern states, *Ca'lahna* included, have almost as many fiddlers and banjo pickers and jawharp players as they have members of ultra-rightwing splinter factions, the party is well-attended. Enter Steve, who has been included in the gathering because he is an industrial botanist—his job is to range through hilly tracts and count all the pine trees thereon, so that the paper companies can estimate the number of days required for the "harvesting" (read *utter devastation*) of a given forest area—who does occasional contract jobs for the University of S.C. at Greaven, and, more importantly, because he's a kick-ass mandolin player.

So picture if you will a woodframe house of moderate size and typical post-Reconstruction design, the kind I've seen and even briefly inhabited on my many visits to Georgia, from whence sprang my mother—a home white and boxy, with front porch and machine-lathed columns made to resemble the wide landings and white plaster columns of cotton and tobacco plantation manor houses, harking back to a heritage for which all confederate flag-waving, fiddle-sawing Southerners yearn with tears of nostalgia. Squirrels gambol in the myrtle trees, cicadas croon among the kudzu, a big coon hound snoozes on the porch. He looks up at you lazily as you walk in and then rests his broad muzzle back down on splayed forepaws and resumes his dream of loping after runaway plantation workers through thickets of sportive wood and across freshets of mountain snowmelt.

Opening the front door, white and heavy with a thousand coats of unstripped enamel, you enter into a thick swirling cloud of smoke from hand-rolled joints and Bugler cigarettes, an airborne particulate mass that seems alive, unicellular, and even macrophagic, so actively does it consume you. Your eyes sting. Your bronchi ache. You are assaulted by a din of loutish laughter, manly whoops of backslapping camaraderie and raucous bleats of female mirth and come-hither teasing. People in various stages of alcoholic ataxia stumble against you roughly, making your route errantly Brownian. Through the shifting strata of smoke, at the far end of the expansive front room, by the red brick fireplace, perhaps twenty musicians sit on hard-backed wooden seats and unpadded metal folding chairs arranged in a loose circle. The players, men and women in approximately the same attire — blue jeans or denim overalls, plaid shirts over T-shirts advertising a tractor or a distillery product, or both — clomp steel-toed workboots on the oak floor, bow fiddles energetically and exchange stoned-out grins as they play.

What you notice first about the music, especially if you are one accustomed to playing and hearing bebop and blues in which one person takes a solo, then another and so on, is that here *everyone* is soloing at once, playing the childlike, repetitive melody almost mechanically, with no room for improvisation. Guitar players accompany the melodists by chunking open-stringed chords of the most rudimentary cowboyish sort in a loose parody of rhythm. Still, there's life there, a joy and celebration of rude, raw vitality and of people's ability to turn fermented hops to sweat and piss, sanctifying themselves in the metabolic furnace. No enemy of sanctification, you grab yourself a Corona from a galvanized tub filled with ice, take a hit or two of locally grown *sinsemilla* as it comes around, and you plop down to listen to the music and let the scene wash over your receptors like a flash flood over the sheltered Mojave.

Time goes by.

The assembled hooters play tune after tune and drink beer after beer until the wee hours, at which point the less hardcore players and the more serious drinkers begin to leave or pass out. The only two musicians left playing are Gin and Steve, who play on until their fingers get too tired to fret another note, and then they start talking. They cover the subject of botanical taxonomies thoroughly, then modulate to stringband music, then ascend to religion. He is a Christian who belongs to a born-again group called the New American Calvary and she confesses that she has a soft spot in her heart for Jesus, his goodness and suffering and so on. [Gin never told me about this particular softness but it makes sense, given the influence of her Bible-thumping grandparents.]

Steve says his favorite foods are burgers and malteds, and Gin says Me too and makes a joke about her current boyfriend, an asthenic Jewboy who won't eat red meat because he believes he'll get fever blisters on his uvula if he does. The man laughs heartily, with the sound of a wide river turning waterfall by plunging into a deep gulch. All subjects are profoundly engaging to both of them. He is sincere, she entranced. Eventually Steve, gentleman that he is, says he hopes he will see her again. She again says Me too [note the absence of Hmns or Noodlies here]. They shake hands at the porch and exchange a look which can be described in no more genteel terms than as a prolonged, portentous, reproachable eyefuck.

Steve reconsiders the goodbye and offers to drive her home. She accepts . . .

SHOE-POLISHING
DAY

～

Y ou don't need an advanced degree in Interpersonal Dynamics to figure out the rest.

My own mental skinflicks, featuring Gin and Steve making the fiddler with two bows on the floor of her as-yet-unfurnished married-student flat, took over at this point in our phone conversation, and, seeing no point in maintaining the thin veneer of civility any longer, I let all the Italianate cells in my body do their reactive fangool. "Let me at the fucker," I shouted into the receiver, "I'll fuckin' rip the motherfucker's motherfuckin' balls out by the fuckin' roots and feed them to the fuckin' dog."

Gin laughed gaily, well beyond the reach of my drasty blusterings. "Oh Duke," she said, at which utterance I noticed that her distinctive honk had mellowed to a tonality which could be described as verging on the feminine. "You don't even have a dog," she tootled.

"Well if I did," I said meaninglessly, fury's first and strongest wave by.

"I know." The awful truth out and the most difficult task accomplished, Gin was relaxing now, even willing to slip back into a little safe noodling. "Hmn," she said.

But my noodling days were behind me forever, and besides

there were still a few time-tested consuetudes to be ritually enacted, most important of which was the ever-popular, "What does he have that I don't have?"

She didn't hesitate in summing it up by explaining, "Steve supports me, and you never did," in a manner that made me feel like a brand of cat litter that had proved to be less than absorbent and had therefore to be replaced by a better.

"I always supported you," I protested. "Didn't I always praise you to the skies for being able to memorize the Latin names for every plant in the world? Didn't I encourage you to pursue all this fish research bullshit in the first place? Didn't the word 'genius' spring to my lips every time you recalled an obscure mote of Celtic or Appalachian folk music?"

Gin said, "Yes, Harmon, and I always appreciated you for it. You gave me something no one ever gave me before."

"You mean I fucked you without putting a burlap sack over your head."

"Yeah," she laughed, recalling without rue her Tennessee days, "and much more . . . "

"So I did support you. You admit it."

"You did." She paused to think, then spoke slowly. "I guess it comes down to that Steve wants to be with me and I never got the feeling you did."

"But I was moving in that direction," I said.

Was this true? At the time we were together, if you had asked me (and if I were of a mind to introspect and answer honestly) I would probably have said No, I couldn't see living with Gin, her rafters full of creepy crawlers, her piles of rumpled clothing and senseless linens, her pervasive nearness. On the other hand, things evolve slowly, and just because I couldn't see it happening didn't mean it wasn't happening. With the latter in mind, I appended, "You didn't give us a chance."

"Three, almost four years, Harmon."

"Well, I'm a slow mover."

"I know some barnacles that move faster."

"Is that a marine biology joke?"

"I suppose. But also an explanation."

"So if I had wanted to live with you, you wouldn't have gone for Steve."

"Yes. I don't know. I probably wouldn't have gone away, so Steve wouldn't have been an issue."

"But now he is."

"Very much."

The adoration in her voice caused a mini-resurgence of my earlier bitterness, like a chile relleno breakfast in reflux. "It's so easy for you," I said. "Just dump Tennessee with a phone call and, *bam!* you're with Harmon. Call Harmon and *bam!* you're with Steve."

"You think this is easy," she said with a dash of rue in the roux this time. "I know I'm giving up a lot."

I had the rare good sense to keep my mouth shut, which allowed Gin to touch upon her own foci of misgiving and vulnerability. Doing so further softened her voice. "It's funny," she confided. "You're much handsomer than Steve, actually. I'm not even that physically attracted to him. He's shorter than you, and he's kind of funny-looking—big ears and crooked teeth."

She delivered this litany of Steve's anatomical shortcomings not critically but rather fondly, as if describing a cherished heirloom—an old cane-backed rocker perhaps, with all its familiar and history-laden nicks and dents. I had, since she initially introduced his loathsome name into the conversation, imagined Steve the Forest Ranger to be a bunyan of a man in plaid Pendleton and well-packed coveralls, a studly mountaineer of turgid biceps and jutting chin and ruddy complexion, so when I found out Steve's vitae fell somewhat short in its listing of macho qualifications, I started warming to the ugly little guy in spite of my fervent desire to think him an unmitigated blister.

"He's skinny," Gin went on, "and his skin is bad from acne when he was a kid, and he certainly doesn't have your bucks. In fact he's in debt up to his eyeballs with government loans from school. Besides," she said, her voice quavering noticeably even though that darn ITT had momentarily interjected a blast of static that made it sound as though we were on a party line and the party of the third part was frying up a panful of calamari in extra-virgin olive oil, "there's no one like you, Duke."

She really said this, crying or at least dry-sobbing all the while, which eased the obloquy of my abandonment to no small degree and made me warm to her as much as I already had to Steve. "Thank God for that," I said with unforced humility and the calm resignation of the foredoomed.

"But Steve really wants me, Harmon," she said solemnly. "He wants to live with me. *Now.*" She came down emphatically on that spondaic foot. "I guess I'm more of a homebody than I thought," she concluded. "Besides, he doesn't mind if I put on a few pounds drinking beers. Steve says he likes 'em fat and happy."

I let slip the opportunity to comment meanly on the Stabler familial predisposition toward porkdom. "I like fat, too," I protested. "I always have." The last involuntary twitching before the endmost rattling breath.

"Yes, but Steve wants me in a way you never could. You know that. I know you do."

Recalling my response to this last statement, I am put in mind of a migrant community of bees that camped out on my front porch one night several years ago. I awoke to a loud humming which I mistook at first to be a prolonged power spike on the high-tension line nearby, but when I went outside to check it out I found what seemed an entire subspecies of bee — a particularly loud and aggressive strain — had selected as its new home one of the four-bys that supported the corrugated fiberglass of my porch awning. Remembering from Cub Scouts that it's safer to be politic and deferential in the company of bees, I eased my way back inside and did what any red-blooded American male would do. I called an exterminator. They guy on the phone told me that bees migrate just like geese, and that if you steer clear of the hive, it will move on its own in a day or two. Sure enough, the very next morning

I went out, and the camp had cleared out, leaving no trace of apian life except for a few stragglers, maybe locals, cruising for a little stamen action around my pyrocantha hedge.

Although I was relieved that I could go in and out without risking anaphylactic shock, I missed the nasty little beezers a little bit, too. Wellsir, the way I figure it, our emotions are just like migrant bees. One moment I was filled with vile, rankling resentment and the next minute it had mostly dissipated, to be replaced by good-natured supportiveness wrought by time and by friendship long standing. "You're right," I said to Gin. "I know it's hard for you. I don't blame you. It hurts me a lot, but I don't blame you at all. In fact, I wish you both well."

Gin interposed a skeptical silence here, waiting for the hammer to fall as it had many times previously.

"No, really, I mean it," I said.

And I did mean it. I may have an infuriating (so I've been told in the past) self-protective tendency to intellectualize and/or to crack wise, so that others sometimes have trouble locating a chink through which they can reach my feelings, but I can serve up sincerity in dollops when I get beyond my own wounded pride and store of orphaned grief.

"Thank you, Harmon, you're a big person," Gin said.

"Actually I'm the same height as Dustin Hoffman," I came back, and when Gin rang off after a few awkward goodbys, I saw myself clearly: a short Italian-Jewish songwriting Strat-wielding dilettantish space-guarding lapsed academic, not only without parents or nucleic family to speak of, but shit out of Stablers as well.

You got that right: Ah, me.

After that conversation, Gin neither called me, nor would she take my calls. I reached out on several occasions, but each time Gin had something more important to do—it was her shoe-polishing day, she said, or her bow-rosining day, or she had a carful of groceries. I guess Steve is the jealous type, or else Gin decided that by never talking with me again, she might spare herself any more ego-deflating reminders of my chronic waffling. Or maybe her detachment was a brutally passive form of reproof. Whatever the reason, it's painful to have been cut off so completely from someone who had been — if nothing else — my best friend, and you don't need to be Holmes to detect in me the traces of barbed acrimony, an emotion which apparently takes longer to decay than PVC trash-can liners in a landfill.

But it's all for the best, I suppose, since it worked out to the benefit of all concerned. Gin is fortunate to have found in Steve a fount whence commitment springs, a main-man who has a mind with no warring subpersonalities competing for hegemony and no misgivings about bringing little fatties into the world. Steve is fortunate to have found Gin when she was ripe for marital plucking, like a plump plum on a sagging branch. Meanwhile I may be fortunate (the jury is still out on this one) to have connected with the elusive Ondine, and it goes without saying that Ondine is fortunate to have such an agreeable chappie as H. Nails III in her business.

So after all is said and done I can honestly say that I do wish Gin and Steve well . . . sometimes, depending on how much sleep I've gotten and how much red meat I've eaten recently. Ondine says that beeves, when slaughtered, eaten and assimilated, are the cause of half our angers and most of our wars, and I'm a fool to argue.

MESSENGERS
OF LOVE

~/~

With Gin migrated to South Carolina, I no
longer had any reason to visit her house or
pond, so I had no occasion to come in contact with Ondine. As it turns out, Ondine
had gotten her own place in town. Even if
I had visited Squalor Holler with the intention of recapturing
that vision of pondside perfection, Ondine wouldn't have
been there. However, the point is moot, since I was in no
frame of mind to pant after redheads or any other tint of female, pondside or otherwise.

I was grieving over my lost Gin.[8]

For several months I stayed pretty much to myself and
avoided social engagements of any kind. I stopped playing
music, not only with Sheebeg and Sheemore but also with myself. Although I hadn't missed a day of practice for many
years, the thought of onanizing over muscle-memorized pen-
tatonic scales or training the bleary eye on dog-eared fake

---

[8]I know living in South Carolina doesn't really qualify as being lost
(doomed, maybe, but not lost) and it was my fault Gin left in the first place,
but it still gave me the ungrounded, hollow sort of blues one gets after love
of long duration ends, or one's kitty runs away.

72

charts brought me no joy, and I didn't have the energy to learn anything new.

Likewise with reading, usually another of my greatest pleasures: I couldn't sustain interest in a book or even a magazine article long enough to get through more than a couple pages without distracting myself with tormented fantasies, such as the one in which a tall conifer is struck by lightning, falls on Steve the Forest Ranger's arm, snapping both ulna and radius like king crab legs within the steel jaws of a nutcracker, crushing ligament and soft tissue beyond repair and causing him to go into a shocky coma from which he never emerges. Likewise with songwriting: I came up with a few smokehouse-flavored lines that expressed my crushing indolence of that period — "Lately I been nowheres/'ceptin where I didn't wanna of been," being the only one I can recall anymore — but I couldn't come up with whole verses, nor did any catchy melodic hooks suggest themselves.

Unable to pursue creative enchantment, and unfortunately still committed to sobriety, I spent most of my time watching TV. I remember distinctly. It was just before the Olympics that Gin informed me of her impending marriage to Steve. I passed several fortnights camped out on my bed, dispassionately observant as healthy young athletic types sprang over pommelhorses and knifed into pallucid waters without a splash, while I had barely the energy to raise my pissjar from dresser-top to dick, or the desire to lift a frozen ScooterPie from my enamelled Ms Pac-Man bed-tray to parched lips. So distrait was I that on one occasion I may even have raised my urine-filled Mott's apple juice jar accidentally to parched lips and then unintentionally touched my fallow prong with a frozen ScooterPie . . . which was the most action I'd had for some time and under the circumstances didn't feel half bad.

But Mistress Time, as she often will, brought me out of my funk somewhat. By the Dodgers' first televised spring exhibition game in Vero Beach, I was beginning to feel some of the old Nails vigor flow back into my extremities. For starters, I began sluicing fruit and protein smoothies in the morning. My cells took up a collective cheer at this thick puree with its promise of meals more substantial than ScooterPies and frozen toaster-waffles. Once back on my feed, I was able to draw myself up out of my bed and walk, at first shambling about the house in rubberized bath sandals, next taking a tentative turn or two around the backyard, then briskly striding the two-mile loop around my neighborhood, and at last returning to my health club where I was able to pedal the Exercycle vigorously for a full forty minutes. Revitalized by a healthful diet and regular exercise, I began accepting offers of musical work.

Carl Petrel was starting a new band and needed a guitar player who was willing to alternate between lead and rhythm. Stormy, as most people called Carl, was my most reliable pill source during my period of applied degeneracy. Well-known in Fiesta City creative circles for providing high-quality drugs to artists, guerilla illusionists, utopians, musicians, street mimes, Green Party eco-saboteurs and ideologues — all at near or below cost — Stormy usually had available a panoply of products, including black-market prescription drugs, weapons-grade Thai Stick and pharmaceutically reliable LSD in several forms — blue-flecked tabs he called Ostrich Bombs, tattoo-blotters with Scrooge McDuck cartoons on them, empty-looking horse caps and transparent gel-squares — along with prodigious amounts of the killer weed in which he specialized: lids of shake-free sinsemilla packaged in brown paper gumdrop sacks which he rubber-stamped with the logo *CONSTANT COMET TEA* alongside a clip-graphic of the longtailed comet Kahoutek.

To Stormy, dealing (I've heard his rap many times) is not the crass money-making venture it has become today. In his mind it's a public service. Stormy believes that for sheer generativity, no human experience before or since has rivaled the original Acid Tests in the mid-sixties. Stormy claims to have been present at all the L.A.-area Tests in 1966, including Compton, Sunset and Pico, and I believe him. He recounts having spent fifteen hours at one of the Tests — the Watts Youth Center, I

believe — lying with his ear pressed to the ground while some
disarranged celebrant dragged a piece of furniture back and
forth across the floor — *FIFTEEN HOURS!* — wooden legs
vibrating like triple-bass strings on hell's own concert grand
while protective metal caps skreeked against concrete or un-
waxed hardwood, putting Stormy in mind (or out) of millen-
nial earth harrowed by saintly garbageworkers.

At some point during this afflux of hallucination, Stormy
believes his nose started to bleed profusely, giving the floor a
lubricative coating which silenced the furniture noise: no
more friction, no more noise, like if you spread mayonnaise
on a fiddle-player's strings in mid-concerto. Or maybe the
stoned-out testee just got tired after fifteen hours and stopped
dragging the infernal chair. It was during that moment of silence that Stormy decided he could find no higher meaning
to his life than playing electric guitar at top volume and
elevating other peoples' consciousness chemically, both of
which he would perform as a sort of sacred beneficence,
providing his patrons the means by which they might turn
their lives into nonstop, garish party-art.

Having identified his calling, Stormy went at it with gleeful
abandon, keeping several generations of Fiesta City indigenes
deafened and delirious, while staying a step ahead of the land-
lord's demands for back rent and the Contra Madera County
Sheriff's Department's Narcotics Task Force — who, despite
Stormy's high profile in certain social circles, seemed to be unaware of his existence. Maybe selective invisibility is a side
effect of ingesting Ostrich Bombs regularly.

I hadn't been a consumer of Ostrich Bombs or Constant
Comet or any other controlled substance since my detox, but
I had still frequent contact with Stormy, since we both play
retro-R & B, and there are only so many clubs in Fiesta City
that support non-top-forty bands. Stormy would come to hear
me play, or I'd find myself hangin' at the Bla or The Merthio-
late Lounge when one of Stormy's many short-lived pickup
groups was performing. Between sets we'd get to reminiscing
fondly about my former intemperance or discussing his cur-

rent projects, the most recent of which was a singer named
Junie Melanchik.

A big, brazen, beamy girl with generous warm bosoms,
eyes the truculent gray of unsheltered ocean at galetide, and
a tangle of hair the same color as sweet corn before you boil
it, Junie Melanchik was singing around town with some garage musicians assembled loosely and calling themselves The
Junie Melanchik Band. That name alone should have been
enough to deter all but the most entertainment-starved locals,
and did: Junie was the best-kept musical secret in Fiesta City,
almost as invisible to the public as Stormy was to the Sheriff's
Department. Still, the Melanchiks did land some small-time
gigs, mostly around campus, and it was at one of these — in
the Olde Pubbe of the university's Student Union — that
Stormy stumbled upon Junie belting out the Janis Joplin/ Big
Brother version of the Big Mama Thornton classic "Piece of My
Heart" with almost as much gritty getdown as Janis herself,
and with a much more provocative outfit: skintight black
leather pants, three-inch spiked heels, a leatherette pushup
halter, a headband of some iridescent synthetic material, and
lots of eyeliner.

Junie dressed, sang and comported herself outrageously,
and Stormy fell in love. After the Melanchiks' last set, he approached Junie, pledged his troth to her, confessing that he
was a simple but good man, that he was a practicing Buddhist
and a guitarist of some skill and a sizeable local following, that
he admired Junie's "great set of pipes," and that if she stuck
with him, baby, he'd make her a star, or at least get her some
decent gigs. He also mentioned in passing that he had the best
dope in town. As it turns out, all this pledging wasn't necessary, since Junie instantly recognized Stormy as Her Type. The
daughter of your basic garden-variety freaks-turned-chiro-
practors, Junie had nursed from her mother's dayglo-painted
tit under blacklight, had shaken her plastic rattle cutely to the
two-drumset beat of The Dead, had potty-trained while Jag-
ger was extolling the virtues of brown sugar, had thrice
travelled the country in a VW van before she started kinder-

garten. If one can believe her account, Junie's first words were, "It's the pigs. Act straight."

All this points to the fact that Junie had grown up among sixties-ish trappings, and so Stormy, who had never left the sixties, was as familiar as her old stuffed Teddy with the eye-buttons missing. Junie instantly loved Stormy's beard and motorcycle cap and shoulder-length hair, thought his beer gut irresistible, found the scent of patchouli oil on his neck profoundly sexual. She was furthermore dazzled by the possibility of getting the musical recognition which she thought her due (and correctly: she does have a great set of pipes). Unlimited access to the best dope in town sounded pretty good, too, since Junie was a chronic insomniac (like me) and used marijuana to induce a euphoric rush followed by a steep descent into sleep. It was therefore not difficult for Stormy to convince Junie to move in with him.

"OK," said Junie.

"*Greeeaaat,*" said Stormy, in the manner of a tripper who's watching his hand make colorful contrails in the clear ether. Stormy always talked as though he were stoned, even when he wasn't.

They moved in together at once. With a line of credit from a struggling local music store (its owners needed the business so badly they were willing to take a risk on Stormy, whose TRW read like the obituary page), they bought a new state-of-the-art P.A. system, complete with sixteen channel mixer, preamp, modular effects system, digital delay, various racks and cables. They trundled all of this stuff to Stormy's house— now their steamy love nest and band headquarters.

Their dining room virtually filled with the latest in consumer electronics, the only thing remaining for Stormy and Junie to complete their band was . . . yes, musicians. At no small additional expense they ran an ad in *The Fiesta City Picayune,* a local free journal which used to feature progressive political analysis but has gradually evolved to favor upscale fashion reviews for young professionals, full-page bikini-wax ads, and a few ill-informed book reviews written by copyboys.

It still has an extensive Classifieds section, though, including an ad that read, somewhat cryptically,

> *CAN YOU SURVIVE*
> *THE MESSENGERS OF LOVE?*
>
> *Dead-icated musicians needed for high-energy*
> *intuitive excursion into light and darkness*
> *Must be ungrounded in Airplane, Cream,*
> *Hendrix, Creedence, all Blues, Big Brother.*
> *Achieving dharmic sisterhood within*
> *the circumference of musical spacetime*
> *is our goal. Bring your own comfort.*

Who could resist such a challenge? In no time they had auditioners aplenty—a gangly youth who looked like a Summer of Love-era Phil Lesh[9] on the steps of 710 Ashbury, his straight blond hair in a shoulder-length Prince Valiant cut, bangs and all; a jackbooted skinhead with ripped Levi's and lightning tattoos on his scalp; several college-age neo-freaks with smooth faces and ponytails and tiedyed T-shirts; and a couple of teenaged thrash-rockers slinging three-quarter-sized Japanese trainer guitars and wearing Metallica T-shirts under unbuttoned plaid flannel shirts. The band had a rented ministorage area in which to conduct auditions and practices, a goal and philosophy (albeit a loony, idiosyncratic confluence of the wisdom of the Far East and the retro-psychedelia of the Fillmore West), and a name—Stormy Petrel and the Messengers of Love, Starring Junie Melanchik—a passably catchy handle, but still an unknown quantity as far as the nightclubbing public was concerned.

To give the enterprise credibility they needed someone who had a reputation for being able to play . . . which, I suppose, is where I came in.

---

[9]Bass player for the Grateful Dead, in case you've been vacationing in Byelorussia for the past twenty years.

CAPTAIN ZZYZX

~~

Did I mention in the previous chapter that, like Junie Melanchik, I'm a chronic insomniac? If I did, I lied. Actually, I've been diagnosed by Dr. Moss as having apnea, a condition in which the sufferer, sleeping peacefully and dreaming of bunnies and puppies, suddenly stops breathing and wakes up with a rude start. In some people this awakening results from a blockage of the nasal airways, while in others like me, the brain simply forgets to tell the lungs to do their stuff, and one soon has the unpleasant sensation that one is being murdered with a pillow over his face.

In point of medical fact, the effect of apnea is exactly the same as that of being murdered with a pillow. In both instances one's brain gets no oxygen, and were this asphyxia to continue for more than a few minutes, one *would* die. But the brain is smart.[10] Sensing its own imminent demise, the brain's Survival Center faxes an urgent mailgram to its Wakeup Center which in turn wires the lungs to start pumping, and one starts breathing again. As you might imagine, all this suffocating and panicked waking gets the adrenals working overtime,

---

[10]Which is why they call smart people brainy.

which in turn leaves me jangled and wide awake, sometimes for as much as four hours. On such nights I have to stay in bed until ten or eleven in the morning just to get the minimum five or six hours of sleep.

It had been one of those nights. I had finally gotten to sleep about four a.m. and was having my recurring dream about the big opossum with the red and white flowers painted on its head, when the phone rang. I had forgotten to turn the ringer off before I went to sleep.

"Harmon," I barely heard a voice say.

"Hnn. What."

"It's Stormy."

I pulled aside the rubber-backed, light-tight shade that enables me to sleep late into the morning when I need to, and I looked out the window. It was sunny, and there were some birds chirping in a cheerful, irritating way. "No it's not," I said, making little effort to conceal my grumpiness. "It's nice out." This seemed like an appropriate place to wind down this pointless chat. "Bye," I said and made ready to hang up the phone.

"Wait a minute, man, it's Carl," the receiver squawked at arm's length from my ear.

"I don't know anybody named Carl," I grumped. Actually this was untrue, since my next door neighbor when I was a kid was named Carl Schwinn. He's the one whose parents used to hold his hand over the stove when he was bad. I hadn't had any contact with Carl Schwinn since he joined the Marines after high school and eagerly went to Vietnam (he came back in a bag) or with anyone else named Carl for that matter; so, while not strictly accurate, my riposte to this morning's caller was understandable.

"Yes you do, man. Carl Petrel. You know, Stormy."

"Oh, Stormy," I said, getting it and resigning myself to the fact that I was awake and probably would remain so for the duration of this loathsome day. "What time is it anyway?" I asked.

"Ten-fifteen. Did I wake you up?"

For some reason, when people wake you up they always ask you if they woke you up, even if they know from your tone of voice that they did wake you up. Even more unreasonably, they always expect you to say something like, "Oh, no, I was already awake. I sound like this because I recently sprained my tongue and I have it taped up." I wasn't about to let Stormy off that easily. "Yes you did," I said emphatically. "I was dreaming about a possum with painted flowers on its head."

Stormy had carefully outlined the strategy by which he would convince me to join his new band, and he wasn't about to be deterred by illustrated opossums. He said, "Possums, that's *greeeat!* Nocturnal, right? Hey, I just got back from Albert King." His plan clearly involved easing me into a performing mood with stories about the concerts he had seen recently.

This was an unfair tactic, and effective. Stormy knew that I had built my own guitar-playing style meticulously upon patterns I had learned from watching Albert King in person and from listening to him on my old Silvertone hi-fi until the grooves in his records were smooth. For a time, I even performed with an unlit cherrywood pipe in my mouth, in emulation of my hero and his trademark briar. At Stormy's mention of Albert I brisked up, as though slapped across both cheeks with antifreeze, and asked, "Oh yeah? How was he?"

"He went between being pissed off and brilliant. The backup band—not his usual for some reason—was really bad. He would start a song and then end up swearing at the drummer, and at one point he threw his pipe at a guy. And then he kind of, you know, let it go for a while and then got pissed off again. They never did get the sound right. Listening to his band was like fucking without a hard-on," he said by way of summing up the evening's entertainment, "but it was still Albert."

"I'm glad I decided not to go," I said. Actually, there had been little decision involved, since I rarely go to concerts any more, not even Albert King's. Too expensive, too much noise, too much smoke in the air, plus you have to put up with drunk or stoned-out kids falling on you all the time, just as I used to do. I'd rather spend my money on recordings nowadays.

"Good move, Elston. It sucked," Stormy said. For a reason known only to Stormy, he had started calling me Elston Howard a couple of years previous and never stopped. "But you've got to see the Arthur Lee tour when they come here. Junie and I went to see them at the Masonic in Oakland, and they were *astouuunding*. They sounded just like themselves. It was uncanny. They sounded so much like themselves I knew it was them."

If you weren't stoned-out or Stormy, you often had no chance of comprehending the precise meaning in some of Stormy's abstractions, but if you allowed yourself to be swept along in the metatextual current, you could get what he was talking about, sort of. It required practice, but I had spent enough time around Stormy to become pretty proficient at it. Here, for instance, he was making a phenomenological observation concerning the way in which sense experience can alter the passage of decades so that the intervening space-time is collapsed into a single mathematical point. In Stormy's mind a past Arthur Lee concert and the present one had merged into one expanded moment, like a dying galaxy drawing in upon itself and sucking all its disparate flesh and plastic and metal back into its own vortex, and for Stormy this was a profound and epiphanic event. He continued reverently, "They did everything I wanted them to do, too. I really couldn't believe it. They did 'Seven Seven Is', and 'Alone Again More' and 'And More Again'."

"I never heard of those songs."

"I guess it's the age difference," he theorized. He was probably right. The years between us placed a late-teenaged Carl Petrel squarely in the Panhandle of Golden Gate Park in '67, dosed out of his mind and dancing in the streets, while Harmon Nails III was still adding mint plate blocks to his stamp collection and feeling no more kinship to the hippies than he did to the aphids or the earthworms. "You must have heard 'My Little Red Book,' though," Stormy postulated.

"Oh sure, on the oldies channel. But I thought it was Tom Jones singing. It sounded like somebody's Vegas act." I knew this would bug him.

"No, man," Stormy cried, "it's heavy! But the best is their obscure, mystical stuff, and they did all that at the show, and there were enough people there who knew what it was to make it a significant thing. There's, you know, lots of people who were there or they're just getting there now, and those are the people we're trying to get to with this thing we're doing."

"Which thing are you talking about?" I asked, beginning to feel as though I were ballooning amid clouds pregnant with vagueness.

"The band, Elston, the band."

"Ah, the band," I said, relieved to have a concrete noun on which I could rest my balloon's gondola before the next Stormy gust of abstraction carried me away again.

"Yes, the band. It's been, you know, developing nicely. This one's been a real learning experience. I've been giving myself weekly assignments, and it's really helped my playing."

"All right!" I enthused. "Anything that helps your playing has to be a good thing."

Sometimes you can't help ribbing Stormy. He's such an R. Crumb cartoon with his big beard and stoney grin and Gautama belly. You know he'll never haul off and slug you, especially over the phone. Usually, Stormy will take a joke aimed directly at him, and he'll either sidestep it with his customary maniacal gush of laughter—"Haha*haaaaaa!*"—or else he'll surprise you by benevolently shooting a good one back at you. To my present jab he offered no response whatever and then went on, "So that's been great. The bass situation is still up in the air. We've been playing with an excellent bass player, but his playing might not be good for blues."

"What might his bass playing be good for? Creating earthquake sounds for disaster movies?" I joshed.

"I don't know. I don't know," Stormy replied seriously. "I guess you'd call it kind of Jazz-Pop-Fusion. He tends to be real busy, you know? On some of the more improvisational-type numbers, like 'Lovelight' where you want to get kind of Dead-ish, he does fine, but like on straight-ahead blues like 'Tore Down' he just bugs the shit out of me."

"That can get on your nerves after a while," I sympathized, because I knew what he meant. A bass player who keeps good time, comes down heavy on the two and four, and uses notes sparingly, is hard to find.

"Eggscrackly," he agreed. "We might be able to make it work, but if he doesn't, there's this other really *greeeat* bass player I know, who coaches the Fiesta City Youth Boxing Club. He's from Bakersfield."

"Ooh, say no more. If he's from Bakersfield, he's got to be good."

Stormy performed a bit of psychic Aikido on this witticism, allowing it to pass by and be consumed by the same negative energy that gave it momentary life. "He's the best bass player I've ever heard in my life, and he's my age, so he already knows all this music. It's his music. He plays it instinctively. The problem is he has all sorts of commitments like with the Boxing Club, plus he works nights as night auditor at the El Conquistador Motor Hotel."

"I don't know what that means, but it sounds pretty im-portant."

"I'm sure it means nothing and it's totally unimportant. Like all jobs." He paused to let the anarchic weight of this last assertion settle, like a big black crow landing noisily on a chimney grate, and then roared, "Hahahaaaa. Haha*hahaha*. Ha*haaaa!*"

It's a curious thing about Stormy. When you hang around him or talk to him for a while, you start to feel as though you've been doing bhang hits off a slab of blond Afghani hash for the past hour. I guess that's what they mean by contact high, because contact with Stormy does unquestionably alter your consciousness, whether he's high or not. You soon find yourself noticing that the world has taken on a slightly tilted, pulsating quality and that you've simultaneously begun to feel as though there's nothing solid on which you can stand, neither your clean, well-dusted living room, nor your ritual pastimes, nor the lull of your own thoughts. Everything seems more cosmically absurd than usual—which is how the world must appear all the time to Stormy—and before long you even start talking like him, even though you're determined not to. *"Greeeeat,"* I said, "Haha*hahaha."*

"Hahahahaha," he agreed, delighted to have someone sharing the vacuum with him. "Anyway," he went on, "the drummer's great, his fills really pump. He's a full-blooded Cherokee, my age with a ponytail. He used to play in bands before he went into the joint for dealing and he's seen it all. Now he's born-again, but not obnoxious about it. The piano player's probably the weakest improviser, cause I got him right out of the music department and all he knows is sight reading Chopin and shit, but he's getting dragged along by the rest of the band and he can play 'Minglewood' just like Pigpen now."

"Sounds like music to me."

"It is. It is. It's *experiential.* Every time we get together there are moments that sound better than some of the moments from the time before, so that's encouraging. But the thing is," he said, pausing and intaking his breath dramatically, "we need you, Elston."

As in the case of his proposal to Junie, Stormy needn't have spent the six preceding pages of dialogue working up to this appeal. I had already made up my mind to play with him, because the enterprise would require no practice on my part. As a guitarist Stormy had no talent for improvisation but an uncanny knack for listening to lead breaks and mimicking them note for note, rest for rest, inflection for inflection, and so on. Therefore, while Stormy was maintaining the song's compositional integrity, I could lay back, comping tasteful triadic sevenths and ninths and fingerpicking rhythm fills, and on the numbers that required some free-form, harmolodic improvisation, all I had to do was hammer down on my overdrive foot switch, crank the Strat's volume pot all the way up, and stretch my fifty-foot shielded cable to the limit as I walked through the crowd wailing, shrieking or crooning through my new Marshall's two twelve-inch JBL's, all of which I knew would be effective discharge for the Gin-sorrow which continued to overtake me in waves. Catharsis, as my former shrink, Liz, might call it.

Furthermore, everyone knows that playing in a band is a *greeeaat* way to meet women, and I was starting to get—how do you say in English?—no, not horny; more like, well, I guess horny comes pretty close. I told Stormy, "Sure, I'll come to a couple practices, see how the chemistry is. One thing, though."

"What?"

"A stipulation. About the name."

"Whose name?"

"The band's name."

"You have a problem with Stormy Petrel and the Messengers of Love, starring Junie Melanchik?" He sounded a freckle wounded.

"I love Stormy Petrel and the Messengers of Love, starring Junie Melanchik. It's just that a while back I made myself a promise that the next time I was in an electric band, it would be called Captain Zzyzx."

"Captain Zizzy?" Stormy sounded bewildered, which for him was a stretch. Most of the time he was merely (and happily) dazed and confused.

"Zzyzx. It's a long story."

The Captain Zzyzx story really isn't that long, compared to some.[11] It involved my former roommate Russ Thrasher, with whom I used to drive to Vegas occasionally, on expeditions to the Stardust Hotel where we played in the five-ten Razz game

---

[11]Such as the story of my childhood Star of David, which went on almost as long as my childhood itself.

they had there. On our first trip, the last bluebooks of spring
semester handed in, we took the Pearblossom cutoff west and
hit I-15 at midday, unaware that even in early June the Mojave
routinely hits a hundred-plus. With no air conditioning in
Geranno (the faded blue Dodge Dart owned by Thrasher for
several months before its cylinder head cracked under the terrible strain of Thrasher's heavy-footed driving), and windows
and wind-wings therefore opened wide to the onrush of su-
perheated desert air, we sank back into the plasticized, non-
bucket front carseat and sweated freely, the sweat drying almost immediately upon its exudation from our pores, so that
gradually a layer of salty urea caked our immovable limbs and
bare torsos.

Stuffed with Bun Boy cheeseburgers and homemade cherry
pie after a roadside stop near Baker (a name as appropriate as
L.A.'s is unfitting), we had most of the drive behind us and
were feeling the same sapless jubilation that old-timey travel-
ers must have felt after a making treacherous passage across
arid badlands and pulling into a Bun Boy in one desiccated
piece. It was around four in the afternoon. I was driving along
stuporously in the slow lane, mouth open, head lolled back
against the seat-top (no headrests in those days), when up
ahead loomed the most peculiar road sign I had ever seen. Actually, it was in every way a normal road sign—green sheet-
metal rectangle having rounded corners and mounted on
parallel-sunk four-bys—and unremarkable except for two
things: its placement in the middle of a desert otherwise devoid of human artifact, and its terse signifier, "Zzyzx Road."

At first I believed the sign to be a delusional symptom of
heatstroke, and I squinted several times to make it go away,
but it didn't. "Zzyzx Road," it still said. As we approached
Zzyzx Road, I found myself compelled, as though caught in
some irresistible flux-vortex, to veer off the highway and onto
the offramp.

"What are you doing?" Thrasher shouted the first words either of us had uttered for a while, it being virtually impossible

to hear over the hot wind rushing into and around Geranno's interior.

"I don't know. I have to check this out," I shouted back.

"Check out what?" Thrasher shouted. "We're almost there." Since we had slowed to twenty or so, there was really no longer any need to shout, but Thrasher kept on shouting anyway.

"Zzyzx Road. I have to get off for a second," I shouted back.

Thrasher shrugged. If ever a soul understood about having to get off, Thrasher did. "Well, if you have to," he said philosophically, no longer shouting.

The offramp curved away perpendicularly from I-15, and we found ourselves on a stretch of single-lane blacktop heading out into the desert with no apparent destination. I followed Zzyzx Road slowly for a while, through a parched moonscape of rakish rubble-drifts and skeletal, gnarled cholla trees. Thrasher looked from me to the passing scenery and back to me again, as though I might have some wisdom to share with him. My mouth was still open, but I wasn't producing wisdoms or anything else audible, although I might have been wheezing subsonically from the dry desert air.

After having driven a couple of miles with no end in sight, I turned Geranno around and headed back onto the highway, while Thrasher with stony impassivity watched the world go by. We picked up speed, and as the wind began to whip and roar again, I laughed out loud, considering: What whimsical highway engineer, what Ionesco or Artaud of asphalt and bridgespan, had the tilted notion to build a road with neither destination nor functional reason for existing, and then, for a name, to assign it a jumble of letters at the end of the alphabet, so that motorists from Orange County might scratch their cruise-controlled collective heads and be transported into mystical realms by the sign's manifold connotations— "Z" for terminality asserted with capital force; "z" for lowercase dead ends within larger terminal sets (suggesting that inside the universe, which will collapse someday, stars die; within star systems, which will burn out someday, planets go

cold; on planets, individuals like you and I are born and disappear; and so on for cells and atoms and zipping muons that
are energy itself); "y" for this vale of plaintive interrogations
without reply; "z" for a final, gentler reminder of finalities,
almost silly in its repetition this time, like a cartoon character
sawing wood in imitation of sleep-sounds; and then the void,
the little "x," the null set to which everything — us, our cars
and burger stands and road signs, our earth and its whirling,
spinning planet neighbors and all the galaxies — must return,
and all you can do is laugh at the prospect, because it's
funny.[12]

"What's so funny?" Thrasher shouted.

"Nothing," I said, but he didn't hear me.

"Drive on, Captain Zzyzx," Thrasher shouted, and for
several months after that he continued to call me Captain
Zzyzx until we both forgot about it.

"Zizzix?" said Stormy.

"Right," I said, "Captain Zzyzx. It's something my old
roommate used to call me."

"What does it mean?"

"Nothing," I said to Stormy, as I had to Thrasher years earlier. Thrasher was dead now. His heart exploded while he was
playing frisbee a couple of years ago — probably aided by the
crystal meth to which he was so partial — which set me back a
bit, rehab-wise. I'm fine now, though. Really I am, and on my
most recent drive back from Vegas, as I passed under the
Zzyzx roadsign, the earlier episode returned to me in a flood
of Pepsi-induced sentimentality, and I promised Thrasher's
memory that I'd call my next band Captain Zzyzx if I ever had

---

[12]For a more historically accurate account of Zzyzx Road, read Rae, Cheri,
East Mojave Desert: A Visitor's Guide (Santa Barbara: Olympus Press,
1989). The real story — something about a utopian developer named Doc
Springer who built an exclusive health spa in the world's most inhospitable
area and then got busted for tax evasion — turns out to be weirder than my
imagined one.

another band. "It is an *incomprehensible,*" I added to Stormy, quoting from *Doctor Syntax.*

I knew this would sway Stormy, who equates incomprehensible with desirable. "Captain Zizzix," he mused. "Well, yes, I like it, hey now, Captain Zizzix. It sounds *greeeaaat!*" he enthused agreeably. "I'll call you with details. Junie will be mindblown. She loves your playing."

"I'm sure Junie already is mindblown, living with you."

"Hahaaahahaha! See you, Elston, you Schimmelpennick Cigar."

I had no more clue as to why he called me a Schimmelpennick Cigar than I had about why he called me Elston Howard, which made his calling me both Elston Howard *and* a Schimmelpennick Cigar unbearably hilarious. "Hahahaaahaha!" I said, and in that moment of abandon I considered once again: As much as we all yearn for security and peace of mind, we must also yearn for a disruptive force in our lives, an adversarial ally whom we allow every now and then to shake things up. For some people dope serves this purpose, and if you can stay loaded without busting a ventricle or parboiling your brain, then say Yes by all means. I can't, and I've seen substances take several good friends down. If you're on the other side of detox like me, you might try playing music, or listening. There's nothing quite like a genial melody or well-turned lyric to loosen one's metaphysical moorings and set one asail in far-flung cosmic regions. If that doesn't work, get a new friend who calls you a Schimmelpennick Cigar — a big, untethered, goofy, spiritual fizzhead of a confrere whose very presence rototills and backhoes the clayey hardpan of your ordinary reality and busts up the crusty clods of your belief systems. In the presence of any piece of heavy grading or trenching machinery, however, one is well advised to be careful, to wear one's hard hat and not take one's drowsymaking allergy pills and so on, and it's the same with Carl Petrel. Toward the end of this conversation I was dangerously close to losing control and, in a jag of laughter, aspirating my own vomitus.

"Hahaaahahaha!" I raged, "Swear to God you kill me, Stormy. See you man. Hahaaahahaha!"

Stormy said placidly, "Drive on, Captain Zzyzx," impossibly intuiting Thrasher's slogan even though I hadn't told him the story.

ONDINE

THE
FUCKPAW [13]

～

ot two days after throwing in with Captain
Zzyzx, I received another invitation, this one
to join a poetry group some local writers were
forming. This puts me in mind of the weather-
man who originally came up with the salty ad-
age, "When it rains It pours." The homeboy who invented
this saying must have been loaded on monoamine oxide inhi-
bitors, or else he never visited Fiesta City. Granted, there are
those occasions when frigid air masses, heavy and asphalt-gray
with moisture picked up along the Alcan highway, bully their
way over the San Gorgonio foothills and into our temperate
Mediterranean balminess. Then It can't do anything but
pour. But more often—for eight months out of the year, in

---

[13]I debated about using this semi-obscene phrase as the leadoff header in
Part Two. I liked its flagrancy but feared that certain deviant personalities
might, upon seeing "Fuckpaw" in the Table of Contents, turn directly to
this chapter, thus skipping the vital exposition that precedes it. Then I
remembered a former prof who said it doesn't matter where you start or
finish a truly contemporary story, since beginnings or endings are only illu-
sions anyway. If it satisfies some readers' curiosity to find out about the Fuckpaw first, who am I to stand in their rutty way?

fact — when it rains It mists, because the land heats up and the warm air rises and draws wet clouds off the ocean. If the cloud cover gets a bit thicker, it drizzles, and sometimes, if the inversion layer drops down to ground level, it lets fall a genuine raindrop and then after a while another, and maybe yet another. Maybe not. It was in this latter precipitative mode that I seemed to be receiving creative opportunities. While I wasn't exactly being deluged by them, they did seem to be falling on out of the sky with some regularity, a single dewy bombard at a time.

At first I had no idea why the writers invited me. Since I'd never had one of my few song lyrics published or performed onstage by anyone, there's no way the charter members of this literary society could have seen any promise in them. As it turned out, Richard Bindhover, one of the Consortium's charter members, was a jazz purist and would-be guitarist and had admired my playing from afar. A long time ago (before I met Gin, even), Richard, a thinnish dude with a face like a muskellunge, used to come up to me between sets at the now-defunct Gander Club and talk about the virtues of partial chords and inversions over fully strummed chords, about the most recent modifications he'd made to his old Gibson ES hollowbody, about scale fingerings he had discovered, and so on, while I would pretend to listen.

In one of these brief chats I must have mentioned that I take quill to scroll from time to time, because it was The Bindhover who was presently calling me and asking if I wanted to participate in the group — tentatively named the Fiesta City Consortium of Poets and Writers. An unfortunate choice of names, I thought. Because of its length and the awkward arrangement of its diphthongs and alliterations and so on, the name fairly begs for truncation, but when stripped down to its essential consonants, FCCPW sounds either masturbatory, like 'Fuckpaw,' or incestuous, like 'Fuck Pa,' or sacrilegious, like 'Fuckpew;' so acronymization is out of the question and you're stuck with the whole bloody pretentious mouthful, unless you like to say Fuckpaw anyway, as I sometimes do.

I responded to The Bindhover's invitation with more ambivalence than when Stormy asked me to join the Messengers.
Historically I've not been prone to joining clubs of any kind,
whether social, literary, political or otherwise. This reluctance
might date back to my negative association with the Cub
Scouts, the meetings of which always seemed to be exercises
in boy's inhumanity to boy. Inevitably at such gatherings the
majority of kids would select one of their number to undergo
some form of quasi-sexual humiliation, the most popular of
these being the infamous "pink belly," in which the unlucky
laddiebuck was forcibly stripped to the waist and pinioned to
the ground by several of the heavier kids, while the two or
three who had their hands free took turns whacking his belly
smartly with their palms until said belly turned pink or until
the kid cried, whichever came last. During such events I, having neither the sort of homophobic rage that would compel
me to torture one of my peers, nor the courage to go up
against an entire troop of Cubs in uniform and neckerchief,
stood off to the side, lobbing pyrocantha berries idly at
Audrey, the sleepy hound who was our den's mascot.

I composed one of my earliest lyrics on such an occasion. A
sort of proto-haiku scribbled on a piece of three-holed, lined
composition paper in one of my gradeschool PeeChee folders,
it went something like,

> *Hurting boys is mean*
> *so stop or Ill kill you*
> *with poisen berrys.*

This promising trifle, if botanically inaccurate,[14] reveals my
sympathy for one whom society has chosen randomly to hu-
miliate, and should be ample evidence that my aversion to
clubs was well developed, even at an early age. By the time I
was an adult, I had become adept at dodging not only such

---

[14]The fruit of the pyrocantha won't kill you, even if you eat handfuls of
them.

obviously dehumanizing organizations as the armed forces, but I was also shunning fraternities, surfing associations, chess clubs, Jane Austen societies, bowling leagues, and even Amnesty International and Oxfam, whose fundamental reverence for freedom and food I shared. Therefore, it should come as no surprise that my first reaction to The Bindhover's invitation to join his poetry group was a spontaneous raising of the soft palate, a retraction of the tongue combined with a contraction of throat muscle and diaphragm—a gag response, with the Fuckpaw playing the role of stimulating digit.

Sometimes, if he's not feeling whipsawed by chemical imbalances, Harmon Nails can rise above his kneejerk conditioned responses. In this case I was able to see beyond my club-revulsion, to recognize my joining this poetry group as an occasion for personal growth. The Fiesta City Consortium of Poets and Writers would force me to start working on songs, it would allow me to plumb the dark, moist, labyrinthine mysteries of my own anima in a confidential and supportive environment, and—most compelling—it would redress my horniness. Being in a poetry group would, I calculated, increase my chances of meeting females of character, literacy, taste and construction.

Consider for a moment the state lottery or the dollar slots in Vegas. With either, your chances of making the Big Hit are, to put it optimistically, negligible (unless you consider thirteen mil to one a shoe-in). But basic probability theory tells us that negligible odds are better than no odds at all, and if you doesn't pay your buck you gots no chance. So it is with meeting members of the opposite sex, and take heed ye readers who are yearning desperately for significant others but don't know how to get yourself one: Put yourself in places which will up your chances of meeting Mr. or Ms. Acceptable. If, for example, you yearn for an outdoorswoman—one who shares your love of tramping up and down hill and dale heedless of sunstroke, snakebite, leaves of three, malaria, encephalitis, or sexual assault at the hands of Beelzebub's Bondsmen or other outlaw bikers you might meet on the trail—then join the Sierra Club. One evening, on returning from a day-long pack into the backcountry, you may find yourself paired up with a robust Nordic wench, a veritable Valkyrie with cheeks like waxed gravensteins, flowing flaxen hair and flanks like a thoroughbred's. You may look into each other's eyes just as the sun dips beneath a violet-hued and jagged horizon, and you'll both know this is finally It, baby. Conversely, if you're more interested in a woman who can free-climb up one side of a sonnet and rappel down the other, who can cook up a villanelle and set it out piping hot and chock full of smiling similes, measured metonymies and feminine rhymes, one who is understated, petite, slightly formal on the exterior but who hides a floe of molten passion beneath her crinolines and stays, then you ought to join a poetry society.

For that reason I said Yes to The Bindhover. I even went so far as to volunteer my drawing room for the regular meeting place of the Fuckpaw. A poetry group must be held in a drawing room, with a variety of herbal teas and almond-flavored Italian toasts within reach of the participants. Besides, if my heart's next dream turned out to be a member of the group, it wouldn't hurt to impress her with my mainland-Chinese throwrugs, my library (which, if lacking in volumes of contemporary verse, does contain an extensive collection of Zap! and Marvel and Scrooge McDuck comix, along with both volumes of the Cromden Anthology of English Poetry), my tiny *microstomichethiobriousbashforddini*, and my collection of living cacti which Gin brought back from the desert. Some women feel secure and trusting when they see that a guy can keep plants for more than a few weeks without killing them. Also, since I wouldn't have to drive my car to my own drawing room, I'd save gas. It doesn't hurt to be frugal, even if you have an inheritance . . . especially when your only paying job consists of two nights at the Holiday Inn, no cover.

~/~

A dismal scene, one worthy of the most depressing Gothic novel by Brontë,[15] was unfolding in the Nails drawing room, where my cacti, my rugs and my tiny *microstomichethiobrious-bashforddini*, instead of basking in the warm regard of a petticoated beauty, were being palpated, downtrodden, or ignored entirely by the assembled poets, semiprecious few of whom were women. I was bummed by the lack of femininity in the room, which just proves a Motto I've only recently discovered and by which I now run my life: Never look forward to anything, and always expect the worst.

This isn't as pessimistic as it sounds. In fact, it's meant to have just the opposite effect. You may have noticed that if you anticipate having a good time at some future event, say a dinner party or poetry gathering, it's more than likely that you'll be disappointed, since Life deals out its good times sparingly and Reality rarely matches one's fantasies of future pleasures. If, on the other hand, you anticipate having an absolutely

---

[15]Or Brönte, or wherever she put the damned umlaut. What was an Englishwoman doing with an umlaut anyway; who did she think she was, some thrash-metal group like Mëgacroüp or Büttdëth?

hideous time at the same event, it's equally likely that you'll be pleasantly surprised, since Life deals out the truly hideous times judiciously, too. In the midst of said event you'll be so happy you're not having a hideous time that you'll think you're having a good time even if you're not, and so you *will* in effect be having a good time. It works for me, anyway.

Unfortunately, the first meeting of the Fuckpaw took place before I discovered this clever mind-trick, so I had eagerly anticipated the gathering. I had believed naïvely[16] that its composition would be heavily and happily weighted on the side of females, since I didn't think most males considered poetry a manly thing to do. As you've already heard me observe, there are certain pursuits, such as dogie-wrestling, prize-fighting and urinating for distance, to which men seem biologically drawn like maggots to mulch, while there are other pursuits from which males seem to steer clear, such as seminars in French language and culture, or classes in tushercise and slymnastics. I had assumed that poetry groups would fall into the second category, since versifying involves a certain sensitivity and neurasthenia which your average puffed up, swaggering macho dude spends much of his life training himself not to reveal, even if he possesses them. However, this preconception about the relative gender-density of poets was a gross error, one which could have been corrected by a single glance at the Cromden Anthology, which reveals—and surprisingly to me—that it was mostly men who have written poetry throughout history. Maybe it's because men, who traditionally repress their feelings more than women, need something safe, cryptic and ambiguous, like a metaphor, in which to couch their expressions. Or maybe it's because, as Ondine insists, the publishing industry is run by piggy sexist males who publish other piggy males like Pope and Pound and so on.

Whatever the reason, the composition of the poetry group on this evening was following historical precedent by running four-to-one in favor of the men . . . which is why I was

---

[16]naivëly?

bummed. Going around the circle of chairs in the same direction that filthy bath water runs down a drainhole — that is, clockwise — one could see: The Bindhover, champing placidly on a mint-filled Milano cookie; Digby Bhowles, a wispy, rum-soaked and prematurely-aged Associate Professor at the U, best known for his habit of walking down the halls while singing operatic arias at full volume or conversing with himself in Italian; Jean Pathingen, also a university lecturer who, having cornered the market in Business English, taught eager young drones-to-be writing techniques crucial for pandering to the military-industrial complex; Dottie St. Cyr, mother of four, who had a master's in library science and worked in the Research Department of the public library downtown and hated the homeless people who slept there; Reed Garth, a construction worker and songwriter who once had a set of lyrics recorded by The Maple Bluff Boys, for which he received a hundred bucks but no royalties or credit; and me, Harmon Nails III, our host, who was busying himself by preparing the herbal teas.

I was standing in the kitchen, with the kettle shrilling and sibilating not far from my ear, which is why I missed the doorbell's ring. I loaded teapot, cups and napkins onto my Ms Pac-Man tray and proceeded to carry same to the other charter Fuckpaws, when, turning the corner from kitchen to dining room, I practically ran into a devastatingly beautiful woman chatting amiably with The Bindhover. I gaped at this stunning newcomer to the party, barely able to accept the testimony of my eyes, which kept insisting on one irrefutable datum: The woman standing before me was Ondine, the same red-headed dozer I had found by Gin's pond, except now she was in my house, her shod feet were on my People's Republic silk rug, and her befreckled hand was extending itself, awaiting the poignant passage of a bone-china teacup from host to guest.

Ondine's hair was still the color of persimmons plumped but not quite ripened on the stalk, but now, instead of being pulled up tightly to one side as it had been when I last saw her, it cascaded in wanton ringlets and brazen coilings about her angular cheekbones and jaw lines. She was a couple of inches shorter than I so that, even though she was standing now instead of lying pondside, she had to look up at me, and her closely-set Easter-blue eyes once again seemed to fix on a point somewhere beyond my skull, heavenward, as though she were receiving a private beatitude from a minor god residing in my attic, among rolls of spun fiberglass insulation. She acknowledged this blessing, or my presence, or both, with a slight widening of the eyes and an almost imperceptible drawing up of the corners of her mouth, like a young child sitting for a portrait, happily patient in her encircling innocence.

Ondine had on a sheath of some kind of pastel-flowered, semi-transparent material which, while it didn't hug her body exactly or accentuate her contours, allowed a diffuse, radiant allure to pour forth, creating a kind of suprasexual nimbus which made her appear divine in an archetypal sort of way, a Diana without the tiny wind-waves frothing and lapping at her delicate ankles or one of those nymphs that you see in ginger ale ads nowadays, except that this woman was on my rug instead of the halfshell. All of which just goes to illustrate another of my Mottoes, a sort of corollary to the previous one: Let go of your expectations and they will be met, sometimes. No sooner had I abandoned all hope of meeting my dream-apparition at this poetry gathering, than she rang the doorbell and walked right into my life, or at least my dining room.

"Hi," she said while I gaped. "You must be Harmon they told me whose house we're in, you look like you're going about your hostly chores." She gestured toward the tea-tray still in my hands. "I'm Ondine."

"I know," I ventured. My tongue seemed to have lost elasticity, my salivary glands their secretiveness, so that my statement came out, *"Anh oh,"* as if I had suddenly lapsed into an obscure Vietnamese dialect.

"You know me?" she asked, genuinely surprised. "How?"

"I saw you once," I said, struggling mightily to articulate the words.

"Where?"

"Up at Squalor Holler."

"Oh yeah? What were you doing up there?"

"My girlfriend — my *former* girlfriend — used to live up
there."

She paused for a moment to reflect. "Ahhh, yeah *yeah.*
You're *that* Harmon, the one who plays guitar. Gin's ex."

"I'm that Harmon." If she didn't remember me, she had at
least heard of my legendary guitar playing, which was better
than nothing. Plus, she knew I was no longer attached to Gin,
which knowledge couldn't hurt my chances with her, either.

"I never made the connection until now, maybe I figured
nobody with a house this nice would be tight with someone
who had a house as tacky as Gin."

Strangely, I felt moved to defend Gin. "Her place wasn't so
bad, really," I said. "Gin's furnishing taste just runs to the early American."

"Early chicken coop is more like it but I'm not making a
judgment, it reminds me of the house I grew up in in St.
Louis, I have fond memories of that place, you know, because
. . . You saw me while you were visiting Gin?" Ondine
sometimes skips over the ends of her would-be sentences, as
though she believes that vocalizing the beginning and middle
of each idea imparts sufficient meaning as to render comple-
tion unnecessary, there being more pressing meanings to impart in subsequent fragments, all of which she concatenates
into one extended, multifoliate, hydra-headed, comma-
spliced syntagm. So many thoughts, so little time.

"No, actually the time I saw you I wasn't going up to visit
Gin," I explained. "I just happened to have misplaced something I needed and I was looking for it, and there you were
by the pond. You were sleeping." I lost myself for a space in
the recollection of that sylvan glade, the soft voice of the
winds, the supreme exhilaration of my spirit at that first sight
of the woman now before me.

"So did you find it?" she said.

"What?" I asked, yanked back to the present by her question, the original context of which had been displaced by my momentary flight of fancy.

"You said you lost something by the pond."

"Ah. Right. I played a job the night before and then I went to Gin's house, and then the next day when I went to practice I didn't have my favorite flatpick, so I thought maybe I dropped it at Gin's somewhere. It was a rare pick, made out of real tortoiseshell. You know how hard those are to come by."

"Oh don't you feel sorry for the tortoises that got killed just so people could pick guitars with them? I think that's *meeean.*" I've since learned that 'mean' is a critical category into which Ondine routinely places any endeavor that doesn't embody the highest expression of human potentiality. If, for example, she watches a news story featuring a deranged ex-Green Beret who just gunned down a playground full of kids with an over-the-counter AK-47, Ondine, apparently having no interest in considering the role Nixon and Agnew might have played in making this poor Joe go over the edge, will make a comment like, "That's so mean, how could someone do something like that, they ought to string him up by the balls."

Similarly, if we're watching a classic film — let's say it's that Bogart flick in which everyone wants the bird statue for some reason which I forget and they're all killing each other for it — Ondine will blind herself to the deeper thematic implications of human greed and ambition and will react only to superficial devices of plotting. "He was mean," she'll whisper to me in the middle of the film. Ondine doesn't care that the perpetrator of said meanness is a character and not a real person, nor does she seem aware that the author is manipulating her feelings toward the 'mean' characters just as I'm manipulating the reader right now to have certain reactions to Ondine (except that Ondine is real, of course). For Ondine, the merit of a particular piece rests solely upon its meanness-to-niceness ratio. Thus, romantic comedies with breezy complications and happy endings are invariably accorded four stars by Ondine, while

cinéma-verité efforts, especially those which attempt to improve us by casting man's baser impulses in harsh light, will
be uniformly panned. "That was stupid," she'll say savagely.
"Everybody was *very* mean."

To her current accusation of meanness on the part of the
tortoiseshell flatpick industry (and my implied complicity in
that meanness), I replied, "I don't think they make tortoiseshell picks anymore. That's why they're so hard to come
by. Besides, I'd never support an industry that killed endangered animals. I won't even kill the little pill bugs that show
up in my bathtub every morning. I take them outside."

This is true, by the way. I don't have a stomach for killing
things and never have. One time when there was no surf, I
went clamming with my friend Robert "Gooey Bob" Hughes
who hated grad school as much as I did, and while I enjoyed
the effort of digging under boulders at low tide, got a thrill
at turning up clams like gold nuggets under wet sand, I never
had the heart to throw the defenseless little smilers into boiling water. I could almost hear their clammy voices upraised in
a polyphony of mortal dread. Moved by their collective distress, I gave them all to Gooey Bob and abandoned my brief
career as a clammer. Same with pill bugs: I don't have the
heart to drown them, inoffensive as they are, so I let them
crawl on my hands and carry them outside and dump them
among the ferns . . . except when I'm in a hurry or have an
edge on from lack of sleep. Then I apologize and wash them
down the drain, back to wherever they came from.

Hearing of my humaneness seemed to bring a sparkle back
to Ondine's mood, which had tarnished somewhat since we
started talking about dead tortoises. "Good for you," she said
exuberantly.

"Pill bugs are crustaceans, by the way, and not really bugs."
Since I was on a roll with the pill bugs, I thought I'd impress
her with a bit of zoological trivia I learned from Gin.

"You mean like crabs?"

"That's right, like crabs and lobsters."

"When I was little I used to think crabs and lobsters were

big bugs that crawled around underwater, I didn't know they were crust stations."

"That's right, bugs are bugs and crabs are crustaceans, and so are pillbugs. They all probably have a common evolutionary ancestor, though." I was getting in over my head here. I really don't know that much about the origin of species, just the usual stuff: Darwin was at home in Surrey cataloguing pigeon varieties when he suddenly got bored and decided to sail around the world, ending up on one of the Galapagos Islands where he came across . . . what? Beagles, I think. That's the extent of my acquaintance with natural selection, a rad idea to be sure, and one which changed the way intelligent people (this necessarily excludes Bible-thumping creationists) think about themselves, but if it's true for beagles, so it must be with bugs and crabs.

Ondine, apparently not fascinated by the ancestry of sow bugs and seafood, threw up a barricade to impede any further progress down this avenue of scientific inquiry. "So did you find it?" she asked.

"Find what?"

"The pick."

"No, and I gave up trying to get another one. They're harder and harder to find, which is a bummer because there's nothing like the feel of real tortoiseshell. There's more friction or bite or something against the string. Do you play?"

"I play guitar some but I never quite got the feel of using a pick so I just use my fingers. And my thumb. It's not quite as loud but it sounds all right, you know what I mean?"

"I'd like to hear you play. Maybe we could play together some time."

"Play together," she said, with a tinge of wariness to her tone.

"Play some music, pick some tunes."

"That would be all right."

"Greeat," I said, doing a barely passable Stormy.

"Great," she said, not enthusiastically but not patronizingly, either. "I used to play music with people a lot before I moved here, but it's kind of hard being in a new place, you know what I mean?"

"I think I do. So how'd you end up here, anyway?"

"Tonight, to the poetry reading?"

"No, Fiesta City. You said you came here from somewhere else."

"Yeah well what specifically brought me here was I was living in Sedona, I moved there because—"

"Sedona . . . " I interjected with an inflection that indicated geographic ignorance.

"You don't know where Sedona is?" she asked, amazed at my lack of New-Age cultural literacy, as though I didn't know what brown rice was.

"Sorry, I don't. Maybe I misplaced it along with my pick."

If she appreciated my attempt at a joke, she didn't indicate it. "Sedona's in Arizona near the Hopi land, I'm surprised you never heard of it, it's where the vibrational currents that run through the planet are supposed to come together, you know there's chakras in the body and Sedona is like a chakra on the planet and what that means is it's a higher vibrational current comes down in the earth there so it's a good place to help you get a lot of your inner work done faster."

Generally when I hear someone mention pyramid power or past lives I excuse myself politely under the pretext of some pressing business—"Aw jeez, I just remembered, I have to clean my oven; it's getting really greasy in there."—or, if I can't get away, I just let my mind go blank and allow the words to pass by like puffy clouds of simple-minded idiocy. But this was Ondine, in my memory an angel right out of some Sistine fresco. She could have told me she was Chair of the local Young Republicans and I wouldn't have budged from my position of rapt adoration. "Oh, *that* Sedona," I said.

"Besides, even if you're not into all that airy-fairy shit, it's just beautiful." I was relieved. It appeared that she didn't take the New-Age business all that seriously, and the mild profanity issuing from the mouth of an angel somehow put me at ease as well. "There's great places to hike, there's a little place called Slide Rock, it's an actual slide made out of rocks . . . "

"Must be where they got the name."

"You're pretty sharp, Harmon, you're catching on," she said. "So you can just slide right down through the rocks and then when you get to the end you can have lunch and take your clothes off and lay naked on the rocks. The sun just penetrates deep into your skin and you feel something happening to your energy body, your pores start to relax and your channels open right up, you know what I mean?"

I didn't know anything about the generative powers of Sedona, Arizona, but as she described herself sunbathing, I did feel something happening to my energy body, although it wasn't exactly my pores opening up — or if they were, I was distracted from enjoying them by a more emphatic distension that was developing elsewhere. Had Ondine continued to soliloquize about her nude body under sunlight — quartzite flesh on weathered, rust-red Arizona slickrock — I might well have gone beyond my ability to conceal my responsiveness with a tea-tray. Luckily, Ondine was distracted from the topic by the other guests. "Hey it looks like the group is getting started," she said.

There was indeed some assembling behavior taking place in the salon, a torpid implosion of poetasters toward the center of that space. I had completely forgotten about poetry, and I wished at this moment that the Fuckpaw would be transported to an ethereal realm of pure beauty and truth, so that I might be left alone here on the physical plane with Ondine. But the group members, quite corporeal to a one, were moving corporeal chairs in a loose parabolic orbit around the drawing room rug and apparently digging in for a literary siege of some length.

"Looks like you're right," I said ruefully.

"I guess we ought to join them."

"I guess so."

Ondine didn't seem to have any trouble disengaging from

me. "Well," she said, "it was nice talking with you, Harmon," and joined the encircling throng, leaving me to trundle the tea tray back to the kitchen. There was no longer any point in bringing it to the group, since the water was certainly lukewarm by now.

⌇

The Bindhover called the Fuckpaw to order with a peremptory, "All right, team, it's time we get down to brass tacks and tackle the task at hand. Nothing overly ambitious, only the discovery of truth and the creation of things of lasting beauty, ha ha ha." Everybody laughed obligingly, including Ondine, and began to shuffle papers and notebooks on their laps.

"Right off the bat," said The Bindhover, "let's establish a few ground rules, shall we? While I in no way perceive myself as the permanent leader of this group, I do feel a certain obligation to steer a course for it tonight, since I feel that I was in some small way responsible for bringing us all together. After this, however, I grant you license to depose me if you so desire, ha ha. Now, what I propose is this. Each week, before we read our own written material, one of us will bring in a piece of poetry which we find especially challenging, and we will discuss it from a critical perspective, in order to help us in the creation of our own poetry. By initially centering our analysis on literary works *not* written by any of those present, there will be no tendency to treat the poetry with kid gloves, as is so often the case, in my experience, in writing workshops of this kind — especially in the beginning stages, when people do not yet feel comfortable with one another. This exercise will also serve to limber us up, so to speak, for the more important task of critiquing each other's written work, which will follow our break for tea. Does this arrangement sound acceptable to all of you?"

Nobody raised any objections. "Wonderful," the Bindhover gushed, "then let's begin. For this evening's get-together I've brought a deceptively simple piece of writing for us to examine, but before we tackle any actual texts, I believe it might be worthwhile for us all to become a little better acquainted, don't you? Let's go around the circle and tell the group our names and one interesting thing about ourselves." Everyone—myself included, even though I couldn't see myself—looked stricken at this suggestion of participating in so humiliating an activity as a social mixer, but The Bindhover didn't seem to notice our discomfort. He said pleasantly and earnestly, "Reed, why don't you begin, and then we'll proceed around the circle in a clockwise direction."

"Tell my name?" Reed Garth asked in a deep, phlegmy voice that put me in mind of pebbles in an industrial rock-polishing tumbler. "I think everybody already knows it."

"Yes, I'm sure many of us do, but we've never been formally introduced, ha ha, and we'd like to know a little bit more about you. Please, Reed, let us hear your name and one interesting thing about yourself." Expectantly, The Bindhover folded his hands in his lap.

"Well, OK," said Reed Garth. He cleared his throat, but it retained that just-quarried quality. "Well, my name is Reed Garth, and I don't know if it's interesting or whatever, but I'm a stock clerk at Sun and Earth here in town."

"You mean the health food store?" asked Ondine. "I think that's *very* interesting, I always go there because it's the only place you can get this herbal tinxture I like to build up my immunity, with echinacea and golden seal in it."

"Yep, that's the place," said Garth, loosening up a bit. "We have plenty of vitamins for sure," he added, speaking directly at Ondine's breasts as if they were camera three and the red light was on. I was starting to dislike this guy. Those were *my* breasts he was talking to — well, not technically mine, since they were attached to Ondine at the time, but I felt possessive of them all the same.

"That seems like it would be a very mellow place to work," Ondine posited.

"Sometimes it is, but sometimes it's a hassle," Garth said seriously. "Like today this old guy comes in and asks me for half a lettuce. Half a head of lettuce! He says, 'I live by myself, so I can't eat a whole head of lettuce. It goes rotten before I finish it.' Now I'm thinking, I don't know if I'm supposed to cut a perfectly good head of lettuce in half, so I go back to the produce manager and I tell him, 'Hey, there's this asshole out there who wants half a head of lettuce.' "

Dottie St. Cyr, seated across the circle, turned bright red at the Garth's mention of the human engine of evacuation, but at this moment Garth didn't seem to notice anything other than Ondine's right breast, the larger and more demanding of attention. "Well," Garth proceeded, "it turns out the old guy followed me back into loading, and he was standing right behind me when I said there's this asshole who wants a half a head of lettuce, so he heard the whole thing. So I said to the manager, 'and this gentleman here wants the other half!' " He laughed heartily and looked up from Ondine's breasts to her face as if seeking her approval. If she got the joke, she wasn't letting on but was instead staring at Garth with a practiced, venomous look that she gives to guys that ogle her shamelessly, like construction workers on scaffolds. Under Ondine's withering gaze, Garth reddened.

Reddening seemed rife, if not rampant, in the Fuckpaw, and at this rate we'd all soon have looked as though we'd suffered simultaneous stroke or were all choking on mint-filled Milanos, had not The Bindhover spared us that rubescent eventuality by saying, "That's an extremely amusing anecdote, Reed, but let's try to refrain from extraneous conversation as much as possible during this introductory period.

We'll have plenty of time to go at each other like cats and dogs, ha ha, when we begin our *explications de texte*."

When I worked at the university I gained a certain notoriety for my undisguised hatred of faculty meetings, toward which I would show my contempt by hiding behind my wraparound Fiorini shades, slumping in my chair, and even wearing a padded mailer — the kind the publishing houses used to send desk copies to us lecturers — as a hat during meetings that veered so wildly from the agenda that there was no hope of reaching closure or resolution within anyone's lifetime. I therefore appreciated The Bindhover's efforts to keep the "extraneous conversation" — i.e. long-winded self-indulgence — to a minimum, and I told him so. The Bindhover replied, with a tone of extreme gratification in his voice, "Thank you, Harmon, why don't you continue with our little exercise."

Good deeds never go unpunished, as Thrasher told me long ago, paraphrasing somebody he was reading at the time. Reluctantly, I gave my name and for my one interesting thing explained how my favorite tortoiseshell flatpick had disappeared under mysterious circumstances. Oddly, nobody expressed sympathy for my tragic loss, but I'm sure that was because The Bindhover had warned them not to talk, and that they were all deeply moved by my tale of tireless, grail-like quest for the pick whence arises tunefulness of the purest sort. Continuing around the circle, Ondine said she wrote songs, not poems exactly, and she hoped that would be OK with the group; Digby Bhowles said he had purchased his cufflinks in Milano, not far from La Scala where they do the operas (at the mention of which Reed Garth observed, in spite The Bindhover's no-interruption rule, "Hey, Milano, like the cookies!"); Jean Pathingen said her husband just finished writing a romance novel; Dottie St. Cyr said two of her children were named Joey and the other two were named Christian; and the Bindhover said he loved to ride his bicycle to school every day: in sum, as unexceptional a group of people as you'll find outside an institution for the criminally dull.

"There, that wasn't so hard, was it, ha ha," said The Bindhover while he pulled a neat stack of papers from his briefcase and passed one to every member of the circle. "Well now. The poem I've brought for us to read today is a work by the Czechoslovak poet Zdnek Stribrncky. I believe it to be representative of much post-brutalist verse that's being produced on the continent right now. I won't tell you any more about it, because I don't want to influence your interpretation, but I will tell you that 'Treed II' is excerpted from a larger *oeuvre* by Stribrncky, each poem of which is based upon a different animal, some wild and some domestic. This particular effort, as you will soon see, is based upon the common house cat, and — oh dear, I don't want to influence your interpretations. Why don't you go ahead and take a few minutes to read it, and then we'll discuss it together." Everyone bent to the task of reading the poem, dittoed purple on the page.

"Oh, and by the way," The Bindhover appended, "the poem is a translation into English from the original Czech. I didn't want this first one to be *too* much of a challenge, ha ha."

I gave the poem a quick first scan. This is how it went (I can reproduce it verbatim, because I kept a copy of it in a manila file labeled *FUCKPAW*):

Treed II

I am a house cat; they call me Boot.
Pat my head, and my ears go back;
my mind is underneath.

I climb up a tree.
From the top branches I see
my own muddy pawprints.

Tell me: why are my paws black
while my body is white?
I am trapped here

among walnuts and dry leaves.
It is too high to climb down.

—Zdenek Stribrncky

I rarely understand poems on a first reading, and it often
takes me several subsequent turns through a text for me to
make any sense of it, but by the second time through I usually
have at least a vague idea of what the writer was trying to get
at. After having read "Treed II" through a second time, however, I felt no closer to unraveling its perplexities than I did
before I read it. I was on my third reading, trying to figure out
how a cat, particularly a house cat—a breed which has always
struck me as incomparably stupid—had the self-awareness to
realize he had a mind (not to mention the linguistic tools requisite to put this insight into words), when The Bindhover
saved me from any further migraine-inducing puzzlement.
"Very well," he piped, "why don't we begin. Before we enter
into a judgment concerning the literary merit of this poem,
though, let's see if we can't arrive at some consensus vis-à-vis
Stribrncky's thematic intention. In other words, what does
this poem mean, and, to paraphrase the late, great John
Ciardi, how does it go about achieving that meaning?"

"Treed II" seemed on a qualitative par with my childhood
poisen berrys piece, so I was certain that nobody present could
make any sense of it. I was wrong. In a painfully loud operatic
contralto, Digby Bhowles began to orate, as if someone had
flipped a switch and brought him to pedantic life. "I am initially struck," he said, "by the discordant qualities of the
words themselves. While this may be the function of a shoddy
translation, I must assume that the translator did justice to the
meter and consonantal interplay of the text, and that
Stribrncky himself had a rich purpose in such discord, that being to mirror the political turmoil in his native land and indeed the spiritual fragmentation of our modern age as well.
From the first line, in which the persona introduces himself
not merely as a cat but as a *house* cat—that is to say, a being

no longer in contact with its own heritage in the wild—he then multiplies this epochal distancing by employing the words 'head' and 'ears,' both of which ring loudly as paleolithic bellowings by his own saber-toothed forebears. By metaphorical extension, then, we can take this to represent all sentient beings, especially our own *homo sapiens*. The entire unwritten record of a people—or, by logical extension, any species—is contained within an impenetrable, highly participatory, and collaborative language represented by the equivocal images that are the heart and soul—not to mention the head and ears, ha ha ha—"

Digby Bhowles laughed so hard at what must to him have been a dynamite joke, that he began wheezing and turned as red as Dottie and Reed had done before him. I thought I might have to administer mouth-to-mouth.[17]

Luckily, Digby Bhowles caught his breath on his own, and he picked up where he left off, "—where was I, ah yes, the head and ears: images that are the stuff of poetry and dream. Very likely, Stribrncky was employing the house cat as an embodiment for the mythic traditions of our own pre-literate ancestors, and from this we can gain insight into modern man as he struggles with issues of authenticity—issues which become more challenging as we move further from our origins and become more fragmented and estranged from ourselves."

I expected the room to lapse into a stunned silence following this windy excursus. That's certainly how I felt: stunned and silent, I mean, as if my wrought-iron chandelier had come loose from its fittings and crashed down on my head. But no sooner had Digby Bhowles concluded his lengthy and emetic analysis than Jean Pathingen, leaning forward earnestly in her chair (my chair, actually), took the ball and started downfield with it, bowling over cogency and restraint as she did so. "Pre-

---

[17] As repulsive an image as I've had since my Aunt Doreen served a particularly fatty brisket a couple of years ago, and my Uncle Ed cut off long strips of skin and fat and sucked them down his throat, making pleasure-sounds like a B-movie bimbo as he did so.

cisely, a-yes, um-hm," she enthused, "the first thing I observed about the poem was the dichotomy between interior and exterior. The speaker, who obviously is not a cat but rather a man who for some reason feels he has been in some way dehumanized, initially describes himself as a being fraught with dualities — in much the same way that Sartre sees the inauthentic man as estranged from himself — from his external features of head and ears, to the name that was given him by some unseen, unnamed outsider, to his very fur, which is unexplainably — "

"I think you're both missing the obvious main point of the poem," Dottie St. Cyr broke in, striking a note of the soul's extreme turbulence in her voice. "You've overlooked the unmistakable parallels between the house cat in the tree and Jesus on the cross."

Heaven help me, I thought, a born-again in our midst. I had had a number — altogether too high — of born-again students in poetry survey classes, members of campus groups like Awaken To Young Life! and Youthful Crusaders For Christ! and every one of these students managed somehow to attach a Biblical interpretation to each poem we read, from Coleridge to cummings, and to impose his interpretation upon the class with a righteous militancy that always put me in mind of the Inquisition. In much the same transport of spirit, Dottie St. Cyr went on, "I see 'Treed II' as a clear and very moving picture of a man who recognizes himself as being different from all other men because he was the son of God, so that at the same time he's declaring his humanity, he's also holding it back, as surely he must, since he will soon rise to heaven. The author wants to remind us that Christ was a mortal man, born of the flesh, and as such is free to think for himself, but at the same time he recognizes full well that he is something more, and the reason that he came to earth was to deliver us all from sin, so that we might all be saved." She smiled beatifically as she said the word "saved," and at that moment I had an almost irresistible urge to leap across the circle and drive a fist into her lily-white, smug, poppin'-fresh frontage, but I folded my hands in my lap instead, Bindhover-style.

"In that way Boot is not free," Dottie concluded. "He has a preordained mission. When he says, 'Why are my paws black/ while my body is white?' Boot is expressing, as eloquently as I've ever seen it done outside the Gospels themselves, the anguish of our Lord Jesus Christ, who was torn between his own humanity and his Godhood."

Inspired by Dottie's far-flung hermeneutics, Reed Garth at this point made an effort to enter the fray by comparing the plight of the stranded kitty to the plot of a Silver Surfer comic he read once, but he was woefully outmatched by the three professional academics and soon lapsed into a species of catatonia, which change in mood, given his former leering at Ondine, I found gratifying.

During the course of these monodies, Ondine was tapping her feet, a habit she has whenever she gets bored, and toward the end of Dottie's little speech I was trying to figure out where in my own house I might find a padded envelope to pull over my head. Meanwhile, Digby Bhowles, wearing the silks of the Hegelian stable, was overtaking Jean Pathingen and Jean-Paul Sartre on the far turn, but Jesus Christ our Lord, with Dottie St. Cyr hysterically applying the whip, was coming up fast on the rail, when The Bindhover said—and I'd never been so glad to hear his voice—"If I may interrupt for a moment."

Paul, Jean and Dottie all looked at The Bindhover with loathing, as though he had walked in on them engaging in some kind of monstrous sexual feeding frenzy, just as they were about to achieve simultaneous climax. "There are a number of extremely ingenious readings here," The Bindhover said supportively if somewhat condescendingly, "and I certainly would not presume to impose my own interpretations upon this learned body. However, I am reminded of an old saying—I'm sure many of you have heard it—which goes, 'If you hear hoofbeats, think horses, not Zebras.'"

By speaking metaphorically of horses and Zebras, The

Bindhover was, I hoped, implying that while the recently im-
parted textual interpretations might be ingenious, they were
also hopelessly obscure and involuted. Unfortunately Reed
Garth missed The Bindhover's implied point entirely, and,
delighted to have a second chance at participation, blurted,
"Not if you're in Africa. If you were in Africa, you'd think it
was Zebras, not horses."

"That's right," I said, seizing upon this opportunity to
throw a subversive monkey-wrench into the gnashing cogs of
pointless debate, "if you were in Africa you'd think of Zebras,
except of course you wouldn't call it a Zebra, since that's
whitey's word. The word for Zebra might be something else
in Swahili," I added. "Like Nbutu."

I thought the others would recognize the parodic intent of
my statement and would be thereby chastened into dropping
their absurd pretensions to erudition, but Digby Bhowles
shocked me by agreeing with me, something which no academic had ever done before, so far as I can recall. "Mr. Nails
is absolutely correct," he said. "If, for example, you were a
black savage who ventured out into the city and was educated
at a western university, then you might call a Zebra something
else entirely."

"Quite true," said Dottie St. Cyr, obviously not as offended
by blatant racism as she was by human rectums. "At the same
time, had our Negro pursued a course of study such as zoology
or animal husbandry, he would likely have developed a keener
appreciation for the diversity of God's creations within his
own environment, so that he might, for instance, know the
hoofbeats to be another animal entirely, neither horses nor
Zebras."

"They could be wildebeests," I said, hoping to shut them
up with a pointless observation.

"It seems to me highly unlikely," Digby Bhowles objected,
"that he would mistake a wildebeest for a Zebra, given that
the wildebeest's head and humped shoulders resemble those
of a buffalo, not to mention its drooping beard and large curv-

ing horns. Its horns are characteristic of both sexes, by the way, which is extremely rare among mammalian species."

"But one *could* mistake wildebeests for Zebras," Jean Pathingen reminded Digby Bhowles, "if one heard their hoof-beats before one had an opportunity to identify them visually. I believe both animals weigh approximately four hundred pounds when fully grown."

Ondine was growing more overwrought by the minute, as evidenced by her having joined the ranks of the facially reddened, and by her feet, which were no longer merely tapping impatiently on the floor but were bouncing so furiously that her papers slipped to the floor. "This is all bullshit!" she shouted. The rest of the group fell silent and gaped at her with shocked indignation, which made them collectively resemble a school of netted bonito recently hauled from the bosom of the sea.

A lesser woman (or man, like me) would have backed down under the intense scrutiny of the group, but Ondine is made of sterner stuff. "I mean," she said, still exercised, "everyone looked at the poem and came up with something different that makes no sense, because everybody's so caught up in their own trips, instead of trying to figure out what the poem means, I mean, let's just figure out what the plain sense of the poem is and try to leave our own trips out of it, you know what I mean, and who cares about wild beasts or how much Zebras weigh?"

With this outburst Ondine's attractiveness to me scaled new heights, and I was just about to throw the full weight of my critical opinion behind this plucky redhead, to support her audacious stand against the seemingly insurmountable forces of dullness, but The Bindhover beat me to words. "Yes," he said slowly and thoughtfully, "Yes, yes, *yes*. Ondine's point is an extremely apt one, I think. In fact, I believe I.A. Richards, in his seminal work, *Practical Criticism,* used that very term, 'plain sense,' to describe what the ultimate end of any responsible literary explication should be: to divorce ourselves as thoroughly as we can from our own preconceptions and theoretical predispositions, and to approach the text *qua* text, that is to say, independent of any biases we might bring to it."

"Certainly that is an admirable ideal," said Digby Bhowles, smelling a philosophical imbroglio on the wind and rising dicklike to the occasion. "However, it is important to keep in mind that poetry does not exist in a vacuum, and it is ludicrous to imagine that any of us is truly capable of stripping himself bare of preconceptions."

Reed Garth at this moment, I noticed, having recovered from his most recent humiliation, looked like he was doing a pretty good job of mentally stripping Ondine bare of her preconceptions, not to mention her outer garments and undies. "We are," Bhowles concluded, "products of a cultural context and carry with us the baggage, for better or worse, of all that we have learned or been taught. We might as well accept our conditioning as a *donné,* and approach any textual analysis accordingly."

"That is unquestionably true," said Dottie St. Cyr, creaming her cords for Christ. "If I hadn't been saved, then I might not have seen the light and . . . " I wish I could recount for you the thrilling conclusion of Dottie's speech, but this was the precise point at which I checked out and started counting the books in my bookcase and singing the words to the Sex Pistols' "Anarchy in the U.K." to myself, over and over. Throughout the next hour[18] I registered only snatches of conversation from the assembled: "We must guard against . . . "; "We have a very human Savior here, one who seems almost guilty for the misdeeds of mankind . . . "; "There can be no resolution to the dilemma presented by the persona, and that is why the title is . . . "; "I am *not* disagreeing with

---

[18]One hour and thirteen minutes to be exact. I can publish that figure with absolute certainly, because I glanced at my Seiko so often that my right arm was sore the next day, as though I had been curling a dumbbell considerably heavier than my usual thirty-five pounds per arm.

you; I am merely suggesting that there is another perspective from which one might . . . "

The Bindhover looked increasingly frazzled, as if a nipping and eager air had blown up in my living room and given his shirt and jacket and hair a not-too-gentle muss job. Strangely, his beard also seemed to have grown considerably more than one would expect in two hours and thirteen minutes, which stubble gave The Bindhover the weathered, sun-dried and grizzled appearance of a Greek sailor on a three-day binge. He tried vainly several times to hoist Dame Reason, all two hundred pounds of her, back up onto Her throne, with various exhortations like, "I think we may be missing my point here;" "we may be losing our textual focus;" and a desperate "Please, please!" that would have put James Brown to shame, but each time, just before he got Her balanced up on the pedestal, a new storm of controversy blew up, the upshot being that we never did get around to reading any of our own poetry. Gamely, trying hard not to appear utterly defeated, The Bindhover said, "I believe we'd best adjourn for tonight, and we'll begin the next session with critiques of our own poetic output."

Yeah, right, I thought to myself. There's as much chance of my joining this group of yahoos again as there is of my becoming a card-carrying member of Awaken To Young Life! Find yourselves another drawing room, bebees, because this one's closed for poetic business, tiny *microstomichethiobriousbashforddini* and all.

Ondine was the last to leave, the rest of the group having filed out with firm handclasps and murmured words of gratitude for my hospitality, except The Bindhover, who stayed to help clean up. "What did you think?" I asked Ondine at the door.

"About the poem? It was stupid," she said angrily. "Very stupid. Cats can't talk. And if they could, they wouldn't talk like *that*."

"I meant the group."

"Oh, I think I'm wasting my brain cells and I have better

things to do with my time than listen to a bunch of tight-ass bookworms jerk each other off."

"You have a way with words," I remarked. "Your diction is piquant, yet it carries with it a suggestion of, how do you say in English . . . ecumenism—or is it eczema, I forget which." Ondine laughed, which was a good sign. She didn't associate me with the foregone excesses of the Fuckpaw. "Anyway," I said, "even if the group was a disaster, I'm glad I got a chance to meet you. Maybe we'll play music sometime."

"May*be*," she said. She turned her body away from me and padded off into the night, calling out as she did so, "I'm in the book. Ondine Scott with two T's." Her name wafted on the air like the heady scent of jasmine on an unseasonably warm spring evening.

After the Bindhover left, I ran posthaste to the *Everything Pages* (as my phone book immodestly calls itself) and found Ondine Scott right where she should have been, amongst the esses. I called the number but got a recording that said her number was no longer in service. Dismayed, I called Information. They told me that Ondine Scott had a new listing. Encouraged, I scribbled it down on the front cover of my Everything Pages. I started to call again and then reconsidered, not wanting to put Ondine off by appearing too anxious.

A couple days later, at precisely 9:48 a.m.,—not too early to wake her, not so late that she'd be gone on some morning errand—I phoned Ondine. She seemed in a rush but said music would be great. Not *greeat*, just great. We made plans for a musical get-together the following Saturday.

Life was fat with promise again.

DIRT IS DIRT

⌐∽

I admit to having had in the past certain shortcomings
with respect to women, most notably in my selection
of prospective partners and in my initial dealings with
them. I remember one of my former shrinks[1] telling
me that I seemed to be fixated on a certain type of female—smart but sexy, cute as the dickens, and quick on the
verbal draw. "Proto-intellectual Nancy Drew-types" I think
was the phrase she used to summarize them. I also remember
this same shrink observing, "You seem somewhat less than
authentic," after I had spent a half-hour role-playing an encounter with one of these women.

This was Liz' charitable way of saying I had acted like a complete jerk, which observation was substantively true. I talked
too fast, my body language was High German or something
equally stilted, and I would resort to delivering unsubtle one-
liners, many of them self-deprecating, in hopes that I might
appeal to some latent maternality in the woman. Liz used a
filmic allusion to describe the way I came across to her: "You

---

[1]Let's say it was Liz Browner, Ph.D., although I can't say for sure because
they all sort of blur together.

talk just like you're Ronnie Reagan reciting lines to June Allyson. What's really going on with you?"

I had never seen a Ronald Reagan movie (I still haven't), but I had enough self-awareness to identify the problem when jammed-up by this pushy clinician. It was simple, really, basic Freudian stuff right out of Psych 101. My ramping libido wanted to jump the babe and nail her without ado. At the same time, one portion of my superego demanded ethics, political correctness, the non-objectifying of women, while at the same time another portion, decorous to a fault, was insisting on a lengthy courtship with much chaste holding of hands and strolling down gravelly paths in tangled English gardens. With these metacognitive forces tangled in a saurian deathmatch, poor Harmie found himself caught in the middle, spending prodigious amounts of psychic juice trying to conceal from the general public—and from the woman at hand—the terrible onslaughts of his subpersonalities on each other. Focused as I was on such emotional isometrics, you can understand how my affect might have been perceived as oaken, dithering, puerile.

Problem was, in many cases my act worked. Because those Nancy Drews reinforced me for acting like a boyish jerk, I kept on acting like one. Even after, on Liz' suggestion, I sought out "someone with a higher real-person quotient"—Virginia Stabler was my first consummated foray into this uncharted realm of female realness—you will recall that I still experienced those difficult moments of fumfering on the grassy knoll above the airport. We probably would never have gotten together without some applied exhibitionism on Gin's part.

Gin was undeniably real, especially in comparison to the women that came before her. She had real hair under her arms, real smells, real appetites. But in Ondine I sensed the most formidable womanhood I had yet encountered. During our first real encounter at the Fuckpaw, her femininity seemed to exert the kind of power on her surroundings that stars exert on planets, or that Saint Francis exerted on pigeons, so that the sum of things in my house—the poetasting humanity, the furniture and knicknacks, the ions and dust-motes in air, the ripples of literary conversation, the very light—seemed to align itself in orbits and eddies and fluxions around Ondine, who managed in some mystical way to occupy a point of centrality, the *focus* if I remember my high school trig, no matter where she moved.

Ondine appeared, however, to have none of the blatancy which is characteristic of women who are beautiful and know it, and who use the mere luck of their fleeting good looks to validate their shallow existences. To the contrary, Ondine's power was so subtle that it appeared unconscious, instinctive to her, which made it all the more intimidating and her all the more challenging. If my intuition was correct, Ondine would see through social games as easily as a sparrow hawk sees through the updrafts that hold her aloft, and any hint of juvenility on my part, intentional or otherwise, would be met with disdain, or worse, dismissal. She wouldn't dig the little kid act, is what I mean, and snappy comebacks about Sedona wouldn't win her respect, let alone her heart. I had to act authentic—nay, I had to *be* authentic and dispense with acting altogether. A righteous challenge if ever there was one, ranking right up there with that Arthurian knight whose mother dressed him up like a harlequin and then told him to go out and foil evil wizards, slay monsters and disempower witches.

With my attention concentrated on warriorly loin-girding, I paid little heed to my surroundings, one result of which is a shortage of descriptive detail I might use to render the scenario now. The doorbell must have rung, I must have opened the door. Most likely it was sunny, as most days are in Fiesta City. Too, there were probably birds chirping away, since scrub jays and mockingbirds seem to enjoy hanging out in the bottle-brush tree by my driveway. I can further surmise with fair reliability that Ondine had on some kind of athletic outfit, since that was what she wore for all but the most elegant occasions or poetry groups, and what she continues to wear to this day. She was probably wearing sweat pants of a butt-clinging synthetic blend, along with her gray Valparaiso University sweatshirt. Ondine never went to Valparaiso University or to any university for that matter, but she does go to yard sales, which is where she picked up the sweatshirt. It was already well-worn when she brought it home, the lettering and school emblem cracked and eroded, but the shirt looked good on her anyway—damned good, in a dressed-down but nevertheless figure-flattering way.

Imagining as I am at this moment, and arousingly, Ondine's conoid, everwhite breasts under gray fleece, I realize I haven't seen that Valparaiso sweatshirt recently. It must have lost its tensile integrity and shredded, as all fabric will eventually do when subjected to the rigors of the Whirlpool Spin-King enough times, or maybe it just decided to take an extended vacation in that overpopulated heaven where one's flatpicks and parents go, never to come back. Whatever its eventual end, it was that Valparaiso University sweatshirt, its ivy-enshrouded emblem disquieted by bosomy swellings, that I faced on my front porch that late morning when Ondine said, "I'm here."

"You're here," I said, confirming her grasp of the situation.

"Am I late, I had a watch I got in L.A. near the airport when I flew in from Arizona, the guy said it was a real Cartier[2] and wanted twenty bucks for it but I talked him down to twelve, I thought that was a pretty good deal cause it had a diamond in it even though I knew it wasn't real, but it stopped running a few days ago so I'm going on internal time, you know what I mean."

So far so good. I hadn't shuffled my feet or made the turtle face I used to put on for grammar school class portraits. I had instead sucked up two lungsful of air in a manly, authentic way, had delivered my greeting with forthrightness and deliberation, and Ondine had responded by doing most of the talking. Believing that Ondine had purposely assumed the greater

---

[2]Ondine pronounced it *Cartière* (rhymes with *party air*), probably because it was a ladies' watch.

portion of conversation to make me more comfortable, I felt grateful, adding one more thermal layer to my already-considerable warmth toward her. As it turns out, Ondine was doing most of the talking not to put me at ease, but because whenever we're together, she always does most of the talking. Why this is I'm not sure. It may attach more to my own reticence than to any tendency toward chattiness on her part. I'm not a glib extemporizer, and even in my Lecturer days I relied upon the participation of students to fill in what would otherwise have been a chilly quietness like that of deep space in its post-Bang infancy. It may be that Ondine feels compelled, when confronted by such yawning conversational gaps, to fill them in with dumpster-loads of words organized no more systematically than junk in a landfill.

On the other hand Ondine may simply be one of those people who think out loud instead of weighing the merits of their thoughts before making them public. We all generate within our melons a good deal of random ideation, impulse and impression, but most of us never verbalize this mundane blather for fear of sounding stupid. But Ondine, by her own testimony, doesn't give a shit what people think about her, so she talks and talks. Some of what comes out is inspired—today, for example, she told me in all seriousness, "I feel so tired and heavy, it must be because the ozone layer is letting more gravity through,"—while much of it boils down to shopping lists, descriptions of lumbar spasms, and gossip about people I don't know. I enjoy her talk—sometimes because it's genuinely engaging and unflaggingly forthright, and sometimes in the same way that one enjoys having the tubie on in the other room, or those garden-advice shows on the car radio. Coming as it does on the hooves of Gin—who, when we weren't noodling, would sit in quiescent, bucket-seated silence during our automobile excursions to the store and elsewhere—Ondine's chattiness was a refreshing change.

"You're not late at all," I assured her amiably.

"I brought my guitar," Ondine said with uncharacteristic terseness.

There was no guitar in sight. The object most closely resembling a guitar was a shrubbery by the side of the driveway, about halfway down its gravelly length. This wan, monotonously leaved plant — I believe Gin once called it a saltbush — had grown, through no intervention by clipper or saw, into a shape somewhat like that of a bass fiddle. Still, it wasn't a guitar, even by the loosest definition of the term. Accordingly I asked, "Where is it?"

"It's in the car, should I go get it?"

"That would be good."

Ondine whacked my arm playfully with a closed fist and said cheerfully, "OK."

Observed from behind (by me) as she walked toward her car, Ondine appeared to glide a millimeter or two off the ground, so little bounce was there to her gait, and her hips — the only part of her body that has ever made the slightest concession to flesh, the rest of her being as leanly muscled as a thoroughbred mare in her prime — swayed with none of the exaggerated, self-conscious rump-jutting of a fashion model crossing the runway but rather with the subtlety of a Geisha padding across a tatami floor, or the easy ebb and flow of seawater in a shallow tidepool lapped by spent waves. Like the primal life in that metaphoric pool, I was stirred by her motion — not jarred into coarse sexual life but rather inspired in the true sense of the word, as when the archetypal Platonic feminine, with a single wave of hand or tilt of pelvis, sends divine breezes blowing down some canyon of heaven.

Once again Ondine perched on my front stoop. She shrugged one of those leanly muscled shoulders, the one attached to the arm from which her guitar was now suspended. Ondine's guitar's hardshell case, as the laws of Newtonian physics might have predicted, rose and then subsided again with the shrugging of her shoulder. "It's kind of heavy," Ondine said, by way of explaining why her guitar had been in the car, "and I was sure you, you know, you'd have a bunch of guitars I could play but I brought. . . . I'm more comfortable playing my own guitar, you know how that is, but then I brought mine instead because I'm more comfortable playing my own guitar than somebody else. Hey," she said, stepping into my foyer and simultaneously into a new sphere of discourse, "your house is really clean."

"I guess it was pretty much of a mess last time you were here, what with all the poets and teacups."

"What's that on your mantle?" she asked, shifting attention like highschoolers shift romantic allegiances.

Ondine has a standard, nondescript midwestern accent, with two exceptions: She always stretches her hard a's into taffy-supple diphthongs, and she sometimes compresses her usually mild m's into cherrybomb p's. Why she does the latter I couldn't say, since I'm a guitarist and not a speech pathologist—perhaps she has some kind of situational obstruction of the nasal passages, or maybe that's the way all people who are born in Detroit talk—but the result was that on this day *mantle* came out sounding more like *peeyantle*. Not yet accustomed to her quirks of pronunciation, I replied, "I don't own a piano," in a tone of mild confusion.

"Not on the piano, on the *meeyantle*," she said with red-haired impatience, gesturing toward my fireplace and a cork-stoppered glass vial that sat atop the mantlepiece.

"Oh, that."

"Yeah that, I noticed it last time, it looks like a jar of hash but I'm sure you wouldn't keep dope out in the open like that."

"I wouldn't keep dope anyplace," I said with a tinge of the pseudo-religious zeal that too often colors the substance-free asseverations of the recovered abuser. "Those are clumps of dirt."

"Why do you have dirt in a jar on your *meeyantle?*" she demanded, a reasonable question if ever there was one.

Her question had an answer, if not an equally reasonable one. "My cousin Bradford went to a little town in Russia called Nemirov when he was on vacation a couple of years ago, and he brought me back some dirt."

"Why?"

"I asked him to. I thought it would be cool to have some dirt from the place in Russia where my family came from. All the relatives on my mother's side of the family come from Nemirov. The soil that nourished my roots so to speak."

"Really, from Russia?" She looked at it more closely, as though to discover some property in the soil which would account for the ideological differences between the two countries. The dirt in the jar was the color of dirt, and it had the consistency of dirt—dirt that had at some time become mud and then dried back into dirt. There were some pallid, veiny roots trapped in a couple of the larger clods. "It looks like the same dirt I have in my backyard," Ondine said.

Inexplicably this struck me as hilarious, and so I laughed. "Well, I suppose dirt is dirt wherever you go," I said sagely, "but this dirt is special to me because it's from the homeland." Actually, since I derive from mixed stock, I have two sources of dirt which one might call homeland, one in Russia and one near Naples, but I figured I'd fill her in on the complex details of my mixed parentage some other time.

"I don't think I have a homeland, I'm one of those Hind 57's, you know, I have relatives here there and everywhere but not any one place I'd identify with as roots, my grandmother came from Germany and my grandfather came from Scotland and then Nova Scotia, no, Prince Edward's Island, no, Nova Scotia that's right, and relatives from Wales and some were native American Indians. Hind 57, but I never got any dirt from those places. It's a nice thought though, and a nice jar."

"It makes me feel good," I said.

Ondine looked at me curiously, as if recognizing my existence for the first time. I guess you don't often meet people in whom dirt inspires a feeling of *bien être*. I formed an impression—one which has since been confirmed—that Ondine used a person's degree of unusualness, along with that of niceness (as opposed to meanness), musicality and several other measures, as criteria for judging whether that person was worthy of more than passing attention. I had already passed the musicality test by dint of my reputation, and the dirt on my mantle was clear testimony to my oddness.

How truly odd I am, of course, she had yet to find out.

"So," Ondine said, dropping the topic of soil as quickly as she had raised it and moving onto one more germane to her presence at my house, "what sort of music do you want to play?"

"Whatever you want. I can play just about anything. I'm a professional," I said in a tone of scarcely veiled sarcastic contempt for the egoism, narrowness and venality implied by professionalism in any creative endeavor, whether it be music or teaching. I've spent more than my share of time with representatives of both castes, and a more raptorial bunch I've never met before or since, let me tell you. They'd shank your Muse soon as look at her.

"I'm not a professional," Ondine said almost apologetically, which attitude surprised me, as it revealed a vulnerable side I hadn't seen before. "The only songs I can play, it's a little embarrassing but all I can play is songs I wrote. Some of them are a little embarrassing."

I reassured her in the manner of a gynecologist talking down to a stirrupped client. "Nothing to be embarrassed about. I wish I could play songs I wrote. I keep trying to write songs, but I haven't done anything I feel really good about. Mostly I just play them after somebody else wrote them."

"I like my songs, but they aren't real songs, you know what I mean?"

"You mean you strum the backside of your guitar and move your mouth without making any sound?"

She laughed at my pleasantry. "No, they're *sonngs*," she stretched out the word melodically, "but they're songs I wrote."

The circularity of our conversation was beginning to give me the same feeling I used to get when I'd ride the Octopus at Pacific Ocean Park after eating corndogs. "Well," I said, cutting to the cob of the issue, "I imagine your songs are good songs, but you're probably just a little self-conscious about them."

She thought about this. "Maybe I can play a nice superficial one to start with," she ventured, "then maybe if I get to know you better and trust you more I can play something more revealing."

I liked the sound of this. I'd have preferred a *when* to an *if*, but her speech portended well. "Sure," I said in a yeasty tone, "whatever makes you comfortable."

"OK," Ondine said.

She didn't make a move to take up her guitar or to break into song.

"OK," I said.

"OK, here I go," Ondine said. She removed her guitar from its hardshell case and applied herself attentively to the task of tuning it. She made a face of intense concentration, chinking up her eyes and mouth simultaneously as she plunked strings and twisted pegs. Unfortunately, rather than improving the instrument's tune, her ministrations had just the opposite effect. It was beginning to sound like one of those middle eastern instruments made out of gourd and goat intestines. Any more tuning and we'd be forced to play some hyper-modern twelve-tone space music, and I didn't think either of us was up to that challenge. Consequently I said, "I think that's pretty good. So which one do you want to play."

She considered for several moments. "How about 'The Many Masks of Love?' " she said finally, as though it were a standard title, one you'd find on any jukebox in any soda shoppe on any interstate across America.

"I don't know it, but it sounds fine to me."

"I'm not sure what key it's in or anything, I just play what I hear in my brain."

"That's all right. Just play, and I'll find the key."

"Really, you can do that?" She sounded impressed by this ability of mine, but it's not hard. You just listen for the root chord and then noodle quietly to yourself until you find the tonic note and then play scales from there.

Ondine began strumming some altered chords to a beat which was uncertain at first but gained in regularity after a few bars. "The Many Masks of Love" was a simple two-chord number whose embellishment took the form of open-stringed inversions and a few hammer-ons. I etched some lead lines around her playing. Two verses into the song she started singing,

> *In the many masks of love I've seen*
> *all the lessons that life will bring*
> *but the hardest lesson that I know*
> *is the pain that comes when you must let go*
> *but you keep on giving it gladly*
> *and it all comes back to you*
> Nobodytoldyoulifeseasy,
> *but it sends you love*
> *love like you never knew*
> *love like you never never knew*
> yabababaldybladdladadadaaaa . . .

Ondine had a lovely voice, high and clear yet with some bottom to it, like a combination of Joni Mitchell in the upper registers and Koko Taylor at the bottom where the soul is, with maybe a touch of—who was it?—Vin Scully perhaps, a dash of midwestern baseball-belt in the brew. The influence of Joni Mitchell on Ondine's phrasing was strongest, however, and undeniable—especially in the *Nobodytoldyou* line, which she spoke rather than sang, and in the warbling scat. I entertained a fleeting vision of Ondine as a twelve year old, sitting in her bedroom, lights off and candle burning, maybe some incense going as well, guitar in a drop-D open tuning for maximum mystic, ballads of preteen angst issuing from her lips. This picture brought me a few years closer to the innocent child in Ondine—that little smiler who had a gift for looking through one's ceilings toward some higher good—and therefore nearer the quantum core of the woman. "The Many Masks of Love" also gave me a greater respect for Ondine, who

had successfully written a song—a creative act I'd been trying
unsuccessfully to accomplish for some time.

Ondine had a natural, sincere voice of the sort you rarely
hear in club singers and never in studio pros, its only flaws being a loss of intonation at the top—that is, a tendency to go
slightly flat at melodic peaks—and a noticeable a loss of volu-
bility in the lower registers. Both of these deficiencies could
certainly have been overcome by practice, but as I've since
learned, Ondine never practices. She hates it and thinks it's
boring, which is a stone shame, because she could be really
good. Still, she derives great joy from her music, and maybe
that's enough, and should be. Perhaps Ondine has, with imaginative prescience, foresuffered all the indignities one can
face in the music biz. You practice, get good, make demo
tapes, sing in smoky dives for a percentage of the bar take,
eventually get noticed, record a song or two, get ripped off by
producers and record company execs, spend what little fortune you accumulate on toot and worse, have a heart attack
or inhale your own vomit or take an overdose of reds, join Jimi
and Janis, my parents and flatpicks, and then where are you?
On a slab, baby. Ondine probably sensed that going pro, for
all but the toughest or luckiest of spirits, has a way of tainting
one's creative enchantment. She had perhaps simply made a
conscious choice, for the sake of mental health, not to take her
art beyond an enlightened amateurism . . . like my own
songwriting, now that I think about it.

The lyrics to "The Many Masks of Love" didn't approach the
precarious linguistic alchemy which distinguishes the best
poets from the plodders, cliché-mongers, rhymers, Hallmark
hacks and writers for the *Fiesta City Picayune*—which isn't to
place Ondine within any of those latter camps. Most good,
even anthologized, contemporary writing also lacks that un-
common sense of risk and numinous discovery. To Ondine's
credit, her little piece had a clear theme—something about
the necessity of transcending one's old wounds and giving of
oneself on the deepest level in order to receive—which could
only have come from the heart. I admired this in her writing,

since I tended to hide my feelings amid wispy clouds of dreamlike imagism and the angular statuary of wordplay. I saw in Ondine's lyric a willingness to wear sorrow and yearning on her sleeve like bloodstains for all to see. There was a lesson, or at least a model, there for me . . . not so much in the language — which was pedestrian though not offensively so — as in the disclosure. "That's a wonderful song," I said. "It's certainly nothing to be embarrassed about."

"Well it's just kind of revealing, I mean you can take it in the universal sense, but I really wrote it as more of a make-myself-feel-better song and integrate it with my last relationship. That's kind of how I ended up here anyway because of breaking up with Kabir and that song, I wanted to play it because it was significant of the point where I was able to like the song says let go and start a new life. That's how I ended up at Squalor Holler, I came out here to get away and I wrote the song when I was staying up there and kind of integrating it all."

Bringing all my powers of paraphrase to the fore, I commented, "So it's a pretty recent song if you wrote it after you came out here."

"Yeah, I wrote it sitting next to that pond by Gin's house, I used to sit there for hours and look into the water and collect myself."

"Where we first met," I reminded her, picking up the dangling thread of our conversation before the Fuckpaw.

"I still don't remember meeting you there," she said without a trace of apology this time.

"We didn't exactly meet. You were sleeping. You woke up and looked at me for a second, and then I went away, because I got — " There was no way I could explain the hunger, the celestial dogsounds and all the rest, so I concluded, " — because you were asleep," which was true.

"Oh *yeaahh*. I thought I had a dream, I remember looking up and seeing someone bending over and then run away so fast. I thought it had to be a dream, no one would ever do something like that in real life without saying hi or something, and I just dismissed it as one of my dreams. I'm an avid dreamer, you know, every night I dream away, it's like going to the movies."

"I dream, too, but I can't remember them usually. Someone once told me I ought to write them down, but it takes too much work." This wasn't the time, I figured, to tell her about my years of psychotherapy, or about the flower-painted opossum that often visits me at night. "Besides," I went on, "I'm a light sleeper and I wake up if I start writing them down, so I never do, but I should."

"You know what they say: Don't 'should' on yourself." Ondine pronounced the "should" like "shit," without which playful punch the aphorism would make no sense. Try saying it yourself, out loud. It's kind of fun.

"Right. If you 'should' on yourself, you'll have to clean up your mess," I played along.

"Exactly," she agreed. "I'm just the opposite, I have a hard time waking up, because my dreams pull me under, so it takes me a little while in the morning to come out of the dream. My body's awake but I'm still half in the dream."

"Well, I wasn't a dream, I was me."

"I can see that now but what I still don't get is why did you run away, you said you didn't want to wake me up, but I was already awake."

Thus soon in our conversation—too soon, if you had polled me at the time—I had reached that single, decisive moment literary critics talk about, the one where the whole of the protagonist's life turns on whatever existential choice he makes. The kid in *Death of a Salesman* could have wimped out and gone into sporting goods, but instead he bucked his family history and became a cowboy. Larry Locomotive, the protagonist of the book my mom used to read me every night before bed, kept going up the track even though he was tired and wanted to return to the roundhouse for a hot meal and a stiff drink. Similarly, although my initial impulse here was to spout some half-truth to explain my having bolted from the pond like a deer who'd walked accidentally into an NRA meeting, I was barred by my commitment to a bolder course of action, one in which such hedging was unacceptable. I therefore swallowed the impulse and fessed up, difficult though it was. "Well," I said, taking two more manly lungsful, "I guess I kind of had a crush on you."

I immediately regretted my choice of diction, and she didn't seem too thrilled about it, either. "A *crush?*"

"OK, I was attracted to you, and I had a girlfriend, you know, so I didn't know what to do."

"So you ran away."

"I ran away."

"Do you always run away from people?"

"No, just women I'm attracted to. That is, I used to. I've changed. I don't anymore."

"I see." She didn't sound any too convinced, and I couldn't blame her. "So," she said summarily. "You were attracted to me?"

"Well, yes, I was. I was attracted to you."

"That's certainly brave of you to say, Harmon."

"Thank you."

"You've got balls," she observed.

What do you say when someone comments on the existence your reproductive apparatus, especially when that someone is a dappled, comma-splicing redhead whom you've imagined cradling that same apparatus in her slender, graceful fingers? What would Lancelot have said, had Guinevere commented on his testicles when he returned home with a tortoiseshell flatpick in his saddlebags? Most likely he would have produced nothing beyond a gurgle — which is what I did now — because as statements go, "You've got balls," has to be one of the most ambiguous you'll ever encounter. Clearly Ondine meant to show appreciation for the courage it took to share my attraction to her, yet she was couching her expression in the same sort of locker-room diction that guys use when talking to other guys about shortstops or speculative short-selling. The way I figured it, she wanted, either consciously or not, to deflect any romantic interest I might still have in her. A few moments before, I had been elated. Now I felt like some thin-skinned fruit, let's say an apricot, that's been pecked to pulp by mockingbirds.

Ondine continued, "I mean that in a good way, I didn't mean to offend you if I did on any level, it's just this tendency I have that seems to run in my family [read *feeamly*] of saying things, so I mean it as a compliment."

I considered covering my distress by wryly congratulating her on having ovaries—organs which, in case you didn't know, are cut from the same piece of genetic cloth as the aforementioned balls. However, I prudently chose instead to praise one of her less intimate structures. "I wasn't offended. You have a nice set of pipes."

"Pipes?" she said, absently palpating her lower abdomen.

"Your voice. It's a hip musician's term."

"*Ohhh,*" she laughed.

"You know, it just occurred to me. The band I'm playing in, maybe you'd want to sit in sometime."

"You mean sing on a stage in a bar, in front of people?" she asked in an inflection that combined gratitude and apprehension, if I'm any judge of inflections.

"Unless you have an aversion to smoky bars and night clubs, which would be perfectly understandable if you did . . . "

"No," she said, "I don't mind those places in small doses, I'm a full spectrum person. I can be comfortable at someplace like the Vedanta temple totally spiritual or in biker bars, it's all scenery on the bus ride. I just never sang in front of people before, strangers I mean, or with a real band."

"This band is extremely loose and the people in it are dilet-tantes and Deadheads mostly—extremely non-judgmental. Sometimes harp players sit in, and Junie sings these Big Broth-er songs that blow out her voice, so I'm sure she'd appreciate having a song or two where she could sit out and have a drink. So if you felt like it, that would be greeeeat."

"I'd love it, I really miss singing," Ondine said. "Plus, if you ever need a drummer, I've been going out with a drummer who's very good on the drums. So if your drummer ever needs a break I'm sure he'd be happy to join in, too."

People's jaws often drop open when they hear such catastrophic news as three hundred point plunges in the Dow or deaths in the family, and I think my jaw did so now. "You're going out with a drummer?" I demanded, aghast.

"Michael Schist, do you know him?"

"You mean the guy that plays with Los Timberwolves?"

"You know him?"

"I don't really know him, but I know who he is. I think I've even talked to him once or twice. Doesn't he have a reputation as being kind of . . . sleazy?" I usually don't resort to defaming the characters of people I barely know, and in truth I couldn't recall ever having heard anything about Mike Schist's character one way or the other. However, if ever there was a situation which demanded the suspension of one's knightly code of honor, this was it. Fuck courtesie and fight dirty, with knees groinward.

Ondine rose to the defense of her current lover. "Michael's a nice person, he's a good person. He wants to heal the planet."

I came this close to asking her which planet he wanted to heal—whether he had discovered venereal warts on the mountains of Venus or something—but I thought better of it. It's dangerous to put the full snide on people you're not yet involved with. Instead I said, with snideness tempered if not altogether eliminated, "I'm sure Mike Schist is one of our leading saints, and what I heard about his cheating and herpes and so on is probably all a pack of lies. But the thing is, we already have a drummer in the band. Do you ever sing without your boyfriend?"

"He's not exactly my boyfriend."

"What is he, *exactly?*" I said, chalking up and putting a little sardonic backspin on the word in spite of my better intentions.

"He's just somebody I've been seeing. It's too soon after

Kabir to get serious with anybody so I'm just going to do research for a while, I think I've made that clear."

"Clear to him?" I asked.

"To who?" she was getting confused, and justifiably.

"Mike Schist, your new boyfriend who's not exactly your boyfriend."

"I told him I'm not ready for anything serious, we like each other and it's a safe healthy place to . . . you know," she said with a coy lilt to her voice.

I knew, and the thought of Ondine being topped by Mike Schist—a tall, lean, athletic percussionist with one of those obscene mid-seventies rock haircuts, long in the back and permed curly on top—depressed me as much as anything since the news that Ford pardoned Nixon. In fact, it put my warrior spirit on tilt, and I fired, "I think it's disgusting that you're going out with Mike Schist."

Ondine's face turned the color of a well-infused hibiscus tea. "Excuse me?" she said with a wintery nip to her voice. "Excuse me?" is a stock phrase from Ondine's lexicon. She uses it whenever she feels wronged somehow and wants to make you feel like a worm, but of course I didn't know that then. Still, I felt a nip or two in the air.

"I mean," I blundered on, "it sounds like you're with this guy more out of convenience than anything else, and it doesn't sound like you're that into him. You ought to be going out with someone you really like if you're going to be monogamous."

She paused to consider. "Someone I really like," she said, sounding a note of skepticism, as though to insinuate the futility of looking for such a someone after the loss of her beloved Kabir.

"Yes," I maintained resolutely.

"Like who for instance."

"I don't know. You know. Like me, maybe. I think I'd make an ideal subject for a research project."

"Boy, Harmon," said Ondine. "You've got more balls than I thought."

As is the case with so many hard lessons, such as driving pop's Ford or donning the prelubricated Fourex, each succeeding episode is less harrowing than the previous, until the thing finally becomes second nature and no longer gives you the absolute pip. So it is with being told by redheads that you have balls. I must have been getting used to it because, while it required every fiber of will, I managed to produce a rather smooth, "Thank you for noticing," another of the many useful phrases I learned in my assertiveness class at the Clinic. "It's not easy for me to just come out and say stuff like that," I added, splitting the infinitive so you know I must still have been somewhat rattled.

"That's why I think you're brave, I always have to hand it to men. I wouldn't want that role, always having to come on to women."

"I wasn't coming on to you, I just wanted to tell you." This subtle moral distinction has blurred for me now, but it seemed perfectly clear at the time.

"I know, I'm just saying. I'm a bottom line kind of person, and I like it when other people are too."

"So where does that leave us?"

She stared at a point on my forehead, somewhere between my cowlick and my third eye, and smiled cryptically.

"About research and development, I mean," I pressed.

Ondine shook her head and laughed. Thankfully she didn't allude to my testicles this time. "I'm with Michael right now," she said, "and I want to be respectful of his feelings, so I guess all I can say is everything in God's time."

Granted, I was young and in shape and had time to burn, but it sounded as though Ondine were suggesting we might not get together until a few minutes before the sounding of the Last Trumpet. The prospect of such a wait was none too appealing, let me tell you, and I fell into a moody distraction that cast the rest of the afternoon in an unreal and afflictive light, as when there's a forest fire nearby and the sun, penetrating the thick chapparal-smoke and bone-ash, bathes the landscape, your car and everything else in a yellowish lassitude.

In such a state I accompanied Ondine absently on a couple more of her tunes, both similar in style to "The Many Masks" but more minor of key and melancholic of mood; I noticed, as we stood mouthing our ritual good-byes, that my doorside potted palm had a spotty fungus or blight on all of its fronds; I heard an ice cream truck somewhere in the neighborhood chime a doppler-eerie melody to "Somewhere My Love"—I kid you not—which faded gradually into inaudibility; and I observed Ondine once more receding down my driveway, only this time I was reminded of the late October afternoon when, as a child, I accidentally opened the door to my parakeets' cage and could only watch helplessly as Ronny and Freddy wheeled and mounted as though caught in an impetuous dust-devil, became smudges on pale sky, then specks of no color, and were gone.

~↙

hree days later The Bindhover was killed. He was pedaling along the southbound Esparta Way bicycle path when a northbound Dodge van with a bumper sticker reading "Insured by Smith & Wesson" veered suddenly across the double-double line and ran head-on into the former leader of the Fuckpaw, projecting him forty feet into a vacant lot overgrown with dry weeds.

The Bindhover had been on his way home from the university, where he had just finished teaching an extension course in seventeenth-century courtly sonnets. The driver of the Dodge van, a Vietnam vet, was unemployed and had been drinking tequila poppers at Snooky's Westside Lounge. The *Fiesta City Morning Bee* (our right-leaning mainstream rag) featured a full-page spread, including a grainy, contrasty still of The Bindhover's mangled tenspeed and one of his tasselled loafers bedded peacefully among weeds. They ran a terse story which began, "Richard C. Bindhover, 31, was killed instantly when . . . ," but I knew it had happened more slowly than that. There must have been a minute epoch of successive instants during which The Bindhover, seeing the van headed his way, shifted his weight mightily, even superhumanly, to remove himself from the path of the oncoming death-vehicle. Upon realizing the futility of his efforts, he must have uttered a harsh, clipped cry and then, feeling hard Detroit steel impact the previously inviolate sacs and brittle casings that had been his body, must have felt no pain but rather a flash of recognition that this was going to be bad, very bad. Maybe he was horrified. Maybe he giggled or got in several silent *Mommities* before the light failed, we'll never know. Then too, there must have followed another interstice of dilated time, when The Bindhover's body went about the shocky business of shutting down shop.

I suppose The Bindhover was my friend. I'm sure he considered me such, although in truth I never gave him or his existence a great deal of thought, and when I did think of him, it was rarely without a certain scorn for his timid, technocratic approach to the making of music, his two button-down shirts and sensible shoes, and his matriarchal governance of the Fuckpaw (an organization which would undoubtedly become —without The Bindhover to organize, make calls, cajole and badger its members—the Ex-Fuckpaw). This made receiving the news of his death rather more difficult. I've had enough experience with deaths in my immediate family to make me something of an adept in grieving for loved ones. I've mastered the correlative arts of bedside sitting and phoneside waiting; steeled my palate to the gristly, unhealthy prebagged burgers and tasteless, overboiled carrots whose like you find only in hospital cafeterias; wept so copiously and with such determined abandon that for several months after my mother died I could not open my eyes without seeing roundish spots like glowing purplish protozoa in my field of vision, until gradually my tear ducts and optic nerves scarred over and the spots went away. Yet none of these exercises in vigilance and discharge prepared me for handling the present death, since in no way could The Bindhover have been considered a loved one, at least by me.

My initial reaction to hearing the news—Dottie St. Cyr, of all people, called to tell me in a funereal tone that "one of our

dear friends has gone to God" — was the customary gladness
that it hadn't been young Harmon who got himself tossed
roadside like somebody's oilrag. I berated myself briefly for
my callous self-centeredness and then reminded myself that
everybody has that initial reaction when they hear somebody
they know has died. Next I indulged in a deep, righteous
loathing for Reinert S. Puehling, 42, the conscienceless
lowlife killer of a human being who was at worst trivial, and
who — barring any closet propensities for icepick murder or
stockbrokering on the part of The Bindhover — had left the
world a richer place for his former presence in it. I imagined
myself howling curses at Reinert S. Puehling as they led him
shackled from the courthouse, imagined myself throwing the
switch and watching him strain for his last breaths as the room
filled with Zyklon-B or whatever high-tech aerosol the practitioners of institutional revenge use nowadays. Then, remembering the tendency of the courts to coddle inebriated hit-
and-run felons by giving them no jail time, a firm hand slap
and three weeks of traffic school, I imagined myself hounding
Reinert S. Puehling until the end of his days with crude
telephonic reminders of his abominable misdeed until he had
no recourse but to loop a length of telephone cord over a joist
and do himself.

My mental snuff-flicks of Reinert S. Puehling's bulging
eyes, his blackened tongue, involuntary erection and slipping
bowels diverted me for a while, but soon my more evolved
social-democratic nature reminded me that Reinert S. Puehling was probably himself a victim, a chemically unbalanced
loser whose father had probably been an alcoholic and his father before him, whose mother had likely attempted to abort
him when she realized the error of his conception, who got
jostled on the school bus for his funny name and his bad haircuts, taunted in the locker room for his tiny dick, fired from
job after job because of his habitual tardiness, drafted into a
peerless horror he didn't understand because nobody (except
the defense contractors who turned a neat profit from the war)
did, shipped back home unceremoniously, vilified by Youth

Movement partisans like myself for having lacked the moral fiber to avoid the draft, fired from more jobs, misunderstood and dumped by wife and former friends, driven deeper into alienation and self-doubt, all the while depending more and more on the solace of substances to take the edge off. I actually started feeling sorry for Reinert S. Puehling, who could have been Yours Truly in my own dark substance-abusive days, except that, even at my most fucked up, I had more sense than to get behind the wheel and take some innocent down with me. But Reinert S. Puehling was beset by demons which you and I can only imagine, and he might, for all I knew, have been struggling to vanquish them at the very moment when he yanked his steering wheel to the left with no apparent reason and unsaddled The Bindhover. Doubtful: The newspapers said he was attempting to change a cassette.

No longer able to execrate poor Reinert but still wroth, I turned once again to berating myself, this time for my own catty, niggling criticisms of The Bindhover's flawed humanity. It wasn't The Bindhover's fault that he'd been a fishface, and besides, aren't we all flawed and subject to criticism . . . I more than most? Had I not at one time or another been, variously: sassy, clutching, morose, stingy, crabby, vindictive, finicky, deceitful, lazy, priapic, aloof and abrupt, just to name a few? I hated myself for my manifold imperfections, hated Reinert S. Puehling for his lack of discipline and his bad aim, hated The Bindhover for being out on the bike path when he should have been home practicing his minor scales, hated LBJ and Nixon for perpetuating a war which, years after its nominal end, was still littering the land with casualties, hated mankind for the routineness of its inhumanity toward its own, and ended up considering that the world would be a much lovelier place if everybody were nuked off its face. I'd push the button if they asked for volunteers.

Misanthropy, when indulged to the limit as I was now doing, is an exhausting workout which neither strengthens the heart nor tones the abs and thighs. Instead, it left me with an uncustomary tightness in my lungs, as though some petty functionary had decided to put the planet on oxygen rationing, with a cranium feeling swollen as an overinflated weather balloon, with a tinnitic skirling in my ears like a company of bagpipers, and the purplish spot in my left eye was threatening to come back. Therefore, when Stormy rang up to remind me that he had booked Captain Zzyzx into the local Holiday Inn and that we were setting up at 7:30, I was less than overjoyed at the prospect. I told him the story of The Bindhover and said I didn't think it would be appropriate to play music right after such a close friend had died. Actually, I cared less than a whit about appropriateness. I just didn't feel like playing.

"Out of the question," I concluded.

Stormy wouldn't have a bit of it. "Hey, man, that's what the blues is all about," he insisted. "When you get down you have to get *down*. It's like going to church."

I told him I had a hard time thinking of the Holiday Inn as church, but he just laughed and said, "The Holiday Inn is a perfect church. It's where The People go to heal their troubled souls. The People," he said, using the term reverently, "see through all the pious bullshit that organized religions have dished out throughout history. They come to the Holiday Inn because they don't want any part of crusades or witch burnings or enslaving entire Native American populations and forcing them to build their missions for them."

I challenged him, "I hate to argue, Stormy, but the bar at the Holiday Inn is where aluminum siding salesmen and middle-aged accountants go to get half-price frozen daiquiris, and maybe a disease from a cocktail waitress if they're real lucky. Those People need Recovery House, not religion."

He didn't disagree. "Eggscrackly, Elston. That's why they need our music, and your guitar playing. To restore them."

"My name's not Elston," I pouted.

"You have every right to be pissed."

"Thank you."

"A tragic thing happened to your friend. No," he reconsidered, "tragic would mean his death had some kind of meaning. Getting killed while you're riding your bike isn't tragic. It's just stupid."

"Right, and that's the kind of shit that happens all the time, and always to the good ones. Like my father, who never hurt a fly in his life and died before he was fifty." This wasn't entirely true, since I distinctly recall my father once buying a sticky, coiled PestStrip and hanging it in our patio. But in general principle it was true. My father was a nice man, and—unless you're a fly—an essentially harmless one. "You notice," I continued, "you never hear about drunken sociopaths getting hit off their bikes by nice families on a Sunday outing. It's always the other way around. The assholes always take out the good people. Or cancer." Whine, whine, whine.

"It may look like that sometimes," said Stormy, "but I remember Leary or maybe it was Ram Dass said at a lecture once that there's always more good than evil in the world, even if it's just one more person doing good than there are people doing bad, so that the world is always tilted toward positivity, even if it's just a few degrees. Which is why you have to play tonight."

"Right, I'm going to heal the planet singlehandedly by playing the blues," I said in a cynical tone, recalling ruefully the New-Agey phrase which Ondine had used to defend her current rival for my affections.

"It couldn't hurt, bubby."

"It couldn't hurt *you,* because it's too late for you to find a replacement guitarist."

"Nobody can replace you, man," he said, laying on the oleo.

"Fuck you."

"Hahaahahahaa, that's funny. Listen, I tell you what. I'll give you a ride. I'll carry your amp."

This was perhaps the most compelling argument he had presented so far, since the one thing I hate about playing amplified music is having to move heavy equipment around. Furthermore, the more I thought about it, the more I realized I

didn't want to be home alone with my morbid thoughts tonight. "And my speaker cabinet, too?" I negotiated.

"And your guitar, and your cords, and your pedal boxes. I'll
carry everything."

"I don't know," I allowed.

Sensing a softening in my position, he pounced. "*Greeat*,
I'll pick you up at six-thirty," he said.

"I'm not lifting finger one to load equipment. I'll get in the
car and that's it."

"I'll do it all. You'll see, it'll be *greeeat!*"

"Greeat." I said as unenthusiastically as a body could.

Even before we started playing, I regretted having allowed
myself to be inveigled by Stormy, because it was clear that pre-
cious little catharsis, religious or otherwise, was going to take
place in the Elbow Room of the Holiday Inn. During the
band's first set, the crowd (a hyperbolic misnomer, since there
were only about ten people in the room) consisted of portly
conventioneers and matronly types, the former clad in polyester leisure suits or white-shoed, plaid-trousered post-golfing
outfits, the latter in bright Hawaiian muumuus or generic K-
Martish bowling garb consisting of sensible patent-leather
pumps, shiny, toilet-white hosiery, midcalf-length skirts of a
pleated synthetic fiber, and shirting so nondescript as to render its wearer virtually invisible from neck to waist. Everyone
at the bar seemed to be deeply immersed in his or her own private desperation—so deeply that even my most impassioned
guitaristic blues-wailing failed to provoke a token reaction
from them. My music fell on embalmed ears, which left me
no alternative but to modify the Nails style, there being no
point in ritually disemboweling oneself if one doesn't have an
audience to appreciate the pinkish contours of each organ as
it slithers forth.

In order to match my playing to the mood of the room, I
had to experiment with different timbres and effects until I
finally hit upon one that seemed to work. By relying heavily
on my chorus and flanger boxes, I was able to create a murky,

tabernacular tone which at length seemed to penetrate the Jovian atmosphere of their gloom. Toward the end of the set they began to indicate that they were at least dimly aware of performers in the room by clapping mechanically, as though they were a collection of those computerized automata the Disneyland technicians created for their jungle safari rides.

As the evening progressed, however, the spirit of the Elbow Room changed so drastically that you wouldn't know it was the same place. I've observed this sort of environmental mutability elsewhere, but usually it's due to some powerful natural force, like the moon's tidal pull which causes the third point at Rincon to change in a few hours from a thick, mushy, barely rideable shorebreak to a long, hollow, lined-up tube into which you drop precipitously and from which you emerge screaming, if you make it. I guess you could say that Captain Zzyzx exerted a similarly looney pull on the Elbow Room of the Fiesta City Holiday Inn, because there was definitely a natural process at work there, a sort of neo-Darwinian survival of the strangest. Gradually the conventioneers and matrons drifted out, either offended by the loudness of our music or drawn to their own rooms by a need to commune privately with gin bottles and toenail clippers.

By the beginning of our last set the audience contained at least one of each of the following: a clot of frathouse clowns singing in chaotic counterpoint to our rendition of the Airplane classic "Somebody to Love"; a solitary drunk staring into his neat Wild Turkey with a fixed intensity, as though he were a young Gregor Mendel and his shotglass were a microscope containing chromosomes on glass slides; an aging freak-couple decked out in vibrant tiedyed T-shirts and sweatpants tucked into tasselated buckskin boots, and requesting "Morning Dew" between each song; a handsome young man in his early twenties, well-muscled and broad-chested, dancing crotch-to-crotch with a granny at least three times his age; a wheelchair-bound vet wearing a frayed, cutoff jean-jacket and performing masterful spins and turns to the music in an otherwise unoccupied corner of the dance floor; a bartender complaining that the music was too loud; and a longhair who, despite standing so close to the P.A. speaker that his hair was moving with the pulse of the sound waves, kept yelling, *"Turn it up!"*

This ambience, which could have been rendered by Bosch,[3] was eminently preferable to that of the first set. In fact, this was my kind of audience, the sort of people by which and for which rock 'n' roll was created. Their mouths uplifted en masse to the Room's pseudo-gaucho chandelier, they shouted with crackling peals and long echoing hoots, they whirled maniacally about the waxed parquet, their outrageous costumes a blur and a trail of color under the primary blues and reds and yellows of the stage lights. Spurred on by the sublimely vulgar life of this place and its inhabitants, I finally cut loose on the extended jam in the middle of the *Wheels of Fire* version of Albert King's "Born Under a Bad Sign," to the doubled and redoubled cheers of the giddy throng. At the high point in my solo — as I grabbed the E-string at the seventeenth fret and stretched it all the way to the opposite edge of the fingerboard, where I gave the note maximum wrist tremolo and, grabbing the whammy bar, sent it swooping, diving and shrieking like a fallen angel on its reluctant way to a Boschian netherworld — the kid who had been standing in front of the P.A. speaker came up and began biting or licking my guitar in the general vicinity of the neck-position humbucking pickup.

Biting the strings or the body of his instrument is, as you know, the highest compliment you can pay a guitar player. I don't doubt that a master like Segovia got his share of toothmarks in the soft pearwood of his resonating chamber from time to time. In me, on this first night at the Elbow Room, that kid's reverent gesture produced an immediate frisson of ecstatic transport, in the throes of which I got down on my knees, arched my back in a surprisingly supple asana-like pose, closed my eyes, and allowed myself to thrum ancient

---

[3] Not the one who makes VW sparkplugs.

wounds buried deeply within my breast. Out of my amp came a wailing for accumulated griefs and losses that I'd held bottled like rare wine for months and years—for Gin, her honking and *hnn*ing forever silenced to the Nails ears; for Fay and Harmon, Jr., as wacky and difficult and lovely a set of parents as any zygote ever had the good sense to visit; for Hendrix and Lennon and my former poker buddy Herb Zierer, a contentious prince of a fellow who was shot with his own pistol by a hitchhiker and then dumped in an alley in Glendale; for The Bindhover, who deserved a better fate than to become just another hunk of roadkill—a lamentation which emanated from within my own tragic sphere, penetrating its fragile surface tension and moving out to salve the wounded humanity of the rabble dancing before me, the beautiful, pathetic, sweatsoaked, glazed, pickled and scarred souls who had nothing better to do on a Saturday night than to be at the Elbow Room of the Fiesta City Holiday Inn, because there was no better place to be than this perfect place at this perfect moment of communion.

Stepping back to let the piano take a solo, I opened my eyes and looked over at Stormy. He was comping some rhythm fills and smiling at me—not his usual big, gadarene grin, all teeth and gibbous cheeks and flashing eyes, but rather an expression you might describe as sympathetic, or empathetic, or maybe both. In one of his eyes, I forget which, a tear welled up and then, spilling over onto his cheek, lost itself in the brambly tangle of his beard, leaving behind it a narrow trail that glowed a faint yellow under a golden beam of stage light, like the painted line on a windy stretch of old mountain road. The sight of Stormy crying gave me the same feeling of mystical exaltation an old-world peasant might have upon seeing blood dripping off a statue of the Virgin Mary, and I got a bit misty myself. Soon I had my own alluvial tributaries running down my face, with little puddles forming on the stage floor, all of which would have presented a distinct danger of electrocution if I hadn't been wearing my rubber-soled Doc Martens.

You'd think that the Weeping Guitarists of Fiesta City

would be miracle enough for one night, and on other nights you'd be right. But there was one more miracle yet to come, the biggest and most miraculous of all. Disengaging from Stormy (we each looked away from the other simultaneously, as though we knew that another instant of such commerce would either dilute the poignancy of the moment or explode our brains), I looked out across the bobbing heads of the audience and saw, in a far corner of the room and toplit by a wall-mounted sconce, the wedge-shaped face, the dreamy, close-set eyes and prominent cheekbones, the profusion of red hair that were so familiar. Chance had placed Ondine in the Elbow Room to witness this maddest of moments in this most unreal of settings, an office she performed not by gazing up and through the ceiling as she had done in the past, but straight at me and nowhere else, with a look I couldn't quite identify.

Her expression seemed a private blend of affective yarbs and spices—a dash of discovery, a glop of surprise, a teaspoon of amusement, a pinch of something which seemed like adulation but which, I convinced myself, must have been something else. After all, this was Ondine, at whose feet I would have prostrated myself if I thought it would accomplish anything beyond grinding dirt into my elbows. It was clear, however, that Ondine was seeing something in me which she hadn't seen before. She had on her face the kind of look that explorers have on their best days, and philosophers, and inventors—the very look that Moses might have had when he saw the Promised Land before everything went condo, or stout Coronado as he checked out the double-overhead waves at Trestles for the first time, or Ms. Curie, who found radium and realized, in a flash of profound insight, that the watchmaking industry would never be the same again.

GOT TO ROLL ME

~~

The cocktail waitress at the Holiday Inn was named Janine. It said so in stitched letters on her red polyester jumper. Janine had probably been working the Elbow Room since they built it in the seventies. Her most striking feature was her hair, which she had hennaed to a very unhairlike color — something closely akin to a high-fructose cranberry drink — and which seemed to have been poured on top of her head in convoluted folds, in the manner of intestines or soft ice cream from the spigot of a Tastee-Freez. Janine seemingly existed but to serve others, and she derived great joy and satisfaction from it.

"Can I help you, Honey?" Janine asked cheerily when we sat down. She had to speak loudly, since in most bars they turn on the jukebox as soon as the band takes a between-set break, so as to sustain the mood of conviviality and good times. An old Creedence tune, "Who'll Stop The Rain," was playing, and several lithic couples were making their way around the dance floor, clinging to each other like the daunted survivors of an apartment fire. It was getting late, and the intensity of the previous set had worn everybody out, except me. I was feeling positively ebullient, partially from the emo-

tional release of the last song, and partially because of Ondine's unexpected presence here.

It wasn't clear to whom Janine's unisex "Honey" was directed, so I took the initiative. "Could you bring me a Perrier,
straight from the bottle, no ice?"

"No ice, Honey? It's warm."

"Warm's perfect. I don't like to get chilled while I'm
working."

"Whatever you say, Honey." She said this in a tone devoid
of judgment and with a smile equally gracious. To Janine's
untroubled mind, the customer truly was Always Right — an
unusual attitude to find in waitpersons nowadays, and a
healthy one. It proves that you can turn the most mundane
job into an expression of creative enchantment, if you tweak
the set-screw on your prejudices. That's why you never hear
cooks at Zen monasteries complaining, I figure. Janine turned
to Ondine. "How about you, Honey?"

"Not right now but I'll keep you informed," said Ondine,
taking a sip of Bourbon, or maybe Scotch. They all look
brown to me.

"You got it," Janine said and scuttled over to the next table.

"Are you sure you don't want another drink?" I asked Ondine. "I can probably get it for free from the bartender, since
I'm in the band and all."

"Well if it's free," she said and chugged the last of her
drink. Ondine can't pass up a bargain, I've since come to understand. If we're on a pleasant Sunday drive through some
tractish neighborhood, she'll impetuously shriek, "YARD
SALE!" and force me to pull over and pick through somebody's unwanted sprockets and chipped crockery. It's kind of
fun, actually, and you can find some real bargains. That's
where I got these pointy black shoes I'm wearing right now,
for instance. They were brand new, Italian, and the guy said
they didn't fit him anymore because his feet had inexplicably
grown two full sizes the previous year. It sounded improbable,
medically speaking, but I didn't argue. Hundred and thirty
dollar Boldoni kicks, only worn twice, for twelve bucks.

"What are you having?" I asked.

"Wild Turkey with ice in it. I don't usually drink because I don't like the way it tastes, but somebody bought me a Wild Turkey once and I like it so much better than beer. I can't stand the way beer tastes, it's disgusting. I think it tastes like urine." She pronounced the last word "yearn," which is how people from Detroit talk, I guess. They must use the two words interchangeably in Detroit.

"Funny, that's what my old roommate Russ Thrasher used to say about beer, too. He called it weasel piss. Didn't stop him from drinking it, though."

"I don't see how people can do that, eat or drink things they think are disgusting, I get physically sick if I do. It's like if I go to someone's house and they offer me a steak the way Michael did last week. I told him, 'That thing's *dead!* Bury it, don't put it in my stomach for Godsakes!' "

I bridled at the mention of Mike Schist, but I was feeling too buoyant to let any petty jealousy hold me under. I reminisced, "Seems to me I remember Thrasher getting sick on beer quite a lot, now that you mention it. Of course he always had at least six beers along with several hot dogs, at least a bag of chips, plus a jar of the hottest salsa, and Twinkies. He loved his Twinkies." I used to love his Twinkies, too, but of course I didn't tell Ondine. If she hated meat, I was almost positive she would object to anything whose main ingredients were refined sugar, Elmer's glue, and several preservatives with unpronounceable names. As it turned out I was wrong. Ondine lives for anything sugary and rich — mocha frosts from The Layover restaurant at the Fiesta City airport are her favorite — and, metabolic freak that she is, always seems to lose weight whenever she eats them.

Ondine made a disapproving face in response to my litany of Thrasher's gastronomic excesses. "Sick," she pronounced. "I hate throwing up."

"Me, too." Splendid, another area of commonality. We both played music and we both hated to vomit. A sound basis for a lasting relationship if ever there was one. "That Wild Turkey's not going to make you sick, is it?"

"Not if I think of it as medicine for healing my body, I use Wild Turkey for a muscle relaxer sometimes if my L-5 S-1 goes out."

I had no idea to what these coordinates might refer, although they brought to mind a fleeting image of the L.A. street mapbook I used to keep by my side when I delivered laundered diapers one summer. Ondine explained. "L-5 S-1, it's one of the vertebra in your lower back where the lumbar meets the sacrum, if it gets subluxated then my hip flares up and my whole side goes numb."

"How do you know so much about anatomy?"

"From Yanáh."

"Yanáh?" I asked, fearing yet another romantic attachment or research project.

To my relief she explained, "He's the chiropractor I've been going to ever since I got in a car accident in Arizona, when I was eighteen I was coming back from the mountains . . . "

"Nude sunbathing at Slippery Rock?"

"Slide Rock. I'm surprised you remembered about it, it was a long time ago I told you about that place."

"I have an excellent selective memory. I couldn't remember who wrote 'The Rape of the Lock' if my life depended on it, but . . . "

"Pope."

"What?"

"Alexander Pope."

"How'd you know that? You weren't an English major in school, were you?" I asked suspiciously.

"No, but I took a few classes at Mesa Community College before I came out here and one of them was called a survey of poetry, that's where I really started to like poetry and writing it, the teacher was great. That makes all the difference for me, if the teacher is good. We had to read that poem by Pope, I thought it was too Shakespeary but it had some good parts like where they go into a cave and it's filled with people who are controlled by their fear and so they have all these incurable diseases, I thought that was right on. Also I remember his name because it's not too long, it reminds me of the Pope in Italy, you know what I mean?"

"That's amazing," I said. "I forgot everything I learned for my Master's orals as soon as the test was over. Some things, though—the important things—I never forget, like the image of you lying out on weathered Arizona shale. That's what I mean by selective memory." Cheeky, I know, but that was the mood I was in.

"Ha!" Ondine's laugh reminded me of a wet locker room towel snapping. "Anyway," she went on, "I was doing a lot of yoga in those days and I was very relaxed. This giant semi didn't see the car and pushed it off the road while I was in the passenger seat and my brother was driving. I flew out of a car at sixty miles an hour and I just rolled down the highway. So now Yanáh says my right leg is an inch longer than my left, and that makes my hip rotate back and pulls the leg up. See, the ligaments are torn."

Ondine ejected from her chair abruptly, like an elf spring-ing out of a toy box during a grade school skit, and came to attention with her hands at her sides and her feet together. "Do you think one of my legs looks like it's shorter than the other?"

"I don't know. I guess, yeah, one of your hips is a little low-er than the other."

"You can tell?" she asked in a tone of dismay, as though I were a neurosurgeon confirming the radiologist's initial finding of a brain tumor on an MRI scan.

"It's nothing awful. It just looks like one side is a bit lower."

"You mean I'm a *de*formed?" she asked, nominalizing a word which, in all my previous experience, had always been contentedly adjectival.

"Maybe you're just standing in a cool sort of way, you know, with a rakish tilt to your pelvis."

Ondine experimented with shifting her weight, thrusting

her pelvis from side to side in a fetching way. "How about now?"

"It looks fine to me." Her hip and its lush, rolling, environs looked better than fine, in fact, and her latest pair of tight-fitting sweats—this one of a grayish color variegated with some pilled-up nubbles, no doubt from repeated washings—did something to me.

She looked relieved and said, "Also I know about bodies and anatomy because I was a massage therapist and a yoga teacher, and I started to become a nurse until I realized I had an aversion to secretions."

"Any secretions?" I asked in alarm, concerned for my own secretional future with her.

"No, mostly just sick people's secretions, like diarrhea all over their sheets and emptying bedpans, you know."

"Nurses do earn their money," I said.

"You couldn't pay me enough to do that anymore, I love my own body too much. Plus standing up for twelve hour shifts, that's why my hip is out and my whole right side is numb, I rearranged the furniture in my front room this afternoon for five hours. I love to move furniture. I don't have an addictive personality, but I can understand how people get to be addicts, moving furniture for me is like an addiction. Once I get started I can't stop until I'm done."

"Even if it makes your right side numb?"

She palpated the area around her floating rib on her side. "It's kind of numb," she said and poked it a few more times with a look of tender solicitude on her face.

When Janine came back with my Perrier I ordered another Wild Turkey on the rocks for Ondine. Janine brought it over, and Ondine took a sip—a hearty gulp, actually—and then sat back in her chair with her arms folded, as though to achieve a better perspective from which to study me. Over her head, affixed somehow to the wall, was a sign stencilled on butcher paper that read,

Fiesta Coolers And All Well Drinks
Half-Price During Fiesta.

Fiesta City, my home for the past few years, derives its name from the Old Hidalgo Days parade through the "Old Town" portion of Market Street, and from the wild party that follows as the parade empties out into the courtyard of our authentic Conquistador-style jail and courthouse complex. It's a moving spectacle to see Anglo women dancing *norteño* polkas in gaily ruffled petticoats while veiny Rotarians in oversized sombreros march proudly down Market Street on high-stepping chestnut mares, leaving well-formed, steaming turds behind them — the horses, I mean, not the Rotarians. The annual Fiesta City Fiesta serves as an occasion for locals from all walks of life to come together as a community once a year, get drunk, holler, *"Viva la Fiesta!"* and beat the shit out of each other. The sign over Ondine reminded me that Fiesta would start in two weeks or so, which meant I'd have to stay indoors as much as possible until it was over.

Ondine, reclining under the sign and studying me, still had the same quizzical, probing sort of look I had observed from the stage. This was something wholly new. At no time during our previous meetings had Ondine burrowed into my very essence with eyes so penetratingly frank. Whether this new attitude was due to the medicinal properties of Wild Turkey or to her reaction to my performance before the break, or to both, I couldn't tell, but there was definitely a heightened interest there, and it boded well.

"I never expected to see you here tonight," I said.

"I remembered you said the name of your band and I might want to sit in sometime, so I looked in the 'Making The Scene' part of the paper and they said you were playing here, so I came down."

"I'm glad," I said. "Do you feel up to sitting in for the last set?"

"I don't know, I don't think so. People don't believe me when I tell them, but I'm really very shy, and that's a pretty tough act to follow, Harmon. You were very . . . real. I was surprised, frankly."

"You mean up until tonight you thought I was a pathetic, sniveling little toad?"

"No, not exactly, let's just say it was a side of you I never saw before or you keep it hidden most of the time. I like it."

"Thanks. I surprised myself, to tell you the truth. I was expecting just to go through the motions tonight, but something happened. Maybe if you sit in something will happen, too."

"I don't know, I've got a lot of conditioning from my mother who would get jealous if I performed anything, plus I wouldn't want to step on anybody's toe, you know what I mean?"

"If you mean Junie, I'm sure she wouldn't mind at all. She and Stormy aren't like most musicians, who are usually egocentric and . . . "

"That means conceited, right?"

I was a bit concerned that Ondine had this gray spot in her vocabulary—not that it's terribly important that a person know what 'egocentric' means. I was glad she was woman enough to admit she wasn't sure about the word. That's how you learn, and I hate it when people pretend to know things they don't know, just because they're afraid of seeming stupid. We're all stupid about something. I don't understand symbolic logic or rabbet joinery, and Ondine had never heard the word 'egocentric.' So what, who cares, it ain't no hangin' matter, was what I said to myself, defending my future love from the imagined slings and arrows of my snobby intellectual friends.

"Yes," I said, "or just insecure about their skills and their self-worth and so they overcompensate by being cliquish and exclusive. I've sat in with bands before, like I'll be sitting out in the audience and the front man will say, 'Hey, there's Harmon Nails out in the audience, come on up and jam with us, man,' and the regular guitar player will get all bent out of shape. Even if he's trying to be gracious, you can just feel it.

But Junie and Stormy are easy, you know. I've never met any musicians — working musicians anyway — who have less ego-stuff about their music, which is I think why I accepted Stormy's offer in the first place."

"Yeah, one of the reasons I never took singing serious is because of all the competitiveness, I guess I'm too sensitive for the games that go on. All I want to do is just express myself and have fun, but tonight I just feel too much pressure or like I'm not in the mood, can you understand that? I'd rather just watch, and listen."

"No pressure. Whenever you feel like it, the offer's open," I said supportively.

"Maybe we could practice some of your band songs together first, at home, so I'd feel more confident up on stage."

"I'd like that," I said.

"Me too, that's a good song on the jukebox, isn't it?" She was moving her shoulders and torso to the cut-time, Chuck Berryish lead-in to a Rolling Stones song with which I was intimately familiar. I've played it a thousand times. "I usually don't like the Stones, they lead such sleazy lifestyles, but I like this song to dance to," Ondine said.

The Stones, with their sleazy lifestyles, their rough licks and swelling chordal textures, not to mention their suggestive and sometimes violent lyrics, were my heroes and also my favorite British band when I was growing up and developing my styles of playing and living, but I didn't tell Ondine this. Everything in its time. Instead I merely allowed, " 'Tumblin' Dice' has always been one of my favorite all-time tunes. It sort of summarizes my basic view of the world. *Got to roll me,*" I sang. I'd sacrifice a vestigial body part to have written something so profoundly ambiguous, suggesting at once sexual turmoil, checks-to-the-wind double-odds crapshoots, and cheese Danish piping hot out of the oven.

Ondine considered all these lyrical shadings, or at least the sexual one. "I can relate to that," she said, not leering but not looking what you'd call monastic, either. "Feel like dancing?"

My composure drained away as fast as dishwater when you

switch on the garbage disposer, and I reverted to my former boyishness. "Um, er, ah, you mean together?"

"Don't play games with me, Harmon," Ondine scolded more than half-seriously. "It's a turnoff."

"Of course it is," I said, recovering my resolve and my speech, if not my composure, "and dancing would certainly be a welcome diversion, giving us the opportunity both to explore in greater depth our mutual . . . "

"Let's *go,*" she said impatiently, springing up again.

When I was a sophomore in junior high school my parents forced me, against my shrill protestations, to attend a class called Cotillion. This was supposed, my mother read me from the flyer, " . . . *to prepare young men and women to comport themselves maturely in all situations requiring social grace and poise.*" I guess my parents thought I lacked social grace and poise, and they were probably right: I was a poiseless strewer of soiled garments, a chopper of harmless earthworms, a diagrammer of sentences, a social inept, a stamp collector. Unfortunately, cotillion cured me of none of these ills. All it prepared me for was sitting timidly on cold, metallic folding chairs and occasionally engaging in some stiff-legged box-stepping with a dampish girl who was no happier than I was about the situation. Now, as Ondine and I moved to the parquet, I was reminded of Cotillion and began to marvel at the idiotic forces which shape our lives, often against our individual wills, but before I had the opportunity to finish my marveling, "Tumblin' Dice" cut off abruptly in the middle of the second verse, and Junie's voice came out over the P.A. speakers.

Whenever I play in bands I'm usually the last to drift back to the stage after between-set breaks, because I hate standing around waiting for people to set up—and because, let's face it, it's cooler that way—so I usually have to be summoned to the stage by the band leader or one of the singers, who often get annoyed by my dallying. Junie, though, is uncommonly good-natured about performing this task. Tonight she put the mike in her mouth and, lowering her voice to make it sound like one of those K-Mart employees who announce big savings on lawn fertilizer, purred, *"Dr. Nails to the operating room. Dr. Nails to the operating room."*

"Damn. Duty presses," I said.

"That's OK, have fun."

"I'll try." I squeezed Ondine's hand meaningfully and, taking the stage, strapped on my axe just as the drummer kicked off his solo introduction to the old Robert Johnson standard, "Crossroad."

THE SECRET WOID

⤴

It was some time after midnight, and the place was clearing out.

Dancing by herself with her eyes closed, Ondine made what appeared to be little *"Tst-tst-tst"* noises with her tongue and upper dentition, even though the loudness of the music made it impossible for me actually to hear her. After a few minutes she sat back down and reassumed her observational position, nursing her third or fourth Wild Turkey and tapping her feet. Ondine has a lot of excess nervous energy, and if she isn't occupied with some task that demands total fixity of attention, you can usually count on her to be tapping her feet or jiggling her knees, or both. Sometimes it's annoying, as when you're trying to enjoy a Laker game and there's this infernal batlike flutter going on in your peripheral vision. Other times it's relaxing, like those vibrating beds you find in cheap motel rooms.

At most cocktail lounges with live entertainment, the last hour or so usually serves as a kind of denouement, settling the audience down easy after the energetic musical output of the previous couple of sets. On this night, given the apical sublimeness of our "Born Under A Bad Sign," the last set seemed especially subdued. The next tune—our last, as it turned out — was a dreamy, introspective interpretation of the usually up-tempo Traffic number, "Mr. Fantasy," with each Zzyzx involved in his or her own solitary improvisational prospecting rather than engaging in a spirit of tonal community. We wound "Mr. Fantasy" down gradually, ending it with a lengthy space jam replete with feedback, chordal dissonances and an extended synth solo by our piano player — the Phil Lesh-looking music major from the auditions, as it turned out. His name was Nick Pananides, and he continued playing a full five minutes after the rest of us stopped. We didn't mind. There was only a handful of customers in the Elbow Room by this time anyway, and they were much too obliterated to care about tight musical endings.

While Nick's keyboard swelled and ebbed on, the other members of Captain Zzyzx went about the business of unplugging and putting away instruments, winding cords, stowing effects pedals and such. Ondine came up on stage and stood next to me. "That was good," she said.

"It was all right." I conceded. "I guess you can't expect to sustain the kind of energy we put out in the last set."

"No, you can't work at high intensity all the time, that would be like having a continuous orgasm, you'd get bored by it after a while."

"I suppose you would," I said, also remarking to myself that I wouldn't mind testing that hypothesis with Ondine as my lab partner.

"Can I help you with that?"

"Eh?" I said, still lost in reverie.

"Move your stuff."

"Ah, yes. My stuff." Technically, this was Stormy's job, since cartage was the carrot he had dangled before my eyes as an incentive to playing. However, I quickly calculated that letting Stormy help me wouldn't increase my chances of getting next to Ondine, while letting *her* help me might. "Only if you really want to," I said.

"Only if you really want me to."

"Sure, if you want to," I said. "Moving stuff is the bad part about playing music. I often thought if I was independently wealthy I'd hire some high school kid to be my roadie. He'd just come and set up for me before a job and pack up after, and all I'd have to do is play."

"Really? I love to move things."

"Right, the furniture."

"And housecleaning and the garden, it makes me feel like I have an impact on the world when I move things, you know what I mean?"

"Everybody has to get that feeling somewhere." This was a deeper pronouncement than I'm used to making in public, but Ondine brings out that kind of talk in people.

Ondine said, "The only problem for me is knowing the boundaries of where it starts affecting my body. Since the accident I don't know how much I can do anymore and not hurt myself. Sometimes I go over the line."

As Ondine flexed her hip again, Nick Pananides finished his solo by resolving to a major chord, which he sustained, organ-like, for several minutes until he got tired of hearing it. Then he began packing up with the rest of us.

"Does that mean you won't carry my amp out to the car?" I asked her.

My Marshall stack, with its twelve-inch JBL woofers, weighs nearly a quarter-ton and, with its sturdy black cabinetry, reinforced corners, and heavy mesh screening, looks like it weighs even more than that. Ondine eyed my amp with mistrust and said, "I may be a furniture junkie but I know my own limitations and if I moved that thing I'd need bodywork for the next two weeks. But I'll carry your guitar for you out to your car," she offered.

Unable to find my car or remember where I had parked it, I experienced a brief spell of disorientation. If you've ever had your car stolen or misplaced it in the Dodger Stadium parking lot, you'll know what I'm talking about. It's a profoundly rootless feeling that recalls every child's anguish at becoming separated from a parent among the mazelike aisles of a five-and-dime. Once the initial confusion had passed, however, I remembered that Stormy had brought me here and that there was a perfectly logical explanation for my car's absence. I told Ondine, "I just realized, I got a ride. My car's not here. It's at home."

Ondine looked at me in the precise way that one person would look at another person who thought he had brought his car but in fact had left his car at home. "Well," she said, "maybe your stuff will fit in mine."

"I *soitenly* hope so," I said, twiddling thumb and forefinger as though flicking a cigar ash, while at the same time raising and letting fall my eyebrows several times in rapid succession—the worst Groucho imitation ever. Ondine was too young to get the allusion anyway. *You Bet Your Life* probably went off the air before Ondine learned how to tie her sneakers.

She had parked her car in a far corner of the parking lot, next to a tree which had a dense crown of foliage at its uppermost reaches and also some leaves growing at the base of its trunk, so that, under artificial lighting, it resembled a leg on one of those horses you see pulling wagons in beer commercials. Ondine's car turned out to be a boxy Nova from the early seventies. It had probably been a metallic aquamarine color when new, but years of oxidation had turned its paint job to a splotchy lichen-gray color, and some of its chrome trim was missing as well.

Bending into my dolly-load like a suburban homeowner pushing a mower with rusted bearings and spindles, I rolled my amplifier up to the car. In one hand Ondine carried my attaché case with the effects pedals in it, and in the other hand my guitar in its gig-bag. Appraising the Nova for size, I adjudged, "There's no way we're going to fit my amp in the trunk. It's too small."

"How about inside the car?"

"Maybe, if we open the back door and lay it sideways across the seat, if you don't think we'll hurt the seats."

"This car's been through hell, I got it from my uncle who

has a used car lot in Algonack, that's near Detroit, there's no way you could possibly damage it more than it is already."

Ondine opened the rear door closest to the curb, and we both tilted the speaker cabinet and slid it in sideways across the back seat, until it made contact with the door on the other side. It fit perfectly, except that it was two inches longer than the width of the car, so the door on the passenger's side wouldn't quite shut. "Shit," I said, "It's so close." I imagined I'd have to ask Stormy for a ride after all, and my evening with Ondine would arrive at an abrupt and unsatisfying terminus.

Ondine had a better idea. "What if you drive and I sit up here and hold the door closed?" she suggested. "It's not that far of a drive back to your house and I could hold the door that far."

Ondine's idea smacked of danger and the deliberate flaunting of legalities, and it therefore appealed to my rasher nature. "It could work," I speculated, "but it seems like it makes more sense for you to drive and for me to hold the door. It *is* your car, after all."

"I'd do anything rather than drive if I don't have to, working the clutch subluxates my back as much as moving things, plus I hate to drive. I'm an unliberated person in that way, I'd always have the man do the driving, not because it's the macho thing or anything like that. I just hate to drive," Ondine repeated, opening the front door on the passenger's side and climbing in.

I got behind the wheel. In order to access the rear door handle with her left arm, Ondine had to kneel on the front seat and cantilever her torso over the seat's back, while at the same time torquing her body in such a way that her rump ended up only inches from my face. Now I admit that I had in the past allowed myself a certain number of fantasies featuring Ondine in various positions and degrees of undress. Any lad of my general age and hormonal imbalance would have done the same. But the present angle was one I'd never considered, and there was more here to inflame the passions than mere novelty. Take for example her magnificent buttocks, their contours

rendered plumply globular by the nubbled but otherwise
sheer fabric of her sweatpants. That garment, straining vainly
to return to its original unexpanded shape, rode up and into
the abscission formed by Ondine's two legs, forming a tightish
crevasse of indeterminate depth and far-reaching moral consequence. As Ondine strained to achieve purchase on the door,
her thighs rubbed together, producing the same lubricious
rustling your lungs make when you have a chest cold, and
there arose—keep in mind that all this was taking place just
inches from my nose—the faintest hint of an occult fragrance
such as the attar of rose and gardenia petals, scents I've since
come to recognize as deriving directly from the floral sachets
in Ondine's underwear drawer.

All of these sense impressions combined to create in young
Harmon a mood of urgent sexuality, and I would undoubtedly have grabbed Ondine by the fleshy handles of her thighs
and driven old Heathcliff home, as I believe is the expression,
had I not been constrained by clothing and custom. We are
not, after all, rutting beasts of the field but rather the refined
products of many centuries' movement toward civilization,
and—except for some congressmen and clergy—we all adhere
to certain principles of decorum. I therefore kept my hands to
myself . . . or, more precisely, to the steering wheel of Ondine's Nova.

"I think that's going to work," Ondine said.

"It's *soitenly* working for me," I said, lamely falling back
upon my Groucho again. I was still a bit shocky from the presence of Ondine's twitching bum in my face, which left me at
a loss for snappier comebacks.

"Say the secret *woid*," said Ondine, flicking her own imagi-
nary cigar with her free hand. That's Ondine, full of surprises.
Just when you've convinced yourself she's culturally deprived,
she turns around and delivers the appropriate epigram or line
of dialogue, complete with a flawless rendering of dialect and
intonation, and if you ask her, "Where'd that come from?"
she'll answer, "My brain," or, "I channeled it." She must have
managed to find some reruns of *You Bet Your Life* late at

night, while Kabir was plotting the heavens with his astrolabe.

"And the duck'll come down and give you a *hunnerd dollas,*" I played along.

"It's a common *woid,*" Ondine concluded. "Something you see every day."

The other band members were loading instruments and accessories into their vehicles and trickling off into the night. Nick Pananides, having loaded amp, stool, keyboard, and self into his van, leaned out the window as he spoke a few inaudible words to Stormy and Junie, and then idled across the lot, the Dodge's engine burbling and its tail pipe breathing grayish puffs into the chilly air. Passing me and Ondine on his way out, Nick saw me and sounded the horn of his car. I waved back. "There goes the Greek," I said to Ondine. "Don't you think he looks like Phil Lesh?"

"Who's Phil Lish?"

"Lesh. He's only been playing bass for the Dead something like twenty years."

"Good old Phil," Ondine said and added with some exigence, "Let's *go.*"

"OK, in a second. Stormy's coming over."

The honking had drawn Stormy's attention away from his P.A.-loading duties, and he was heading in our direction. Having completed his transect of the parking lot, Stormy peered into the car, where Ondine was still in her kneeling position, I behind the wheel. I rolled down the window.

" *'Ello, 'ello, 'ello!*" Stormy affected a fake accent which was supposed to sound Cockney but more closely approximated Portuguese. His beard was suffused with Constant Comet residue, so that the Nova began smelling like a control burn at the county landfill. "What 'ave we 'ere?" Stormy said.

I said with some impatience, "My friend offered to give me a ride home with my amp, and I graciously accepted. Ondine, this is my friend Carl Petrel, better known as Stormy. Stormy, this is my friend Ondine."

"Pleased to meet you," said Ondine, craning her neck in

such a way that she was able to look at Stormy. "I'm holding the door closed," she added, by way of explaining her unusual posture.

Stormy bowed deeply, managing to keep his eyes on Ondine throughout the bow's entire range of motion. "The pleasure is entirely mine," he said with extreme unction.

"I like the way you played," Ondine said.

"You are most gracious, dear girl."

"Ondine's giving me a ride home," I reasserted in a pointedly louder voice, hoping that Stormy would take the hint and bugger off, taking his ridiculous accent and annoying leer with him.

"You said that already, Elston Howard," he said, not departing but at least dropping the accent. He pointed his shaggy, aromatic chin in the direction of Ondine and said to me, "I take it you're not sorry you came tonight after all."

It seemed long ago that I had received word of The Bindhover's death, and I had a pang of guilt at not having given my dead friend so much as a thought over the past several hours. But I've dealt with enough passings to know that even when those closest to you die, you can't grieve all the time. Sometimes you grieve, and sometimes you forget for a while.[4]

---

[4]When I die, I want to make grieving easy. I want all my musical friends to hire a room and jam with a passion, and I want my non-musical friends to dance with roses in their teeth and umbrellas in their hands. I want each of my poker buds to withdraw a thousand bucks from my estate and make a junket to the Stardust Hotel in Vegas, site of my favorite cardroom, where they'll either blow the money in no-limit hold-em and have the time of their gambling lives doing it, or parlay it into a meaningful fortune. I want everybody to drive to the end of Zzyzx Road and throw my ashes into the desert wind. Standing in the middle of a hot nowhere, I want everybody to reminisce about what a puzzlingly contradictory but basically righteous and amusing cove I was — as was the Bindhover, I'm sure — and wish I was still here. I've never written a will because I consider it bad luck, but you can take this as a will if I'm dead and you're wondering how to dispose of the Nails fortune. The rest can go to whatever needful relatives, environmental and human rights causes you see fit.

"Nope, you were right," I conceded.

"Damn straight. So don't forget, tomorrow night, same time," Stormy said.

"Huh?"

" 'Captain Zzyzx, nine o'clock, Elbow Room.' It's in *The Picayune.* "

"We're playing here again tomorrow?" I moaned.

"I told you before, we're booked weekends for the whole month."

"You never told me that, because I would have said no for sure. I hate playing two nights in a row, you know that. I need a day in between jobs to recharge."

"I'm sure I told you, Elston, and you said it would be *greeeat.*"

"Never did."

"Well, it's only two nights a week, and it's only for this month. Besides, you saw how much fun you had tonight. And you're still having," he added, again leering in Ondine's direction. "It will be . . . "

"Greeat," I said sarcastically.

"A stone gas," he corrected me.

"Can we get going?" Ondine broke in. "My rotator cup is starting to swell up." "Have a nice evening, you kids," Stormy said. "See you tomorrow night, Elston. Don't do anything I wouldn't do."

"Killer advice, Stormy," I said, thinking that even if I ate three cans of nutmeg and a handful of morning glory seeds, as my ex-roommate Thrasher did once when the supply of synthetic psychedelics temporarily dried up in L.A., I still couldn't imagine anything that Stormy wouldn't do at least twice, just to make sure the first time wasn't a fluke. Zany characters I have known. Stormy strolled back to his truck and continued loading P.A. columns into it, the efficiency of his labors hampered somewhat by Junie, who came up behind him and, putting her arms around his neck, climbed onto his back. They were both laughing as Stormy, big, amiable waltzing bear of a man, toted his consort around the parking lot as he continued his equipment-loading chores.

I started Ondine's car and guided the Nova out of the parking lot. The fog had settled in thickly, as it does almost every night during the summer months in Fiesta City, rendering headlamps all but ineffective. It appeared as though twin projectors were casting beams of white light on a screen of dingy cotton three feet in front of us.

"Why does he call you Ellison Howard?" Ondine asked.

"Elston. That's just Stormy."

"I like that, it means you can have two different personalities to go with your names. I change personalities all the time, I have eight fire planets."

"That's a lot of fire planets," I observed, figuring this was an astrological reference but being clueless as to what it signified.

"I know, it means I'm a very lively babe. Turn right here."

I suppose in every relationship that moment must inevitably arrive when your mate gets on your nerves for the first time. In the olden days, it probably didn't come until after the couple was married, but nowadays it can come at any time, as when your partner gives you directions to a house which you've occupied for years and driven to without ever having gotten lost, not once, not even in fog so thick that tonight's three feet would seem unlimited visibility by comparison. "That's not how I go to my house," I told her a trifle testily. "I take Reddick."

"It's faster down Malterwood," she insisted.

"Maybe so, but it's more relaxing to go the long way," I said. "It's kind of like a ritual with me."

Ondine mulled over in her mind the notion that Reddick Way might in some way be considered sacramental and seemed finally to accept that this was valid. She admitted, "I do everything fast, maybe even too fast for my body sometimes," and at this brave self-disclosure my irritation passed. I wish I could add, "never to return," but I can't. Ondine continues to tell me what streets to take, what parking spots I've passed by, and so on, and each time I have an urge to jam a ballpoint pen in her ear. But those little annoyances exist in every relationship, I'm sure, and part of "maturing into intimacy," as they say on the self-help book covers, must be learning how to let that shit roll off.

"We have to go slow tonight anyway, with all the fog," I said.

"It's funny how it can be so hot in the day here and then the fog comes in and it gets cold. I've never lived in a place that did that before. I love Fiesta City, it's one of the most special places on the planet, and I've been to every state but two. I can't imagine any place like this, with the mountains and the ocean and the people seem much more open-minded than other places I've been to. Like tonight, if we were somewhere else and a woman came to a bar by herself and then leaves with you like I did, people just jump to conclusions and fill in the blanks about what they think they're doing, like it has to be some kind of sexual thing."

Since she brought the matter up, I thought it only fair that I pursue it. "I wasn't going to say anything, but now that you mention it, I was kind of wondering about that myself. How come Mike Schist didn't come down with you tonight."

"It's a free country, isn't it?"

"If you've got the money," I said. "But that's not the point. I thought you guys were tight."

"What's your definition of tight?" Ondine was sounding a tad defensive to one admittedly untrained in counseling psychology.

"You said you were monogamous with Mike Schist. That means tight to me."

"Well I had a good talk with Michael yesterday and I told him he was getting more involved emotionally and forming attachments I'm really not ready for on that level. I told him because I care for him so much, I really needed to shift it into a friendship because it wasn't fair to him. Or to myself, because we're just at different stages, it's too soon after Kabir, so I just decided to be friends with him. Besides all that, there

were just too many differences between us, he eats meat and
drinks too much and likes to hang around bars even when he's
not playing drums for a job."

"Are you telling me you gave Mike Schist the gate?" I asked
perhaps a trifle too brightly, unable to conceal my glee.

Ondine returned a smile which seemed surprisingly con-
spiratorial. "It sounds mean when you say it like that, but I
told him it would be better if we were friends."

"So that means you're not with him anymore?"

"I guess so," Ondine smiled.

THE LOVE BARGE

⌁

Thrilled to the brink of superconductivity by Ondine's disclosure, I wanted to turn my eyes
heavenward and praise Him. Instead I had to
keep my eyes on the road, which was getting nar-
rower and steeper as we wound down into the
canyon near my house.

We dipped down below the fog bank, and all at once we
could see. The Nova's headlights, whose beams had up to now
been limited by the verging mists, were allowed to extend
themselves fully, and the contrast between the two-dimen-
sional fogscape and the sudden opening out into unclouded
visibility gave the passing scenery an illusion of unnatural
depth. The cloudbank which recently had enveloped us now
lay overhead like a vast, dingy roll of comforter batting. Those
details of locale—hedges and tiled rooftops and gnarled olive
trees—which were not thrown into sharp relief by the Nova's
headlights, seemed to glow with a diffuse light that sifted
down from on high, as though they'd had a recent dusting
with luminescent talc.

I pulled the car up to the curb in front of my house. My
porch light, which operates automatically by a light-sensor,
was on. All was still at the Nails estate, except for an anarchic

assembly of moths which had been drawn to the light and, having achieved it, were freaking out. I let the Nova idle, unsure what the next step should be. "We're here," I said.

Ondine let go of the back door handle with a sigh and sat down next to me. She looked out the window, so that I couldn't see her face at all, only the back of her head. Her red hair appeared unsprung and limp, perhaps from the moisture in the air. I'm no beautician (nor do I have any aspirations toward becoming one), but I think moist air does that: takes the bounce and vim out of one's hair, I mean. It was the first time I could remember Ondine having been quiet for any length of time, and it made me uncomfortable. "What's going on?" I said. I learned that nettlesome technique from Liz the shrink, who used to fire similar open-ended prompts at me all the time.

Ondine turned to look at me. She seemed sad. "I started thinking," she said.

"What about?"

"I don't know, how people didn't use to move so quickly."

"Quickly as in bullet trains and supersonic transports?" I asked.

"No, I mean in relationships, they used to hold hands and go on walks and take their time."

"Like during the Victorian period, for instance," I offered, attempting to draw from my droughty reservoir of knowledge about literary and social history.

"Was that in Shakespeare's time?"

"No, Shakespeare was the Elizabethan period. Different queen entirely. The Victorian period was more recent, around the turn of this century in fact. They were pretty repressed as a group, but their form of romance was sort of like what you describe, I think. I know they had long courtships."

"It sounds appealing, like something I've never done but I should try it. Why don't you turn off the car, we could run out of gas before we're through talking, plus we're polluting the air."

"Good idea."

I did so, and all became quiet. On the greensward without, one could hear multitudinous crickets all wrapped up in their contrapuntal chirping, along with the occasional faraway roar and shrill airbraking of medium-sized jetliners.

Ondine broke the silence. "Did you ever wonder what it would be like to be a Victorian?" she said.

"You mean wear a top hat and lament the world made alien by industrial progress?" You could tell I was feeling more relaxed with Ondine, because my wit was coming back, sharp-edged as plastic picnic cutlery.

"I mean how it would be to go slow with someone on purpose, make a point of getting to know them before you get in over your head."

"To tell you the truth, I never gave it much thought, probably because all my courtships have been pretty long anyway. I'm generally shy with women until I get to know them," I confessed.

"That's hard to believe, you haven't seemed shy with me at all. Frankly you've been pretty outrageous if you don't mind my saying, and I've known some very outrageous guys before. What I do is just the opposite, I go out on one date and end up living with the guy. But now I'm to a point in my life where I'd like to explore going slow, being friends, read poems to each other . . . be Victorian." She had an earnest, animated look on her face now, her closely-set eyes alive with eight fire planets full of possibility, and all their rings and spinning moons.

"I know a few Victorian poems," I said.

"I guess if you used to be an English teacher you would."

"It's true. In fact, I'm a Victorian expert," I exaggerated. "I did my Ph.D. dissertation on them. I was writing about a novelist named George Eliot, but Robert Browning was in there, too. He was a Victorian. In the end, it ended up being not so much a dissertation as a ridiculous story I made up about these books I inherited that got stolen, but they gave me my degree anyway, I think because they were sick of me. I also did an oral report on John Stuart Mill."

"That's interesting," Ondine responded. I detected a trace of sarcasm.

"So we could do it together," I ventured.

"Do what together?" Ondine gets this Detroit street-wise wariness in her voice whenever a suggestion that might have a sexual component is directed her way—a learned survival response, I'm sure.

"Be Victorian. Hold hands and walk on the beach and whatever else you want to do."

"That sounds fine, but what about sex?" Leave it to Ondine always to drill right down into the porous shale of the issue.

"Here, in the front seat?" I said, always the kidder. I kill myself sometimes.

"Disgusting male pig," said Ondine without rancor. "No, I mean how do we deal with our attraction?"

"Which attraction is that?"

"Don't play dumb, Harmon, you're not dumb. I'm attracted to you, you're attracted to me, so what do we do about it?"

"You're attracted to *me?*" I said in stunned disbelief.

She looked at me like I was the most gaping butthole that ever surfed. "Why do you think I hung around the sleazy smoky Holiday Inn all night? I hate bars."

"I don't know, I thought you might be looking for bargains in Fiesta Coolers or something. It seemed too much like a dream that you'd be waiting around for me."

"It *is* a dream. You dreamed me into your dream, you know what I mean?"

"And you dreamed me into yours?"

"Well maybe I dreamed you, too," she allowed, "but that still doesn't answer my question what are we going to do about sex, sex always comes into the picture, it distorts your perception and ruins everything."

Things were going too fast—attraction, Victorian courtships, disastrous sex, all within the compass of a fogbound drive home. I couldn't think. I wanted to say, "Ruining everything with sex sounds like a hell of a good time to me," but I intuited that might have negative consequences, so instead,

in a spirit of jocund magnanimity, I came up with this proposition: "We could never have sex."

Ondine stared at me, her mouth open. Even in the dim
light I could see the freckles on her lips.

"Sure," I forged ahead, "we could remain chaste and pure
and look in each other's eyes with tragical yearning until we
get old and die in each other's arms, never having so much as
touched a single erogenous zone."

Ondine said, "You *are* crazy, you know that, Harmon?"
but she looked as pleasantly surprised by my crazy suggestion
of a sexless union as she had when she saw me cutting loose
on stage for the first time. Clearly I had said the right thing,
had distinguished myself from the garden-variety slavering,
singlemindedly cock-steered male. Actually, I intended the
suggestion at least partially as a joke and was probably at that
moment as fixated, genitally speaking, as the next guy — or
the next ten guys — but hey: That's why they call it gambling.
"It sounds appealing to me, in a Tantric way," she concluded.

"Tantric?" I had heard that word before, but I wasn't sure
what it meant. "Is that like a mantra?"

Ondine rolled her eyes. "It's yoga where you use sexual
energy as a way to wake up the Kundalini life force at the base
of your spine. You never have orgasms, but you recycle that
energy back into your aura to take you to higher levels."

"Oh, *Tantric,*" I said. "We used to do that all the time in
high school, but we had another name for it: 'Blue Balls.' "

"You probably weren't seriously focused on raising the
energy out of your first chakra, or your balls would have never
turned blue."

Somehow our conversation was revisiting my scrotum, and
I was none too comfortable with it there. "Actually I never
even kissed a girl until my last year in high school," I admitted, "so even though I heard about Blue Balls, I never had that
particular affliction myself. When I think about it, I'm a past
master at being Victorian. It's what I've done most of my life,
though not out of choice."

"Not me, I have Venus in Taurus. Kabir said because I'm

an Aries with Venus in Taurus it makes for a very impulsive
and stubborn person, that's why I always ended up living with
guys after one date."

"You don't really believe in all that horoscope stuff, do
you?" I chafed. I can put up with a lot of silliness—reading
essays (usually about dorm food) written by college freshmen
developed that invaluable skill in me—but these constant
references to astrology, a science that ranks right up there with
drilling holes in people's skulls to let the offending humours
drain out, were pushing me over the line.

"I used to more before I was with Kabir, I'm pretty open-
minded but he took everything too serious. Kabir had a teacher and he lived by the stars. I like to get a little light from the
stars, but I can't imagine letting it run your life. I have a little
knowledge about a lot of different subjects, and astrology is
one of them, like for instance you're a Leo but where's your
Venus? That would tell me a lot about how according to astrology you'd be in romantic love."

"Well, you've hung out with me for a little while now.
What do you think about my Venus?" I asked.

Ondine considered the question seriously. "I'm not sure
about your Venus. I see a part of you that's warm and open,
and another part that likes to be alone and craves solitude, like
one of those crabs that carry their shell around on their back
and goes into it all the time."

An incisive assessment. In one swift stroke Ondine had
penetrated to the molten, convective fuse that underlies the
mantle of my indecision, especially in relation to women. The
accuracy of this insight, while making me admire Ondine for
her powers of perception, also fostered in me much the same
shrinking impulse as when any private part is suddenly laid
bare, whitish and shriveled, for all the world to see. And what
do you do when someone, especially a redheaded jeweler, ex-
poses such intimate details of your person? The only thing you
can do: You keep the subject focused on invertebrate taxono-
my. "Hermit crabs," I said.

"Whatever, I never remember names, I don't care as much

about words as feelings I guess. Your Venus must be in Cancer."

"My mother died of cancer," I said, making the intentionally irrelevant connection as a playful reminder to Ondine that I found most mystical speculation fatuous.

"Well, there you have it," she said, playing along. "There's cancer all around you."

"You don't have to tell me."

"I shouldn't make jokes about that anyway, I'm sorry your mother died."

"It's all right," I said. "I've worked through it. After years of therapy I can make jokes."

"I like people who do their inner work."

"That's me," I said. "I've done so much inner work, my major organs all have calluses."

"Ooh, I'd like to see that," Ondine joked back.

"How about tonight?" I asked hopefully.

"Maybe later," she said.

"So where does that leave us now?" I forged on. "This Victorian business sounds a bit like being boyfriend and girlfriend in junior high, you know, sipping a chocolate malt through two straws at the Sweet Shoppe. Is that what we're talking about here, reading Elizabeth Barrett Browning to each other while watching sunsets on the cliff overlooking Hanley's Cove?"

"I don't know, I never read her. Is she any good?"

"She does have some pretty schmaltzy love poems, if you like that sort of thing,"

"I love love," Ondine effused. "There's enough mean people in the world without having to put it into poems, too."

"Then you'll love Elizabeth Barrett Browning," I said. "Love always wins out in the end."

"Like on *The Love Barge*, how all the couples get together," Ondine said, making a trenchant literary connection.

"Elizabeth Barrett Browning's poetry is just like *The Love Barge*," I agreed, and then, to the amazement of both Ondine and myself, I broke into the theme song from the sitcom of the same name.

The Love Barge — and I make this admission at the risk of disgracing myself before my hipster friends — used to be my favorite show when I was recovering from my post-divorce breakdown. My mother would bring me soft-boiled eggs in a little Pyrex bowl made out of clear glass with edges like a pie crust, and the combination of warm, oozy eggs and predictably happy resolutions always left me feeling reassured that the good times do follow hard times, if only on TV, for an hour. Toward the end of my recovery, on my more corky days I would mimic the singer, a soppy lounge-act refugee who had the voice of an angel . . . that is, if the firmament contains singers with larynxes ravaged by chain-smoking filterless Camels, tin ears, and vibrato like that of a siren warning a sleepy populace of imminent nuclear attack.

That enchantingly wretched voice came back to me tonight, even after many years of not having practiced it, and thus did I camp it up for Ondine:

> *Romance won't harm you today*
> *It's a wide, wide grin*
> *in a cozy bay . . .*
> *Romance!*
> *Come on aboard, it's ro, ro, MANCE!*

THE THING ABOUT
RASHES

⌇

Did you ever wake up with flatpicks on your mind, and little tadpoles swimming up and down your spine?

I did, this morning.

In a dream I had been paging through a dusty old copy of the *New World Dictionary* in order to find the correct spelling of a particular word I wanted to use in a song lyric. The word was *gorbeneezer*. I don't remember why it was so crucial to me that I find the spelling for this word, since *gorbeneezer* doesn't exactly trip off the tongue and has the additional drawback of meaning absolutely nothing, but dreams have their own logic. When I did eventually find *gorbeneezer* in the dictionary, I received the thrill of a dream-lifetime. There was my lost tortoiseshell flatpick, a radiant chit of translucent, honey-amber flecked with opaque, cork-colored poolings. It had been somehow lodged between the yellowed, dog-eared pages of the dictionary, and when I opened to *gorbeneezer*, the pick literally flew out of the book and toward my face—remember, this was a dream, and in dreams, flatpicks and other customarily inert bits of matter are often seen zipping about like hummingbirds—gaining in size as it approached my face until, just before I woke up, the flatpick filled my entire visual screen, a vast, expanse of mottled brown and gold.

I came awake with limbs tensed, spine atingle, and my heart in sinus tach, as often happens when one receives a jolt within a dream, even a pleasant one. Still half-awake at most, I hastened immediately to my *Oxford English Dictionary* which resides on the desk in my study, with the intention of looking up the word *gorbeneezer*. As it turns out, the word doesn't exist, at least not in standard modern usage. In fact, there is a shocking absence of words between *goral*[5] and *gorcock*, which, I don't need to remind you, is a cock of the moors.[6]

Life being usually much crueler than dreams, my lost tortoiseshell flatpick was likewise nowhere to be found in or around my dictionary, which left me with the same destitution as I have sometimes when in dream I receive a phone call from my father. He calls to tell me he never really died but was just visiting relatives in New Jersey, and then I wake up and find him still dead.[7]

In my distraction at the absence of my flatpick in realtime, I started pawing through all the papers on top of my desk in search of the dear departed item. I didn't find it, but I did happen upon a handwritten manuscript of something I wrote to Ondine during our Victorian phase. I had started out to write a love ballad, so that I could perform it on her birthday at the Elbow Room, but this is what came out instead:

---

[5]In case you're writing your own dictionary, a goral is a goat antelope, *Naemorhedus,* that inhabits mountainous terrain of southeastern Asia, having horns shorter than their distance apart. Those are some short horns, baby.

[6]In the process of writing the aforementioned dictionary, you might think about filling in the space between *goral* and *gorcock* with some 90's neologisms. *Gorby-mania,* while already dated, is one of my favorites.

[7]Not all that different from being in New Jersey, now that I think on it.

HEALTH HINTS FOR THE DEEPLY LIKED
Leave rough cut quartz out at night
amid potted cactuses and morning glories,
where the crystals will drain tall tumblers
of star nectar and full moon vinegar,
and words will dream themselves to life,
she said. Do barefoot nuns really speak
in white noise, through your electric fan
at the medium setting, to suggest these rites?
Why then I'll fit my house with every
contrivance designed to move air,
furnace bellows and packing house blowers,
and I'll bury buffed minerals in my hair.
More than happy endings I crave no endings
or, at worst, beginnings without lesions.
Is this a song? If so, the formula works.

I was pretty proud of "Health Hints" when I wrote it, since it was my first creative output in months. Ondine loved it, as most people do when other people write occasional verse about them. However, in reading it now, I realize it's also evasive and painfully self-conscious. The narrator talks around the issue of love by resorting to obscure imagisms and ends up asking if he wrote a song. What a stupid question! After reading the last line, I'm moved to shout, "No, *no, NO!*" like some spinsterish piano instructor infuriated at her six-year-old pupil's inability to make his fingers operate like little hammers, and I want to rework the whole thing from top to bottom. But there it must remain, inviolate, a historical artifact and useful as such. From this one piece I can reconstruct my Victorian period with Ondine, in the manner of an archaeologist plaster-casting the skull of a primitive hominid from an otherwise unremarkable shard of fossilized mandible.

First off, the "Deeply Liked" phrase in the title refers to a brief conversation Ondine and I had around the midway point of our Victorian phase. We had just taken a walk through the portion of the Fiesta City botanical garden where tall evergreens, trunks as thick as whisky casks and bark like rough-out leather, tower overhead so that the path between them is sheltered from the sun, creating a nubilous atmosphere, soft and pungent with resins, while soft brown needles cushion one's tread. Passing out of that stand of lofty trees we came at last to the stream — actually a lesser tributary of La Purisima Creek that somehow manages to run year-round despite the notoriously rainless summers hereabouts. Even at the height of August, with the last significant precipitation three months behind us, the stream was gushing vigorously with cool, unpolluted snowmelt from some faraway mountain range, playing swiftly over rock-filled narrows, and eddying in waist-deep pools.

Finding a sandstone boulder that was large enough to hold two people comfortably, Ondine and I stretched ourselves out on it. Upstream from our position, the waters dropped abruptly over a course of boulders, freefell several yards and then spilled onto a tilted slab of granite. Below us, the stream flattened out and disappeared lazily in a tangle of untended, overhanging sycamore, plumed sprays of fountain grass, and dense mugwort.

As she did on that day when I first espied her, Ondine partially immersed herself in fresh water. This time, however, it was her foot and not her arm that was submerged. Her foot (even on that delicate extremity there was a sparse sprinkling of tan freckles) stirred up the clear water, prompting several water striders to skate for cover.

I was feeling exhilarated from our walk, and lying by this bubbling freshet gave me a feeling of carelessness. The combination of these two feelings, along with a desire for Ondine that was mounting geometrically with every passing hour, prompted me to ask, *"Sooo?"* in a tone pregnant with import.

"So?" Ondine responded amiably.

"So . . . how do you feel?"

"About what?" Ondine seemed more interested in studying the concentric patterns formed by her foot in the pool than in responding to apparently aimless probings.

"About us . . . me."

Ondine withdrew her foot from the water, and the wave-rings grew diametrically until they lapped against the muddy fringes of our pool, which became still. "I like you very much," she said in a matter-of-fact tone.

"That sounds like I'm a breakfast food or something," I said, although without the whining that one might have expected coming from me in this situation. "You like a prune Danish very much, not a person."

"I don't like prunes," Ondine objected. "They make me gag."

"You know what I mean," I said, still with good humor to spare.

"Well you're nothing like a Danish as far as I'm concerned except you're sweet. You're a sweet Buckle."

Some days earlier Ondine had taken to calling me Buckle, one of those awful pet names that had evolved gradually, be-ginning with Bucko—I believe she originally had said some-thing like, "Darn right, Bucko," and liked the way it sounded-and had proceeded through the intermediary stages of Buck, Bucky, Buck-Buck, Buck-Buck-Bacaw, Buck-Buck, Buck (again), Bucket, Buckethead, Bucket, and Buckleberry before it took its current form. "Thanks," I said, adding with forced nonchalance, "What if I said I loved you?"

It would be impossible to overestimate the amount of cour-age it required for me to pose such a question. Love is, after all, the truly secret *woid*, the one at whose utterance all other words blench and throw down their significations. I couldn't remember the last time I had, with any degree of conviction, expressed such emotion to anyone not in my immediate fam-ily. It had been a long time, for sure.

Ondine, for her part, seemed to appreciate my sincerity while not trusting my underlying motives. Why should she trust? She'd probably heard the word many times before, only to have her dreams and ideals dashed each time like so much driftwood against the Third Jetty with a northwest swell pumping. Of the eight guys she lived with before me, one had tried to strangle her out of jealousy, one had an affair with her best friend from high school, one joined up with a Tibetan Rimpoche named Chrumpam, one was incarcerated on child molestation charges, one is now married with three beautiful girls, and her most recent, Kabir, in one of his frequent rages slammed his astrolabe into a sheetrock wall, leaving a goodish hole and causing them to forfeit their cleaning deposit when they separated and moved out.

Given such failures of love to live up to its ideal form, most women would, upon hearing familiar declarations from yet another suitor, laugh in their faces or shout, *"Love?* Lord above! Now you're trying to trick me . . . !" et cetera, like that song Junie Melanchik sings in Captain Zzyzx's second club set. Yet Ondine, while suspicious, was by no means jaded and cynical. I guess we have her version of God to thank for that; must be the hand of Higher Love. At any rate, she said, in a voice at once antiseptic and ouchless, like Bactine: "I don't think I believe in that word any more, but it's OK if you say it, I'm not offended, I've been disappointed too many times. I really do like you very much, though."

"Prunes and more prunes," I came back without dispirit. Despite this mild deflation I was much too happy in the midst of our summery idyll to let Ondine's hyperviligance get me down. Besides, I was in no position to insist on the point, and one thing you can say about Harmon Nails is that he doesn't hammer at an issue, leaving little moon-crescents of miff in the sensitive soft knotty. "Isn't there something that falls in the crack, something more than like and less than love?" I proceeded hopefully.

"I think so, but I'm not sure there's a word for it. All can say is I like you deeply."

While this wasn't love, it was something. Satisfied, at least for the nonce, I said, "I can live with that. I'm in deep like with you, too."

Ondine laughed, and at that moment two courting dragonflies traced a twining path as though caught in an updraft and then, coupling in midair, landed on a nearby rock where they remained motionless, at least to the observing human eye. Nature, when not presenting us with insoluble mysteries such as infinity or the way the wind always blows barbecue smoke up your nose, is often just plain unsubtle.

Next, the "Health Hints" reference, also in the title. During our Victorian period, we did exactly what we decided to do during our talk in Ondine's Nova after that first gig at the Holiday Inn. That is, we read poetry to each other — as straightforward a bit of sexual sublimation as you'll find outside a monastery or pole vaulting contest. In my choice of readings I stuck to the more cerebral of my favorites, such as Yeats and Eliot, while Ondine ranged far afield, with offerings by several poets who for some reason had only one name — such as Kobler, Basho, Üllr, and a Turkish writer named Kabir (I had never heard of him) from whom her former love had lifted his own *nom d'astrologue* — along with a smattering of those English romantics who combine sensual evocation with a kind of amorphous spirituality, Wordsworth being the most notable of the bunch.

Unfortunately, while all this poetry-reading was going on, my own songwriting output dropped to zero, and I was damned concerned about it. Not that I had been waxing anything close to fluent before I got together with Ondine, but I at least had a few ideas and inspirations, even if I didn't always follow up on them. I posed my creative plight to Ondine, who instructed me to place crystals in several locations known to be particularly conducive to songwriting — one in the pick-holder section of my guitar case, and one in the breast pocket of my T-shirt, in the vicinity of my heart chakra.

Ondine believes quartz has the power to focus and harmonize cosmic vibrations, thereby healing anything, from the smallest germ cell beset by virions to entire hatred-plagued and overindustrialized worlds. I followed her advice partially to humor her since she takes this stuff so seriously, partially because it didn't cost me anything (she lent me several crystals from her own extensive collection), but mostly because I'm as

superstitious as the next guy. In fact, I've been known to sit
at the poker table with a small, ebonite Laughing Buddha in
front of my chips, and to rub him for luck when I need to
make a particularly crucial draw. I followed Ondine's instructions to use her crystals, and "Health Hints for Deeply Liked"
followed shortly thereafter — not a song exactly, but lyrical
output nevertheless. Whether "Health Hints for Deeply
Liked" occurred as a direct causal result of crystal-channeled
psychic energies, or whether it would have come anyway, we'll
never know, but that's the reason for the crystal image.

"Barefoot nuns" in the following line refers to a beach walk
Ondine took shortly after our conversation in the car. By her
account, she was shaken by the prospect of getting involved
with yet another male, even in such a sexless arrangement as
the one we had agreed upon, and she went to the beach to ask
God whether she should be in a relationship again. She was
looking down, perhaps noticing a shapely cowrie in the wet
sand, when, looking up, she espied two nuns approaching
her. These were by no means your modern, liberated nuns in
blue jeans and Springsteen T-shirts. They were fully habited,
in cowls and cassocks and whatnot, but they had removed
their shoes, which they were carrying in their hands as they
happily dabbled their skim milk-white feet in the Moreton
Beach shallows. Ondine took the apparition of the Barefoot
Nuns of Moreton Beach as a sign that she should pursue a life
of celibacy, free from the entanglements and inevitable disap-
pointments of romance. "I like inner peace and the nuns
affirmed for me that was the way to go," Ondine said.[8]

The image, "White noise," is a direct allusion to Ondine's
electric fan, a squarish, knee-high, plastic-screened General
Electric model without which she can't sleep. Her attachment
to this appliance seems to have less to do with circulating fresh
air than with generating sound. The fan, with its droning mo-

---

[8]I remember thinking several times during our Victorian period that the
world would be a much better place if nuns didn't spend so much time at
the beach.

tor and whirring blades, drowns out all noisy distractions from the outside world and creates a soothing, womblike atmosphere—which, she conjectures, is what dying and going to God must be like. Because of this connection in Ondine's mind between her fan and God, I took a bit of artistic license and combined her nuns with the fan, the result of which I now find hopelessly obscure. Still, it works pretty well as a transition, leading directly into the "Why then I'll fit . . . " passage, an unabashed plagiarism of Eliot's *The Waste Land*, which was the first poem I read to Ondine—how romantic can you get, a poem about cactuses and parched earth.

I added the part about "no endings" to reassure her that I was in no way like all the other guys she'd been with, and that a relationship with me didn't have to end in purplish bruises, gaping holes in sheetrock, or inky fingerprints on some police blotter—or better, that it didn't have to end at all.

Lastly, I don't remember what I meant by "lesions." Probably it was just my usual preoccupation with mortifications of the flesh, or it might be that the willful act of repressing my sexuality for three weeks gave me a rash. I can't remember. That's the thing about rashes. While you have them, they occupy the forefront of your awareness, but as soon as they go away, it's as though you never had one.

THE
REPRODUCTIVE CYCLE
OF WOOD TICKS

⌁

The big Fiesta City fiesta parade, culminant to a month of volleyball tournaments, chili cookoffs, rodeos, gridlocked downtown streets, pale-limbed tourists in Bermuda shorts and black socks, whitewashed plywood tamale stands, half-price well drinks and projectile vomiting, always takes place on the last Sunday in August. That's how I can remember it was a Sunday—around nine p.m. on the evening of August 26 to be more precise—that Ondine and I made our first stabs at consummation.

Ondine and I had been together mere weeks, yet we had already developed certain rituals, as happens with couples the longer they remain coupled. On those nights when I didn't have to play jobs with Captain Zzyzx, I'd drive across town to Ondine's house, where we'd engage in some activity of mutual interest, such as poetry-reading or music, or our then-current favorite, rummy five hundred. Unlike Gin, who had been a selfless card player and thus an extremely irritating one, Ondine turned out to be just the opposite: fiercely competitive and therefore much more satisfying as an opponent, although she took the contest so seriously that several times she accused me of cheating.

I was deeply insulted, as you can imagine. If I'm anything, it's a gambler of honor who'd never cheat at cards, especially if my opponent were a prospective lover against whom I was playing for a mere penny a point. Even at higher stakes — say ten and twenty Omaha — in smoky cardrooms and against complete strangers, I've never made an active effort to cheat, although I might on a couple of junkets to Vegas have neglected to inform some half-drunk conventioneer sitting next to me at the poker table that he was inadvertently flashing his cards for all to see, or to point out to him that certain subtle tells, such as swearing violently at the turn of the river card or spilling his chips on the floor as he went to make a bet, might be undermining the effectiveness of his bluffs: not exactly cheating on my part, but not altogether gentlemanly, either.

Ondine had grown up with three brothers, all older, who no doubt cheated mercilessly at cards, and so she naturally learned to mistrust all opponents, especially male ones. In consequence, although Ondine's broadsides against my better nature wounded me deeply on occasion, I understood where they came from and could forgive. Ondine was a natural player besides, and caught on quickly to the subtleties of rummy, learning without any instruction on my part how to salt the discard pile by sacrificing cards from melds in her own hand, and how to wait until the discard pile had swelled to full ripeness before picking up the discarded ringer with a flourish verging on the malicious, and an aggressive, "I'm going to whack the stack!"

Even though I hate to lose, I love it when Ondine talks like that.

Ondine had a housemate named Andrea, with whom she shared rent for their cozy two-bedroom cottage on the East Side of town, conveniently close to the hospital.[9] On the Sunday night in question, however, Ondine had the place to herself. Consequently, as we sat at the inlaid parquet table in the

[9]You can never be too close to an emergency room, is one of my many mottoes.

dining room and shot rummy, Ondine and I were able to engage in table talk even more loudly than usual. We had taken recently to hurling invectives whenever one of us made a particularly aggressive lay-down or went out with the other holding a handful of points. When Andrea was in the house we'd have to berate each other in hoarse whispers so as not to disrupt her studies — Andrea was in her last year at the university, finishing up a degree in accounting or economics or something equally life-threatening — but tonight, with Andrea away, the small, wood-framed bungalow fairly rang with our cries of "Damn your bones!" and, *"Vrrrr!"*

The latter was a curse Ondine developed as a child, in response to situations in which she found herself physically overmatched by her big brothers. In timbre much like the warning sound a wolf pup might make when threatened, *Vrrrr!* is always accompanied by a hand gesture that reminds me of Zeus firing a thunderbolt of around thirty thousand volts at some insolent mortal who's soon going to find himself more briquet than man.

Having tired of cards and curses[10] we steamed some veggies, ate, and then retired to Ondine's bedroom with the intention of watching TV and reading, as was our ritual. During the previous several Victorian weeks, we had gotten into the habit of camping for long stretches of time on Ondine's bed, where we would read, chat, watch her tubie, eat barbeque-flavored potato chips, and occasionally brush the Nails wrist upon Ondine's befreckled wristflesh in a most tantalizing way. Toward the end of each evening, Ondine would disappear into the bathroom, whence she'd emerge clad in flannel pajamas, her face shiny with exotic unguents from the orient or Walgreen's. We'd lie next to each other with the lights off, she under the covers and I on top of them, until Ondine's breathing would become shallow and regular. As I held her hand, Ondine's

---

[10]Actually, I suggested that we quit, since Ondine, in a bold ambush lay-down, had just caught me with three unlaid melds in my hand, to the tune of about two hundred points, and I was plenty mad.

graceful fingers would twitch softly, like the wings of a caught butterfly. Sometimes, as she descended into a deeper sleep, her jactations would become urgent, more akin to a tuna struggling against sturdy purse-sein netting than a butterfly in hand.

After she'd fall asleep I'd rise carefully so as not to disturb her, give her a dry peck on the lips and turn on her G.E. fan — always to the medium setting, of course. She'd murmur, "'Night, Buckleface," at which point I'd pad out of her room in my stockinged feet, slip on my high-tops without tying them, double bolt the front door, and drive home.

If I claimed never to have entertained erotic fantasies during those late-night tuck-in sessions, you might accuse me of being a lying flat of mushroom-growing medium, and you might be right. Fact is, I had to draw upon every last drop of my Better Nature to restrain myself from tearing back the fathomless layers of fabric and fluff that were her bedclothes and going at the dreamy Ondine like a he-Pekinese on the neighborhood bitch's estrus day. But I knew that the only way to get close to Ondine was to rein in my ramping passions and let time erode her reticence gradually, like wind-blown sands on an outcropping of feldspar. Besides . . . Ondine looks so thoroughly innocent and childlike and vulnerable when she's asleep that the violent impulses of even the most debased rapist would be tamed by such a sight.

Whether Ondine was racked by desire similar to my own was difficult to tell, because Ondine has an uncanny knack for keeping things clean when she wants to. If she makes up her mind she's not going to be sexual with you, there's no way you're going to find an avenue of ingress. I found this quality somewhat bewildering while I was courting her, but I take comfort in it now, since there are legions of stout men who'd gleefully slide Ondine's calf-length Spandex workout pants down over those ample thighs, were Ondine not a past master at the slip. Take the other night as an example. Captain Zzyzx was playing at Elena's Underground, a cabaret on lower C Street, and Ondine came down to watch our second set and nurse a Wild Turkey. She was sitting at the bar, digging Junie's tongue-in-cheek rendition of "Mannish Boy," when a muscular stud, wearing tan, double-knit pants with creases that could slice a pot-roast, pointy cowboy boots made from the skin of some endangered desert reptile, a pair of awful wrap-around shades, and a generous topping of blow-dried hair came up to her at the bar and said unctuously, "Hello, beautiful, I'm Larry. Do you know where a man can find a beautiful woman around here?" As I was observing from the stage, I obviously couldn't hear this dialogue. Ondine filled me in later.

Ondine looked at him directly in the eyes and responded agreeably, "At the hospital."

The cat looked stupefied, which couldn't have been easy for him, since he had already looked pretty stupid before this interchange transpired. He could only manage a strained, "The *hospital?*"

"Yes," Ondine said, "at the hospital. There's lots of beautiful nurses there." I don't know where she comes up with dumbfounding antilogies like this one,[11] but they work. The guy got up from the bar and walked out of the room, mumbling to himself. Ondine turned my way and smiled proudly, and I, in my turn, flashed a broad grin and took my picking hand off the guitar long enough to shoot a *Vrrrr!* salute to the guy as he left. I dropped my pick on the floor in the process, but no matter. It was one of those barely acceptable substitutes for my lost tortoiseshell flatpick. Plastic Fender mediums are a dime a dozen — well, actually, two for a quarter, but the point is, they're cheap. I carry a bunch of spares to all my gigs.

Before I continue with the story of that fateful August night, I need to finish describing Ondine's bedding. Where I prefer the Spartan, clean-lined look of polyfoam mattress and rough-spun, thick-yarned cotton spread, Ondine's bed resembles a multi-layered French pastry, with silk sheets, sateen comforters, flannel sheets, eiderdown mattress, cotton shikibutons and paddings, so that when you lie on top of her

---

[11]Probably her brain again.

bed, you sink down in softness and never hit bottom, as though you were suspended in one of those sensory deprivation tanks where you feel as though you're floating in space, and if you stay there long enough you discover universal truths or go mad. On that Fiesta Sunday, therefore, I was not so much lying down as floating on my side, when Ondine flipped to a page marker in her leather-bound *Poetry from the Immortals* and said, "I'll read one."

"What's it called?" I wanted to know, lifting my head.

" 'Tintern Abbey.' " She pronounced it *Tintinabby,* as though it were one word, possibly a coinage by Poe. "I found it this morning."

"Wordsworth," I said sagely and, laying back, sank further into goose down and satin, so that only my nose and knees were exposed to light and air.

"You know it?" she said, sounding surprised and impressed that I knew the poem's author.

Since I enjoy being the object of Ondine's admiration, however fleeting, I neglected to tell her that every English undergraduate has, at some point in his ignominious career, had to memorize "Tintern Abbey" and to recite it aloud, in front of a classroom filled with bored or mocking peers. It should therefore have come as no surprise that I had heard of the poem. "I may have read it," I allowed and proceeded to recite from memory: " 'Five somethings have something, with the something of something.' " I wasn't faking my present ignorance of the text. It had been years since my most recent collision with the historical ballad.

"That's right," Ondine said, clearly impressed by my powers of recall. " 'Five years have passed,' " she read and then added, "I was there."

"Tintern Abbey?"

"Uh-huh," she said with a flossy lilt to her voice.

"Really?" Now it was my turn to be impressed. Because I hate flying and have trouble sleeping in alien bedrooms, the longest trips I ever take are to Vegas maybe once or twice a year, and then only for a couple of days — usually weekdays, when the hotel rates are cheaper and the highways aren't crowded. The fact that Ondine had recently trod the same ground upon which the Immortals had wandered lonely as clouds and bumped their foreheads on overhanging lime trees in their bowers, filled me with reverence . . . or possibly my blood sugar had dropped off. "Do you have any M & M's," I asked.

"No."

"I'd like a delicious treat."

"I'll tell you about my trip," she said. Ondine had learned quickly that if you accede to my demands for delicious treats, then you're soon spending all your time flitting to and fro like a mother sparrow digging up grubs for pink-faced Junior, who's never satisfied no matter how many plump wrigglers he gets. Gin, who enjoyed food even more than I do and could eat most linebackers under the table, never minded having cakes, colas, and Coffee-nips on hand for all times, but Ondine, who doesn't equate fatness with happiness, wouldn't play along.

"So last year, or was it the year before," she faltered, "anyway, just before I broke up with Kabir and came here, I went all through England and Wales and Scotland. My family comes from Scotland, I visited some relatives there that I had never seen in a little town called Glenrothes but there's no, like, town area to it, the only place to do any shopping is the city center which is the most hideous, I don't know, fifties or sixties architecture and never been upgraded, and all these unemployed people hanging around that look depressed. That's the only place you can go unless you like Bingo, which is always filled with smoke, so I didn't stay long. But other parts of England, like Tintinabby, were beautiful. You go through this little village, I think it was Bristol, I'm not good with names. I've been so many places, I see them all vivid in my mind but if you ask me to tell you the name. . . . And all the village children running down cobblestone streets and the village women in their bubuschkas. And then coming down this road and rounding the bend and feeling like the

fullness of life, the life of the village, the everyday reflecting
back on my own life back home that was about to change. I
felt full, like I could burst at the seams with love at this moment. And then seeing Tintern Abbey, it comes up like this,"
she raised her right arm and brought it down with an arcing
motion, "with one wall, there's holes where the windows
were, and the light streaming down through them, the bus
was going creepy slow because this was a small road, you
know, it was very slow so it felt like this was all in slow motion.
When I read it earlier today, the poem kind of felt that way,
too, like Wordsworth was stretching out time on purpose with
his words or something."

She began reading the poem.

> *Five years have passed: five summers, with the length*
> *Of five long winters! and again I hear*
> *These waters . . .*

I had read "Tintern Abbey" more times than I could
remember, been forced to commit its mossy lines to memory,
but as Ondine read them now, I realized I had never heard
them. Partially this new appreciation for the poem's true gist
must have been due to Ondine's delivery, which had none of
the arthritic pomp and histrionic posturing I'm used to hearing from professionals steeped in notions of transcendence and
Bergsonian time and who cares what all. Ondine, who had no
corrosive background in higher education, was able to read
the thing with an easy, colloquial, sparsely inflected delivery.
This must have been what Wordsworth himself was shooting
for—something about the language used by real people being
the only form of expression that a person of sensibility should
consider valid. If Ondine is anything, she's real.

Ondine read on, and I let myself get lost among the groves
and the copses and caves and houseless woods, until she came
to,

> . . . *These beauteous forms,*
> *Through a long absence, have not been to me*
> *As is a landscape to a blind man's eye,*

and stopped to comment. "This part brings back all those pictures, like Hay on Wye," she said, "it's another little village because the Wye River goes right by there too, and just this feeling he's talking about I feel the same way, like you can't let your heart be stopped or clouded by the things of the world or the mundane, the unhappy endings, you can't let it cloud up your clarity."

"Was that after you broke up with Kabir?"

"No, we were still together but internally the gears had already shifted, alls I found out on that trip was that I had the strength to do what I needed to do, I had proved to myself that I could hang in there with him through thick and thin, and I didn't need to anymore. They also have this cream tea in a lot of the little villages like Tintinabby, places that are like bed and breakfast places in a way, little houses with like little cafés in their front rooms and things, little tables. It's called cream tea, and they bring you out some homemade biscuits with this clotted cream and honey on the side, and a cup of tea, and they put this thick, almost like it's a cross between whip cream and butter. It's whipped up cream but its closer to butter than whip cream."

"We could make some right now," I suggested, the bright promise of treats springing eternal within the Nails belly.

"It's not the same, you have to be there," Ondine said definitively. She read on for a while longer and then said, "Can you finish, my voice is getting tired."

"Sure," I said. I took the proffered book from Ondine and started reading where she left off. I was doing fine, interpreting the lines with a liquidity and a new depth of feeling inspired by Ondine's natural rendition. I got through the parts about "gleams of half-extinguished thought" and "in this moment there is life and food / For future years," and then, wholly without warning, a funny thing happened to me, something that had never happened to me before with poetry.

I was on the part about his sister, and every time I'd bump up against the famous passage about Nature (it must be famous, because it sounded sort of familiar to me), the one that goes,

> . . . *for she can so inform*
> *The mind that is within us, so impress*
> *With quietness and beauty, and so feed*
> *With lofty thoughts, that neither evil tongues,*
> *Rash judgments, nor the sneers of selfish me,*
> *Nor greetings where no kindness is, nor all*
> *The dreary intercourse of daily life,*
> *Shall e'er prevail against us, or disturb*
> *Our cheerful faith . . .*

my throat became constricted, my breath strained, and tears welled up in my eyes. I tried to get through it a couple of times, somewhat embarrassed since I'm not used to bawling in front of other people except when close relatives have just died or, more recently, when I'm playing guitar on stage. I mean, be serious: crying at Wordsworth? The only feeling I could remember Wordsworth having previously elicited in me was fear and maybe some reflux esophagitis, but here he was bringing out deep-seated griefs that Liz the therapist and others had tried to unearth for years and failed. The harder I tried to calm the quaking in my voice and the heavings in my chest, the more recalcitrant those organs became. It was as though they had a will of their own and would *make* me cry.

Ondine put her arms around me and with a soothing, "That's, OK, just let it happen," rocked me gently into a deep reservoir of pain, most likely the same one I had dipped into that night at the Elbow Room but now it was my Self and not my Strat that was the engine of this extraordinary access and release of emotion, and I was delving deeper, to an exquisite, impersonal stillness at the source: a single point which burned and fused below my navel, swallowing civilizations whole; a mass at once critical, morbid, irresistibly attractive, and sublimely restorative to touch.

I rocked and shook with what must have looked to Ondine like a cataleptic fit, and then, just as strangely, a deep, rolling, musical laughter—which I can only describe as ancient and collective, since there was certainly nothing funny happening in Ondine's bedroom—started gushing and upwelling, and I pictured my mother's father, my Zaydeh who, while on a visit from Atlanta to our house (he must have been eighty; I was ten) fell on the step to our garage and broke his hip. For a while he lay there motionless, whimpering with the pain and the helplessness of it, and all at once he spread his arms in a surprising gesture of all-acceptance, as though he were floating on quicksand. He looked up at my mother and me, and from his lips came the wisdom of the ages. My grandfather said to us, in his Fulton County accent inflected with Yiddish and Russian, "Take it easy, you wouldn't get dizzy."

After his operation they kept him in the recovery room at Breitman Memorial Hospital until he stabilized, and then they brought him to a private room. I was standing at his bedside when he came out from under the anaesthetic. Ma was checking on Zaydeh's meds at the nurses' station, so I was the only one there when he opened his eyes for the first time. "Harmon," he said. His voice surprised me with its strength.

"Yes."

"Where am I?"

"You're in the hospital, Zaydeh," I said.

"Where's the dogs?" he said. My grandfather had two small mutts, Josh and Manny, who were his constant companions ever since my grandmother died.

I said, "The dogs are at home in Atlanta, Zaydeh. You're in the hospital."

"What are those dogs doing in the hospital?" he demanded, and in so loud a voice that an orderly who happened to be passing by his room stopped and looked around with a worried expression, as though a pack of hounds might at any mo-

ment come skittering down the immaculately waxed halls in
this most dignified of Jewish hospitals, leaving behind deep
scratches and muddy pawprints. At the absurdity of this image I started laughing, which in turn started my grandfather
laughing: not a rollicking, hearty laugh as at a great pun, but
a knowing chuckle, as when you see an abstract painting in a
museum and you get what the artist was saying. Laughing, we
looked into each other's eyes, and my Zaydeh laughed himself
back to sleep.

Now, as I lay still in Ondine's arms and remembered Zaydeh and his dogs, my laughter turned into a kind of rhythmic
whimpering which subsided eventually, and I was quiet. Ondine didn't stir, either, but continued to hold me. "Sheesh,"
I said after a while. "I wonder where all that came from."

"It doesn't matter," Ondine said. "It was real."

"It was that," I agreed.

"I never saw a man cry like that," she said.

"Neither did I. Not even me."

"I think you're brave."

"For what? All I did was cry." Actually I knew what she was
getting at, but I wanted to hear it from her.

"I mean men get taught they're never supposed to cry, so
you have to be brave and take risks to get back to the innocence you had before you got all that bullshit programming
about big boys never cry."

"Well, I wasn't trying to be brave."

"I don't believe that, I think you were. Real braveness is a
conscious thing, otherwise you're just acting on impulses. It's
hard to let yourself be a crybaby, and you're the biggest crybaby I ever saw."

"Wonderful," I said.

"No, I mean that as a compliment, I wish I could be like
you around human emotions, I have the spiritual covered but
I'm like in kindiegarden on the emotional plane, I know I've
got a lot to learn on that level."

"And you think you're going to learn it from me?" I said
incredulously.

"Not just from you but yes, from you. I think you're braver than you know."

What a concept.

After a few more moments of thoughtful quietude, Ondine asked, "What were the tears about, can you put it into words?"

"I don't think so."

"Try."

"I don't think I can. It must have something to do with the essentially good nature I believe people have but don't show it as often as I wish they would, because they—we—get caught up in having more things, or territory, or power or sex, it always comes down to sex or else we lash out because we've been wounded in the past—basic pre-evolutionary stuff," I rambled with an unaccountably Ondine-esque tempo and slackness of association. Perhaps crying has the same effect on the central nervous system as a glass of Champagne or an overdose of Altione, producing a diminishment in motor coordination and a looseness of tongue.

"But in addition to those vestiges," I blathered on, "each of us has a capacity for being reasonable and imaginative, and silly but in a good way, and for making art, which is what Wordsworth seems to be affirming in the poem, especially in the relationship between himself and his sister. I never had a sister, which is kind of sad, and I had almost complete isolation imposed on me as an only kid in a kidless neighborhood, which is sadder, and maybe I continue to impose that isolation on myself because that's how I grew up and so I'm most comfortable that way—by myself, alone with my furniture just so and my little rituals and habits—and that's the reason I haven't even considered living with anyone since Brenny left, which alone is worth a few hours' of uncontrollable sobbing if I thought about it—an emotional release I never indulge in, for the reason you just saw: There's a mountain of grief behind those floodgates," I said, in what has to be one of the most broadly misconceived metaphors in the history of speech, "and it scares me, it looks overwhelming."

"Plus," I rambled unchecked, "there's something else there, along the lines of a spiritual core. Wordsworth took special care not to call it God but you probably would, and maybe I would, too, if that word didn't have such negative associations for me, of crusades and people burning at stakes, and every other blasphemy that's been committed throughout history in the name of organized religion."

"I don't know about history," Ondine said in response to this soliloquy, perhaps the longest speech I've given in my life unless you count the oral report I had to do on the reproductive cycle of wood-ticks for my eighth-grade science class, "and I'm not big on organized religion, but I love God, it's a presence you feel and I call it God because that's an easy word and everybody knows it means something like a greater power."

"I feel that sometimes, too," I confessed, "like when I'm out in the water and the sun's going down and there's a warm Santa Ana blowing, and the surf is glassing off, and there's only a couple of guys left out, and you just feel . . . peaceful."

"In harmony."

"All's right with the world sort of thing."

"Right on. That's God."

"Neuroscientists would say it's just your body reacting to a stimulus and making endorphins that are getting you mildly and pleasantly stoned."

"Do you think that's all it is?" she asked didactically — if didactically's the word I'm looking for here.

"Partly, but sometimes I do feel as though there's something else going on — that presence you were talking about."

"Well that's what Tintinabby does, you can feel a presence there. It's a special place, like a power center."

"Mm," I said.

"Speaking of powerful presences," Ondine said with a touch of humor infusing her voice.

"What about them?"

"I'm feeling one right now."

"You are?"

"Yes. It's pressing my thigh."

Intense emotional discharge must loosen more than the tongue, because Ondine was right. Although I hadn't been paying it any mind, I had materialized a chertlike outcropping which was indeed pressing itself impertinently into Ondine's flannel jammies at the general vicinity of her outer thigh.

"Ah," I said, and thus, with this visitation from on low, did our Victorian period draw to a close, not with aesthetic movements or Diamond Jubilees, but instead with the rapid emergence of a large, unsophisticated, hard-working private.

O*ww!* You're on my hair."
"Better?"
"No, now it's under your elbow."
"There."
"Ah. Ootch."
"Wait, I'll move. Got it?"
"I think so."
"Wait, shit, your earring."
"I'll move."
"Gracefully accomplished."
"I was a dancer."
"I thought you might have been, the way you can bend your body around like that."
"Just a second, you're pressing my bladder."
"There."
"Ootchy."
"Sorry."
"You did that on purpose."
"Did not."
"Did so."
"I said I was sorry."
"Here, try it like this."

"That's it."

"Wait."

"There. Ah."

"Nope. That's not getting it either."

"There."

"Nope."

"I guess not."

"Damn, I thought we had a chance there for a minute."

"That's OK," she said.

My unshirted back was drenched in an ever-widening slick of sweat, clammy and chill. I felt like I might be coming down with something. "Can you pull one of those sheets on top of me?" I asked.

"Cold?"

"No, thanks, I'm already coming down with one." The lamest comeback in the book, and perfectly appropriate to this situation.

"There, better?"

"Thanks."

"No problem."

"Shall we try again?" I suggested gamely, although my heart wasn't really in it.

"No, I think that's the problem, too much trying," Ondine theorized. "You started out totally in your heart, crying about the poem and your childhood and all, and then as soon as you start to think, you seem so nervous and not sure of yourself or something, and your body was kind of like this, you started moving like a robot."

"Well, I was nervous. I've waited a long time for this."

"I'll say you were nervous, no one ever did anything like that to me before."

"Hey, I was just trying to make you feel good, forgive me if I've sinned. Anyway, there's supposed to be a spot."

"A spot?"

"Um-hm."

"What kind of a spot?"

"A make-you-feel-good kind of a spot."

"Where?"

"Right there."

"Hey, take it easy, I'm not a stuffed turkey or something."

"Oh, really? I thought you were."

"Ow."

"Relax. There."

"I don't feel anything, except like I have a b.m."

"It's there, I swear it."

"No way."

"Yes."

"Are you sure?"

"Positive. I got it from a book."

"What kind of a book would tell you to do that?" she said, demonstrating the movement obscenely with her thumb and tongue.

"Would you cut that out."

"Well that's what it felt like."

"OK, I get the point. Please accept my sincerest apologies: I thought you'd like it, and I was wrong."

"That's the problem with thoughts, they're all in your head, and the last place you want to be when you're making love is in your head."

"I know that," I said in a blustery tone that Liz would probably have insisted was defensive. "It may come as a shock to you, but this has never been a problem for me before." This was not mere groundless braggadocio. OK, maybe there was that one other time back in ought-six, but it's hardly worth mentioning. Besides, I was luded-out that time. "And furthermore," I countered, "you're not exactly dripping with lubricative secretions either, you know."

"Well it's not exactly a turn-on when you start kissing me, and then you just suddenly stop and look at me and you go, 'OK, now what do you want to do?' in an very awkward and nervous way. I mean, alls I can think is, 'Oh my God, this was a big mistake. Let's call the whole thing off.' "

"Oh, great, well then let's just call it off then," I said, wounded manliness overcoming my higher nature. "I mean, it sounds you're putting all the blame on me, and it's not. It's a fifty-fifty thing, and it's as much your fault as mine. If you had just taken your rings off first, before—"

"I wasn't putting it all on you and it isn't anybody's fault, it's just something that happens."

"Not to me."

"It sure seemed like you, if it wasn't you then there's a mad raper running around who looks just like you. And he can't keep it up," she added unnecessarily.

"Nice." I climbed off and turned over on my side to sulk. "Funny."

"Look," she said with a placating reasonableness I'd never noticed in her before—but then we'd never really hassled before. "Why don't we just start over, we can just lay with our peepholes touching."

This was a term I had never come across in any anatomy textbook. "Peepholes: Is that some pseudo-esoteric mystical term, like my third eye?" I asked, my testiness muffled by one of her satin-encased down pillows, so that 'third eye' came out sounding like 'Burl Ives.'

"No, the third eye's a real thing from yoga, but your peephole, it's like a tunnel that your caring and connection goes in and out of. It can override the mind, so when you have a fight about something, you connect peepholes and then you feel better."

"We're not fighting," I insisted, bringing the bottom of my fist down into her mattress, which immediately enveloped my fist, wrist, forearm and elbow in feathery softness. Dust rose.

"We're not?"

"We are engaged in a civil discussion," I said, not quite civilly.

"That's just sematics," she said. "We're having a fight."

"You call this a fight?"

"Seems like a fight to me. Our first fight, and we can choose to escalate or release it. Here," she demonstrated, pressing her palm to her naked abdomen, smooth, white, and lean, "put your hand between your bellybutton and your hara." Since I

didn't know where my hara was (as I now do), I laid my hand
against the area on my abdomen which corresponded to the
area she was touching on her body. "Don't you feel it sort of
warm and flowing?" she asked.

I replied, "I feel something moving in there, but it feels
more like my dinner churning around than compassion," and
then, remembering that formerly devoured meal, I had a flash
of realization. "Dinner!" I exclaimed brightly. "That's the
whole problem. You know how they tell you don't go swimming right after you eat, because all your blood goes to your
stomach while you're digesting, and if you go swimming, then
you'll get a cramp?"

"Yes," she allowed uncertainly.

"Don't you see, that's what's happening here: I ate food before we started reading 'Tintern Abbey,' and now it's being
digested, and so all the blood that would ordinarily have gone
to—well, all that blood's gone to my stomach and intestines
instead."

Any last wisps of romantic mood that had been hovering in
the room were certainly dispelled by this talk of secreted
chymotrypsin and bile and intestinal flora acting on boluses
of masticated gouda and apples, but I had an important point
to make. "If you were a dick," I hypothesized, "what would
you do in similar circumstances?"

"If I was a dick?" She looked appalled at the suggestion.

"Right."

"Anybody's dick?"

"Yes, yes," I said impatiently, "you could be anybody's
dick, but let's for the sake of argument imagine you're my
dick."

"Let me get this straight."

"It's not that difficult."

"I'm your dick."

"Right, and as my dick what would you do if your good
friend, Mr. Stomach, required the lion's share of the blood in
order to digest a sizeable ration of food?"

"I'd wait 'til he finished?" she ventured timidly, like a

schoolgirl who had raised her hand and then, when called, realized she wasn't at all sure of her answer.

"Precisely," I exalted. "You'd hang around all relaxed, waiting for your friend to finish with the blood, so that you could get back to the business of rogering young redheads."

Ondine looked doubtful, but since my hypothesis was clearly putting me in a more positive frame of mind, she didn't argue. Instead, she deftly steered the conversation away from the awkward subject of hypothetical dicks and back around to one with which she was more comfortable: peepholes. "Well," she said, "while we're waiting for your stomach to finish with the blood, let's just lay together."

Ondine climbed out from under the covers, seized me by the ribcage with both of her hands and rolled me over so that I lay supine, causing my disgraced member to be caressed and further shrunk—if such a thing were possible—by a cool breeze from her fan. I did not remain thus exposed for long, however, because Ondine climbed on top of me forthwith and stretched herself out in a prone position, her head turned sideways and cradled in the crook of my neck. She made some subtle shifts in her body's position over mine, until she was satisfied. With my arms at my side I lay there in a kind of passive deflation, feeling more martyred than mellowed by Ondine's latest move. "OK, now breathe," she commanded.

"I'm pretty sure I already was."

"I know but now I want you to follow your breaths in and out, and when you breathe out, concentrate on sending energy out through your peephole and into my peephole."

"Where are they again?"

She interposed her hand between our two bellies, just below the navel. "Right there."

"So what do I do now?"

"Just concentrate on your breathing and tune out everything else so your concentration is fixed on that one point, and just let the juice flow. You can count your breaths if it helps you to concentrate."

I breathed in and out. "How's that?" I said.

"Don't talk," she dictated and then, lowering and modulating her voice so that it resembled that of a stage hypnotist who's about to make some poor schmuck from the audience cluck like a chicken, she said, "just breathe. Breathe the red light of life force in through your nostrils, let it move down your spine, slowly down your spine, let it fill your arms and legs with life force as it moves, breathe the life force down your spine and then breathe it out your peephole and into mine, let your energy flow out of your peephole and fill up my peephole with energy as you breathe out, feeling the energy flow out of my body and into yours, filling you up with healing, nurturing energy, now take another breath . . . "

On and on she went in this droning, chowdery voice. I followed Ondine's instructions as best I could, given my chronically reactive airways which go into spasm whenever I come into contact with house dust, leaf mold, and mystical mumbo-jumbo, and yet I had to admit it: Something was happening. Whether or not it was energy moving I couldn't say, but there did seem to be a kind of spreading warmth between our bodies, as though a capricious sprite had emerged from Ondine's hot-water bottle and wedged a wafer-thin heating element between our two abdomens. I was counting my breaths and remarking to myself upon this unusual warmness, when — around thirty-eight — I began to observe a tingling sensation, more chilly than warm but not exactly cold, either, that seemed to extend out beyond my own fleshly boundaries, almost as though I were aware of vital workings inside Ondine's body as well as my own. Preposterous of course; Ondine has her body, and I have mine. I wrote this chimeric scrap of out-of-body apperception off as mere fatigue brought about by the frustrating exertions of the previous hour and, no longer conscious of my inhalations and exhalations, let myself drift into a sleepy state of semiconsciousness, during which half-waking reverie there came to me an odd visual picture, a bleared, powdery, soft-edged image of Ondine and myself, in which we resembled one of those cell mitosis

charts you see in high school biology — the panel labeled Inter-
mediate, where the cells are not yet separated but almost.

I became aware too of distant pastoral sounds, like young
beeves lowing under dark skies pushed about by winds that
were our shared breaths, and lambs bleating to ancient druid-
ic drums that were our synchronous heartbeats, and when my
breath stopped (as my apnea often causes it to do when I'm
on the edge of sleep), I half-awoke to find that my own formerly withered stump, which had been dozing snugly in the
furry hollow formed by the juncture of Ondine's legs, had
sprung to life and was insinuating itself into a cavity no longer
sandpaper-dry but rather syrupy and siphonic, drawing me
slickly into the life of things. I chinked open my eyes just
enough to espy Ondine, who had been lying on top of me all
this time, sit up astraddle my flanks, her hands on my shoulders and her breasts both of a dangle.

Ondine had her eyes closed and was making pleasure
sounds. "Pull me down," she ordered with some urgency, still
with her eyes closed. I reached up behind her shoulders and,
with the left corner of my upper lip raised and contorted in
that snarling cur-like expression that generations of Impaglia-
tore and Nails men must have made before me, and epochs
of upright hominids before them, I tilted my pelvis skyward
and brought Ondine down hard against the present moment.

"Nrgh," I said.

As it turns out, Ondine — unlike many women with whom
I've had passing sexual acquaintance — doesn't enjoy in-out
friction so much as the slow deep grind, building up to a climax whose force might be likened to a volcanic eruption that
blows away mountaintops and fells forests. Because there was
so little sustained friction involved in our coupling, I was able
to maintain good form without ever surrendering my seed and
thereby losing momentum, while Ondine shuddered and
writhed until, finally, she let her torso topple down heavily on
my own, in a splash of commingled pheromones. Gasping for
breath, she managed to say, "Enough, I'm numb and my legs
are shaking."

"Sure?" I asked with a rough Latinate pride in my voice.

"Yes, positive, now it's your turn."

"If you insist."

I reached my left arm under Ondine's waist and, managing with practiced skillfulness not to disengage, hoisted her and flipped her over on her back, whereupon I abandoned the deep grind in favor of a more direct and expeditious pounding. Ondine lent her tacit consent to this endeavor by grabbing my rump with both hands and slamming me repeatedly against her, which brought me right up to the brink of manumission . . . at which point she abruptly pushed me off her, with the strength and terrible swiftness of a heavyweight judo-Ka executing a throw. I was surprised, and my Boswell poked at the air tentatively, like an eyeless, legless newt in search of a cozy nesting place. However, none of this surprised me half as much as when Ondine climbed off the bed, got down on all fours and growled, "Fuck me like a dog," in a bestial, Stygian voice.

"I beg your pardon," I said, to tease and infuriate, thus arousing her passions to an even higher pitch. This stuff comes naturally to me, by the way. You don't get it from no books.

"I said fuck me like a dog," she snarled assertively.

"You appear to be suggesting that I fuck you like a dog," I said placidly as I climbed up behind her.

"Exactly," she said. "Ram it to me, you bastard."

"Nice diction." I said.

S O   M A N Y
L I G H T   S T A N D A R D S

~/~

I awoke with Ondine beneath me. She was lying on her belly, still on the floor of the bedroom, her body cold and quaking like hilly icescape beset by tremors. She was crying — either that, or she was performing some kind of yogic exercise which combined sharp, shallow breathing with a simultaneous lowering of the core body temperature. Crying seemed more likely.

I rolled off and lay beside Ondine with the intention of lavishing solicitude upon her, but she turned her head away from me.

"What's wrong?" I asked.

"Nothing." The crying had stopped. Her voice was masonite.

I attempted to lighten the proceeding. "People have had a lot of reactions to my lovemaking before," I quipped, "but this is the first time anyone started weeping uncontrollably."

"I'm not crying."

"You were."

"So?" she said, in a tone that might have implied an addendum along the lines of: *What's it to you, goatsucker?*

"So what's wrong?" I asked again, undaunted. Perilous

commerce: Sometimes when you ask questions you get answers.

Ondine sat up on the side of the bed and wrapped her torso in one of her many sheets, this one of thick flannel with pastel blue flowers on it. I sat next to her. She sucked in breath and held it, in the same way I've done on numerous occasions while duck-diving under a sneak closeout set, and then she blew it out again. "It's just, it's hard for me to say this, I don't even know how to say it, but I've been with different people and I'm not meant to be with anybody anymore, you understand?"

"Huh?" I said, rendered dumb by her statement, which, smacking of rejection as it did, seemed wholly inappropriate in light of recent developments. Not only had we just been lovers, we had been mitotic cells together. Certainly that must signify a connection of the most germinal sort. Rediscovering speech, I protested, "I thought we already talked about that and decided it was OK for you not to love me yet, that you'd just like me deeply for a while."

"See, you say *yet* as though I'm going to be in love with you sometime, but what I'm saying is I'm not capable of loving anybody," she said with plaintive inflection.

"You seemed pretty loving to me." I reached under the sheets and brought up a fingerful of our intermingled love-glop. "See?"

"That's different, that's not personal."

"You're telling me *that's* not personal?" I demanded, waving said finger, on which our exudata had already hardened into a waxen glaze, in front of her face. "If that's not, then what is?"

"I mean it is personal, but it's sex, not love. It's like I only feel universal love, things at a distance I love, like animals and old ladies and friends and all, but I don't feel personal love between a man and a woman. I can't. It doesn't suit me, I don't think it works, and I don't know how to do it."

"You don't have to do anything," I said, as if I were an expert on the subject. "It just happens."

"Bot for *me.*"

"Did you say, 'Bot?' "

"Not."

"You mean you've never loved anyone?"

"No, I've loved too many people and each time I thought it happened, but when I really looked at it it wasn't happening. So now I know I just can't love on a personal level, like I'm missing a cromozone or something."

"Chromosome," I said helpfully.

"You know, I've got to tell you it really bugs me when you correct me all the time," she said. There was behind her anger a generous helping of that fierce intensity by which people stereotype women of the red-haired order. Ondine's eyes were wide, unblinking and steady as they trained themselves on that vulnerable area just below my third eye: the bridge of the nose, made from bone so thin and brittle that a redhead, if driven to the brink of insanity by a picky philologue, could cleave it in half with a single ridge-hand blow and then, with an upward thrust of her palm, jam it up into my brain, causing instant paralysis and—if she did it just right—a horrible, gurgling death.

In the face of such gruesome prospects I humbled myself abjectly. "Sorry, it's an old habit, a hangover from my English teacher days. Besides, I don't correct you all the time."

"Yeah well I'm not one of your students," she said, clearly not mollified. "I just talk how I talk and I'm sick of judgments. People are so judgmental and superior sometimes, like they're greater than everybody else just because they know how to talk with correct grammar or whatever, I've got news for you man, there's plenty of great people in the world who get along just fine without knowing any fuckin' grammar rules, I'll take Sister Teresa any day over people who are intellectual and sit around writing articles nobody reads except other anal-retentive intellectual types." She spat out the words *grammar* and *intellectual* as though they were chunks of putrefied animal flesh that had found their way into her mouth.

"For your information there's a lot of things a lot more important in the world than being smart," she continued, "like being a good person for starters who care about other people and aren't mean, I know a lot of smart people who are the biggest cheats, slimebags, scum of the earth I ever knew, and I know plenty of uneducated people who are great people, and I'll take great people any day over slime."[12] Her eyes were blue-gray meteors of some unearthly element, blazing away.

"Well, bad English bugs *me*," I countered. "It's a violation of one of the few things I hold sacred. You know how you love God? That's how I feel about language, and you'd probably be annoyed if I kept mispronouncing God's name all the time, like if I referred to Him as Gob or something. I can't help it, I get this gut reaction whenever I see a misspelled word — it's as though I've received a hard kick to the solar plexus — but in the future I'll make every effort to refrain from correcting you. I had no idea you were so touchy about it."

"You'd be touchy too, if one of your old boyfriends tried to strangle you and another one tried to rip off your fuckin' ear."

"Somebody tried to rip off your ear for dangling a participle?"

"No, but it's just restimulating of guys who always want you to change something about yourself, they never think you're all right the way you are, and then if you show like one ounce of being human, you don't fit their picture of what the good little wife or whatever should be, or like if you watch a fuckin'

---

[12]Her reaction to my compulsive grammaticasting was certainly justified, and her point about professional intellectuals well taken. At the university, I used to work under the tutelage of some of the biggest minds of this and previous generations, reflective practitioners who could scan the spondaic stuffing out of a verse line, who could expatiate eloquently and protractedly on the aesthetic versus the didactic properties of allegory in Bunyan's *Pilgrim's Progress* but who used, almost in the same breath, to refer to their undergraduate students as "foot traffic," and who routinely took advantage of underage boys and girls under their desks.

soap opera on TV or you don't keep the kitchen absolutely spotless every minute, or worst of all, you talk to a man, just some guy on the street who you feel compassion for because he has MS, totally safe and unthreatening, then they totally wig out and get violently jealous or out of control."

"*Ahhhh,*" I said, the scales falling from my eyes (as I believe the expression goes). "*Ah-haaaaaa!* So *that's* what this is all about. Hey," I said, taking her face gently between my two palms and holding it a few inches from my own face, so that I went amblyopic for a brief space until I backed off a bit, "look at me." She had been looking at me anyway, but I found the opportunity to engage in such high melodrama irresistible. "Tell me. Who do you see?"

Ondine, child of grace that she is, didn't hock a lugie in my face or wrench her head violently out of my grasp or even remind me that I should have said, "whom." She merely looked at me with a kind of simmering resentment, as one might watch a CHP officer while he's writing you up for excessive show of speed on the Coast Highway. "You," she said blandly.

"Correct," I said, releasing her face. "You see me. Otherwise known as Harmon Nails III. Not Kabir, not Fred, not anybody but Harmon. I'm not your old boyfriends, I'm not anything like them. I've never ripped off anybody's ear in my life—" I caught myself in mid-speech, realizing this statement was not entirely true. "—that is, except Marlew."

"I knew it," Ondine said, despondency rising. "Who's Marlew, one of your old girlfriends?"

"No, my teddy bear I got when I was two. His real name was Marshall, but I couldn't say Marshall, so I called him Marlew. I must have been four or five when his ear came off. I was swinging Marlew around by the ear, and he just kind of came apart. His ear ripped off and then all the stuffing came flying out of his head. It wasn't a pretty sight. He ended up looking more like an old oven mitt than a beloved companion, and he was too old and fragile to fix. I was clinically depressed for a week, so my parents bought me a land tortoise as a pet. I named him Finger and used to melt candles on his shell and follow him around at night with the lights off. Did I ever tell you about Finger before? I can't remember if it was you or. . . . "

"You try to make it sound funny with teddy bears and everything," Ondine cut in, not noticeably softened by my playful tale of juvenile doll-dismemberment, "but that's what they all told me, too: 'I'm different from all the other guys.' They tell you they're going to be different, they act all nice and loving and things go along fine for a while, and then they start picking at little things, like you leave the cap off the toothpaste tube or do a perfectly clean massage exchange with another man, and you make adjustments trying to be big and encompass their trips because nobody's perfect and you want things to work out, but pretty soon you realize you're not being who you really are, you've invested five and a half years out of your life and you've got nothing to show for it. Excuse me for saying it but from my experience, men — even the ones who mean well and have good hearts — are a bunch of demanding, insecure babies who want to follow their dick around and then project that onto you and get all jealous, or else they let their dishes pile up for two weeks in the sink and their hairs all over the toilet and then get all wigged out if you leave a coffee cup on the table. I can't encompass that sort of shit anymore, I started having heart palpitations before I broke up with Kabir and the doctor said I have a prolapsed mitral valve, and any kind of stress makes it act up. Frankly I'm scared you're going to turn out to be just another asshole that ends up kicking holes in the wall and breaking things and jumping up and down, and my heart can't take it," she said, and the crying recommenced, but in earnest this time.

Reliving former bad times — abusive lovers unnamed and long discarded, her recent split from Kabir the aloof astrologer, her mother who committed suicide after a lengthy bout with lupus, her father who took to the consolations of the bottle after his wife's death, her own recently diagnosed leaking heart — Ondine ran her hands distractedly through her hair and made rhythmic, sepulchral sounds, drawing air in large gulps between her sobs and suspirations. Ondine attempted to talk while all this bawling and sighing and nasal discharging was going on, so that she sounded as though she'd come under the influence of several stiff tequila shooters: "*Ass why I dever wadda be idda relashudship,* oorp, *the's oiees so buch drawba,* oonnh, *nass why I ca't love you odd a persoddal level,* hunnh, oonnh. See?"

I held Ondine close, and when her storm of emotion blew over, asked her, "Need a Kleenex?"

"Please." Taking a few sheets from my proffered box of generic tissues, she applied one to her nose. *"Blaaart,"* she said and then laughed, the kind of laugh you make at the tail end of a weepy jag, when the distinctions between grief and hilarity become blurred. "I hate to cry," Ondine said, laughing. "The only thing I hate more than crying is to throw up. It gives me a headache."

"I hate to throw up, too." We had already established our shared aversion to vomiting some months earlier, when Ondine came to visit me at the Elbow Room that first night, but it seemed appropriate to reassert this rare tidbit of commonality now.

Lying in silence on Ondine's bed, under a bank of comforters, we contemplated the profundity of this shared human experience for a brief spell, which Ondine eventually broke with a single syllable: "Hnn."

"Did you say, 'Hnn?' "

"Yes, 'Hnn,' " she said, a hint of defensiveness infusing her voice. "That's not grammatically wrong, is it?"

"No, you just reminded me for a second of someone I know who used to say, 'Hnn,' a lot."

"Gin," she said with authority.

"How'd you know?"

"I'm telepathic."

I couldn't tell if Ondine was kidding or not, but I wasn't about to challenge her on the issue of her supernatural powers. "I forgot you even knew Gin," I said.

"I didn't really know her. I used to say hi to her and talk about her chickens."

"She killed them," I recalled. "With her hands. Wrung them by the neck until dead."

"Gross. That's mean."

"Probably more callous than mean, actually."

"Well that's just sematics."

I almost informed Ondine that her last word lacked a vital consonant, but her recent speech about anal-retentive intellectual slime had an effect on me. Maybe the formal elements of speech *are* less important than the meanings they impart, I considered, and let the offense pass, leaving molar indentations in my tongue.

"Frankly I can't see you with Gin," Ondine said.

"I can't either. She's in South Carolina and won't even take my calls."

"I mean I could never see what you saw in her."

"I guess we had a lot in common. We liked all the same music and food, and we had a sort of unspoken language that we invented together."

"So why'd you split up?"

"I wonder about that myself sometimes. I think I was originally attracted more to what she represented than who she was."

"Did you think she was sexy?"

"At first I did, but later not so much."

"That's how I felt about Kabir. I loved him, but more like a brother, he always seemed like such a little boy to me and not a man. Did she have orgasms?"

"Gin?"

"Yes."

"You're asking an awful lot of questions, aren't you?"

"I just want to know."

I answered, somewhat reluctantly, "Sure, she had them, but it sometimes took several hours of hard manual labor to get there."

"Really? I can come after just a few minutes of making love, if it's with intention."

"You could come by looking at a light standard with intention, if you don't mind my saying."

She laughed again. "I can't imagine how some women can't come."

"My, don't *we* sound self-satisfied. Psychic and multi-orgasmic, too," I said in a tone of affable challenge.

"I'm not putting them down, I'm just glad I can come easy," she said, but despite her denial I could tell I had opened her eyes to a side of herself which had rarely been pointed out to her before (at least by someone who wasn't trying to throttle her or kick down her house at the same time): a certain pride and superiority and failure of empathy, the very things she criticizes most in other people.

"Me, too," I said, choosing not to press the issue because at that moment I was visited by an insight, and I don't have them all that often. "Hey, remember when you said all that stuff about chromosomes and little old ladies and not being able to love on a personal level?"

"Um-hm."

"Well, it just occurred to me that maybe loving somebody on a personal level doesn't have anything to do with all the pictures you have about what that means. Maybe it just means telling them that you're scared to love them because you've been deeply hurt by a bunch of assholes you've been involved with. It's like a paradox, because by telling me you can't love me on a personal level, you *are* loving me on a personal level. Get it?"

"I don't know." She sounded skeptical.

"It's not something you can know or think about," I said with another pinch of the idiot savant in my voice. "Someone once told me, as soon as you start using your head, you lose your heart."

"I think it was your hard-on you were losing," Ondine had to go and remind me, the brat.

"Anyway," I concluded, trying not to let the memory of my

former dysfunction detach me from the thread of my idea, " 'I'm scared' is as good a place as any for you to start loving on a personal level, as you put it."

She looked reflective. "You might be right," she said, and that little smiler's smile flickered across her face. "How about you?"

"How about me what?"

"Are you scared, too?"

"Do I look like the kind of guy who gets scared?" I asked, flexing my biceps and attempting to throw my chest out, which had the unfortunate effect of pinching a nerve between my shoulder blades. "Ow," I said.

"Don't strain yourself, little man. I need you in shape."

"Oh, whatever for?" I asked coyly.

"A woman can only look at so many light standards," Ondine said, a motto we might all do well to keep in mind during these troubled times.

CHICKENS LOVE
EVERYTHING

~~

Ondine and I became increasingly what you might call a couple, especially if you saw us walking down California Street arm in arm, Ondine occasionally slipping a hand into one of my back pockets, grabbing one of my glutes and giving it a firm squeeze in that delightfully common way she has. We saw each other every day, with me continuing to drive over to her house, where we'd eat rice cakes and ripe bananas, shoot rummy, *Vrr!* each other, and pass the balance of our free time energetically, then sleepily, among her sheets and blankets and comforters. Ondine continued to confront her own internal demons, those lurking fears and suspicions born of past disillusionments and injuries, and for a while she managed to keep them at bay. However, during a particularly trying period of work-related stress (she decided to expand her jewelry business to include the production of modally-tuned wind chimes, an enterprise which required a significant cash outlay for metal tubing, treatment vats and chemicals, not to mention the hiring of two assistants to cut, anodize, and assemble the chimes), her demons got the upper hand, and without warning she drew back from me.

On that terrible day I had approached her precisely in the

way she had trained me: I went first for the back of her neck with a bit of lip-and-tongue work, followed by some bold caresses of flanks and torso, then a teasing dalliance of fingertips at the downtown four-level interchange. In the past, this routine had always set Ondine to wriggling, but on this day she merely shrugged her shoulders and said flatly, "I don't feel like it."

While I was naturally surprised by this unwonted response, I wasn't offended. I remember once not being in the mood myself, so I could accept this rebuff with only minor pangs of rejection. However, the exact thing happened three or four days running, and I started to feel like the family pooch who suddenly and unexpectedly finds himself dumped in a remote parking lot without so much as a Liv-A-Snak as a token of appreciation for his years of unflagging loyalty. Worst of all, when I asked Ondine what was going on, she gave me a motto instead of an explanation. "Sometimes the tide's in and sometimes it's out," is what she said. While this may have been a sound piece of oceanography, it carried an ominous suggestion when applied to our love life. What Ondine was saying, if I understood her correctly, was that we were about to embark upon a sexual ebb of unspecified—and possibly lengthy—duration. Talk about your goings-around coming around. Not since my marriage had I spent more than the occasional one-nighter with a sexually aloof woman, and in more recent relationships, my killer ambiguity had always made *me* be the one to withdraw, as I did with Gin. Yet here I was, less than a year later, on the receiving end of the very aloofness I'd been dishing out.

Having had no experience with sustained rejection, I didn't know how to cope with Ondine's new attitude. Gin, I recalled, had responded to my emotional low-tides by cooking pot pies, playing tunes, and waiting for my mood to change. But, being one of the impetuous Nailses, I'm cut from a more impatient bolt of fabric than Gin. I endeavored to win back Ondine's affection by action. Wooing her with generosity, I bought her one of the biggest crystals you'll ever see outside the Museum of Science and Industry. I drove her to the wedding of one of girlfriends in San Diego and even sat through the grisly, flower-bedecked affair. I gave her my old quadraphonic stereo, which, although somewhat dated and clunky, worked fine. I cooked meals and took out her trash, the latter being a chore I've despised ever since my mother forced my childlike self to do it weekly. Moreover, as all this self-sacrifice was going on, I attempted to allay Ondine's fears regarding my character by assuring her repeatedly of our future as a coupled unit.

Pursuit at first left me glowing with ruddy good health. It's much more invigorating to be the pursuer than to be the one who feels trapped and wants out. But Ondine's detachment and coldness, to which she clung with a passion matched only by her former lust for the diversions of the bedchamber, gradually wore down my steadfast faithfulness, until one day I found myself almost having an affair with someone I met at a lawn party following the wedding of Nick Pananides to a Miss Anabelle Grayson. I was munching on a rice-stuffed grape leaf, when a youngish woman walked over. I had a feeling that I had met her before, but I was distracted from making a positive identification by her rare loveliness.

If Gin was a potato and Ondine a pearl onion, this woman was an iris or narcissus without the bulb attached. Rangy she was, tall, lissome and lithe, with straight, neck-length hair the lucitic amber of clover honey, suede-brown eyes, and lips that, though untainted by stick or gloss, were as richly roseate as any vine-ripened raspberry I've ever plucked and popped into mouth. She wore a dress of a clingy material which, while it didn't hug her body exactly or accentuate her contours in the obvious way that Ondine's Spandex pants and halters sometimes do, still gave one a thrill on the glandular level. She looked directly at me, extended her hand, and delivered a salutation with puzzling informality: "Hello, teach. Long time no see."

"You know me?" I asked.

"Yes, I know you," she said, with a slightly mocking edge to her voice. "Remember Keeshan Hall, the ladder?"

Keeshan Hall!

Hardly were those words out of her mouth when it all came back to me in one of those floods of recollection that were so popular in French novels a few years back, only this one wasn't inspired by sweet rolls but rather by the evocative presence of a woman standing before and looming above me with talk of halls and ladders. This woman, I recalled—Lucie Rideout was her name—had been a student in the first composition class I ever taught when I was a graduate teaching assistant. In those days she was more gawky than lithe, more lanky than lissome, but she was the smartest kid in class and had a remarkably sharp wit for one so young, with ethics to match: She hated all the right things—sororities, South Africa, oil platforms —and, unlike your average sophomore who has ambitions of getting a job as loan officer in a major financial institution, Lucie dreamed of majoring in studio art, perhaps the most impractical and therefore the most admirable of all enchantment-pursuits.

Lucie used to sit in the front of the classroom, where she kept crossing and uncrossing her long, tanned legs. If you're a teacher yourself, you know how distracting it can be when you're trying to conduct class discussion on the hunting imagery in Hemingway's "The Short Happy Life of Francis Macomber" and you find yourself staring down the barrel of an art majorette's loaded gym shorts, but it's a pleasant kind of distraction, not like horseflies or bronchospasms. That she had more than a mild crush on me was obvious partly because of all the leg action, and partly because whenever she came to talk with me in my office—which she did with much more frequency than did the rest of the students—she always sat so close to me that I could smell her perfume, could see the rims of her contact lenses outlined against her corneae. That's close, baby, and it worked the usual mysterious chemistry on me. I was attracted to her—How could I help it? Am I not a man? — but of course never acted on it while she was in my class because it's unethical and illegal. Besides, I thought our age difference too great: I was a grizzled and hoary twenty-two, she a downy nineteen.

During a class session midway through the quarter, one of my less enterprising students, a torpid brat who had bad skin, a pug nose, a buzz-cut, and who usually propped himself up against the wall in the back of the classroom, asked me with half-closed eyes if I was going to give a quiz on the next reading assignment. We had just finished the short story portion of the course, and I had assigned *The Stranger* as their first novel, because it seemed neither too long nor too inaccessible, most of its words containing no more than two syllables. In those days I subscribed to the progressive axiom that students will read assigned texts because they have a natural curiosity and desire to learn for the sake of learning, so I had no intention of forcing them to prove that they had read the novel by testing them on it. I therefore dismissed the brat's question with a breezy, "The day I give a pop quiz on *The Stranger* will be the day I come to class through the window." Since the classroom was on the second story of Keeshan Hall, a venerable, ivy-covered dowager of a building, he and the rest of the class took my statement to mean exactly what I intended it to mean. There would be no pop quiz on *The Stranger*.

I don't know where I acquired this silly-ass attitude about learning for its own sake. *I* certainly never read anything out of curiosity when I was an undergrad, except maybe Ionesco's *The Bald Soprano* because it was easy and its absurdity paralleled my own worldview with astonishing consistency. Everything else I read only because I was under threat of imminent testing or quizzing. This seemed to have been the case with my comp students as well. Since they had assumed there was to be no quiz, they hadn't read *The Stranger*. There's nothing more alienating than standing in front of a room of blank young faces and asking questions to which one gets no response other than an uncomfortable bowing of heads, a nervous shuffling of papers, and a quietude you could cut with a chainsaw. So shaken was I by my failure to generate lively class discussion, or any class discussion, that I let them go a half an hour early. They received this news with whoops, cheers, and a massed rushing for the door.

In retrospect, I realize I should have harangued my students mercilessly for their negligence—they certainly deserved it—but, being a neophyte in the teaching ranks and lacking therefore the necessary self-confidence to wade into them with the twin rods of indignance and self-righteousness, I worked out a diabolically passive-aggressive scheme. I borrowed an aluminum stepladder from my neighbors, loaded it into Velma[13] and brought it to school just before the next class session. Appareled in the Levis and plaid flannel shirtings of a groundskeeper so as to minimize attention that might be aimed in my direction, I carried the ladder resolutely to Keeshan hall, where, after trudging through some furze and gorse, I reached the venerable brick wall. I extended the ladder to its full length—it came in three sections—and, having leaned it against the wall, climbed up to the second story window which was always cracked open, since the ventilation in Keeshan Hall was notoriously bad. I pushed hard on the window, which swung inwards noiselessly, I lifted the dusty Venetian blinds with my free hand, and I announced loudly, "Clear your desks, boys and girls. We're gonna take a quiz!" and climbed into the classroom.

My fenestral entry was met with a variety of student reactions. Some—most likely the few who had read *The Stranger*—laughed unrestrainedly and appreciatively (Lucie was one of these). Others sat disbelieving, with expressions like those you might find on a family of opossums startled in the act of stealing your cat's food or painting flowers on their heads. The snotty kid complained, "But you said we weren't gonna have a test on *The Stranger*."

"To the contrary, my man," I replied in a tone of good-natured reproof, "I said the day I'd test you on *The Stranger*

---

[13]The old VW van I owned in those days.

would be the day I came in through the window." I gestured grandly to the open window, where the Venetian blinds were still swaying back and forth languidly, like coastal palms being caressed by warm afternoon onshores. I drew a stack of mimeographed quiz-sheets from my daypack with a flourish and said, "Go to it, kids. You have the whole class period to finish, although some of you may not need it."

If you ever have to choose between being a student taking quizzes or a teacher administering them, be the teacher. It's a much more reposeful setup, believe me. As I sat in the front of the class, cozily enveloped in some distracting piece of contemporary fiction, the students bent to their quizzy task with considerable grumbling and groaning *sotto voce*, running of fingers through hair, gnawing of ball-point caps, and so on. About halfway through the class period the most hopelessly clueless of the students turned in their quizzes and oozed dejectedly out of the room, and I began grading papers with an effortless loosing of D's and F's like sharp little darts into the hearts of their grade-point averages. There were, however, three students — presumably the ones who read the novel — who received good grades: Two got B's and one got an A. Lucie Rideout was of course the one who aced the test, and not because I liked her, either. She got every question right, and even discussed Camus' notion of authenticity as it pertained to some of the short stories we had read earlier.

The second-story window episode deepened the bond between Lucie and me. She came to see me as a taker of outlandish creative risks — just the kind of person to whom freshman art-studio majors are attracted — while I came to appreciate her complete personage: not merely her friendliness, her quick wit, her long legs and the beckoning recesses of her shorts, but also her unusually ripe intellect, the extent of whose depths she hinted at in her quiz. At the end of the quarter she turned in her last essay by slipping it under the door of my office with a small, lemon custard-colored envelope stapled to it. Inside the envelope was a small, lemon custard-colored square of paper on which was handwritten,

Dear Dr. Nails,
  Here is your last chance to critically appraise and evaluate me.
How lucky you are! I really enjoyed your class, and I hope we are
able to stay friends. If you have any questions about the sources
I used for my paper, or if you want to get together for tennis or
lunch over the summer, you can call me at 966–4590. I'll be
here all summer working at a day camp.
  Thank you very much,

and she signed her name, *Lucie,* embellishing it with one of
those smiling faces that all underclasswomen, even deeply
reflective art-studio majors, must put by their names. It's a
law.

As long as Lucie was a student in a class of mine, any response on my part to this unsubtle come-on would have
been—and should have been—branded as sexual harassment,
a breach of collegiality, and an offense to the eyes and ears of
all persons with more than a dash of moral rectitude. Once
having turned in the final grades for that class, however, the
rules would change. My students would become my *former*
students, from which plasma-pool of youthful humanity I was
free to dip liberally if so moved. With this in mind, I gave my
final papers what those in the trade call a holistic reading,
meaning that I skimmed the first and last paragraphs, omitting the body of each essay entirely under the assumption that
the middle paragraphs are usually exactly the same as the first
and last anyway. I marked all the papers within three days of
the final exam, filled out the appropriate grading forms,
dashed down the hall and handed them breathlessly to the
departmental secretary, who expressed surprise at my having
gotten my grades in so quickly. I was the first instructor to
finish, she said, adding that I hadn't given her the impression
that I was such a 'go-getter' until now.

My quarter officially over, I dialed her number with a finger
palsied by anticipation of earthly delights. If it's true, as T-
Bone Billups sings, that Love always rides a slow train, then
Lust always has a bulging pocketful of quarters for the express

uptown. Calamitously, instead of hearing Lucie Rideout's cheery halloo, I got the electronically processed voice of a phone company operator, who said, "The number you have reached has been changed. Please hang up and dial again." After the school year was over Lucie must have moved, I reasoned, and, having not heard from me for three days, must have inaccurately assumed that I wasn't interested in her in *that* way. I called information, was given the out-of-service number I already had. I called the registrar at the university to find out if Lucie had left a forwarding address or phone, which she hadn't. At a loss for further avenues of enquiry, I kicked myself all summer for not having called Lucie immediately upon receipt of her note, and I consoled myself with the prospect of seeing her again the following school year. I didn't. See her, I mean. When I again enquired at the Registrar's office in the fall, under the pretext of needing to contact Lucie to discuss a grade change, they told me she had been accepted by the Study Abroad Program to spend the following year in Aix-en-Provence. I never saw Lucie Rideout again, and gradually her willowy image faded from my mind . . . that is, until Nick's wedding.

Having placed her, I exclaimed, "Lucie Rideout! You've changed!" It was true. The intervening years had fleshed her out in all the right places, and her face reflected the wisdom, cynicism, and good-humored acceptance that one gains between ages nineteen and twenty-five or -seven, if one doesn't drink a quart of Jim Beam every day.

"So have you, Mr. Nails."

"Please. Call me Harmon," I said suavely.

"Harmon." she said, smiling at our new-found familiarity. "I see you don't have your moustache any more."

"No, it was cool in the seventies, but the past few years I started looking more like a highway patrolman than a left-wing social democrat, so I cut it off. Hey," I said, calling up a vivid scrap memory, "do you still sign your name with those little smiley faces?"

"No," she said with a gamesome smile. "Do you still get away with teaching Beatle lyrics as poetry in your classes?"

"I don't lecture any more." I said somberly. "I gave up teaching."

"Why? You were a great teacher."

"Thanks, but I hated the bullshit that went along with it. Good teaching, caring about kids, teaching them how to write and think was never a priority with the Anguish Department. They wanted you to do research — jump through hoops, play the game, boost their image in the academic community — and I hated research. The only thing I hated more than research was researchers."

"So what do you do now?"

"Play music."

"That's it?"

"No, but that's a lot. That's also how I know Nick. He's in my band, maybe you've heard of us. Captain Zzyzx."

"*You're* in Capain Zzyzx?" she asked admiringly.

"I *am* Captain Zzyzx," I replied, flashing wistfully on Thrasher and the desert. I told Lucie Rideout she should come hear us sometime. Lucie promised she would and gave me her new phone number, joking that I'd better use it this time. I took it.

That night, I mentioned to Ondine that I had run into an old school friend, which was true, although I thoughtfully omitted the trivial details about her raspberry lips and so on. Ondine indicated approval, saying she had lots of 'man friends' who were like brothers to her. She said she'd feel more comfortable seeing these so-called brothers if I had women who were my friends. That way, she figured, I'd have no reason to get jealous of her friends, as so many of her previous lovers had unreasonably done. Spurred on by Ondine's encouragement (and, I have to be honest, by the memory of her shorts), I called Lucie. We had lunch together. We went to a Saturday matinee. We went to the beach and, bathingsuited, lay side-by-side on a towel, upon which narrow piece of red terry fabric something happened.

I told Ondine about it that night. Actually, she kind of pried it out of me, but I would have told her about it if she hadn't, I'm pretty sure. However, that's what our lawyer friends would call a moot point, because I never got a chance to broach the subject. Almost as soon as I walked in her door that night, Ondine asked me pointedly, "Correct me if I'm wrong, but have you been fucking that Lucie?" — ironically, almost the very phrase Gin had used to pump me for information about Ondine many months earlier.

Women are amazing. How they can smell a potential affair, even when one's assignations are rigorously clandestine, I have no idea. Maybe they really are telepathic, or else I'm as transparent as the cellophane on a pack of ribbed Ramses. In either case, I told Ondine no, I hadn't been fucking that Lucie, which was true. I hoped Ondine would be satisfied and drop the subject right there, but she wasn't, and didn't. She asked me if Lucie and I had been physical at all, and I had to admit that we had spent a day on the beach, during which time some incidental caressing took place, although it fell short of what any reputable dictionary or sex-ed manual would call lovemaking. She asked me if, during this 'incidental contact' I got aroused, and I had to admit I did. Ondine called me a 'walking hard-on' and then we had this huge fight in which Ondine said that I was like all the men she ever knew who let their dicks lead them around, along with some other unflattering stuff that I won't repeat here because some of it's true. I accused her of having pushed me into Lucie's arms by going frigid on me. She said that was bullshit and I should take responsibility for my own dick, all the while bashing me with satin-encased pillows and lavishing upon me all manner of rude epithet, which must have roused my Italian nature to violent life, because in one great paroxysm of rage and frustration I overturned her bed, fell back against the wall, sprained my wrist in the process, kicked a bottle of Ondine's echinacea and golden seal herbal tincture against a wall, where it shattered and left a stain of the most vibrant chartreuse.

Ondine rebutted this outburst by shrieking incoherencies

at the top of her lungs, then telling me she thought I was disgusting, out of control like a mad dog, an idiot, neurotic and the slime of the earth. I reminded her that she was an airhead, that all her family was airheads, that she was a loser as a musician because she was undisciplined, and that she didn't have a creative bone in her body. She said that was good information about what I thought about her, and she'd never be in a relationship with someone who thought she was an undisciplined airhead, also informing me that I knew nothing about discipline; at age fourteen, she said, she was working at the Dairy Queen as a waitress to help make her family's house payments, while I was lifting my feet off the floor so the maid could vacuum. She had a point there. I said I didn't really mean it, that I had called her an airhead because she called me a neurotic idiot, and whatever name she came up with, I could go her one better, but I'd rather not indulge in name-calling as it often creates wounds that take a long time healing. She called me a game-playing pig and said she didn't have anything more to say to me. She turned away and started studying the elephant plant in her corner again. I accused her of giving me the silent treatment like a little babyish juvenile infant, and I sang the famous "You are a baby" song to her, right up in her face. She said I was the biggest baby she ever knew and punched my arm, but with her rage somewhat abated, it seemed to me. I said, "Ow, that hurts," and admitted that I was scared she was going to abandon me. She said she was scared I was going to push her away by being unfaithful and untruthful. I said I was trying hard to be truthful, that I never cheated on her and told her what was going on with Lucie Rideout as soon as I realized what was happening. She said, "I know, it's just restimulating," and then she cried, and I cried, and we both cried like the big, babyish, juvenile infants we are. I'm sure I've cried more with Ondine in less than two years than I did in all the rest of my life put together. Whether this bodes well for the future of our relationship I'm not sure, but it feels good, as though a great septic abscess of grief and mistrust has been lanced and all the reeky toxins released—a revolting image, I know, but handy. As often happens, all this teary pustule-draining was accompanied by a stirring up of the libido,[14] which is what happened now. I started to get all starchy in the loins, to which Ondine responded with a gushing fervor she hadn't exhibited since the onset of the sexual drought several weeks previous.

As Ondine and I were getting down to it once more with wholehearted abandon, I found myself being repeatedly lacerated on the cheek by some sharp foreign object. I'm sure there are people who go in for that sort of thing, cuffs and thongs and hot tapioca geysers, but the sight of blood, particularly my own, makes me more queasy than aroused. "Jesus," I complained. "What's cutting my face?"

"Oh, it must be my earring. Wait a second." She tossed her red hair back and exposed one of her more original jewelry creations, an imposing bibelot whose central mass was an ovoid hunk of copper or stainless steel anodized into a blobby prismatic design that resembled a pooling of Pennzoil on a rain-slicked street. From this central metallic hub hung a milky, faceted gem on a small chain, a couple of medium-sized feathers, and on the face of the metal, at its approximate center, was glued a tan-colored flat object of a somewhat triangular shape. Taken as an assemblage, the earring resembled a lure that one might use to catch a good-sized grouper or seabass.

"Egad, what's that!" I cried.

"It's an earring I made," she said, adding suspiciously, "You don't like it?"

"I think it's very attractive, and I know a few bottom fish who would, too. But what did you make it out of?"

"I don't know, some silver wire and solder, some feathers, a little crystal Katie O'Gordon gave me, and this piece of am-

---

[14]Ondine calls this the 'fight-and-fuck syndrome,' a common phenomenon she claims to have learned about on a daytime talk show while running the treadmill at her health club, although they probably used a slightly less vulgar term on TV.

ber or old plastic I found while I was staying out at Squalor Holler. Isn't it pretty?"

"Pretty! Of course it's pretty: It's my pick!"

"Your what?"

"My lost tortoiseshell flatpick, the one I've been looking for all year." I grabbed the earring by its dangling crystal and tugged on it.

"Hey!" She pinched my wrist as she is so fond of doing. "You promised you wouldn't rip my ear off, remember?"

"Oh, right, sorry, it's just that when a guy finds his long-lost tortoiseshell flatpick, he's bound to get a bit overanxious. Where'd you find it?"

"I don't know, near Gin's chicken coop, I guess. I went in there to get some feathers, and this thing was on the ground. I thought it was pretty."

"The chicken coop!" I exclaimed, the feathers falling from my eyes. "Of course, I went in there the night I lost my pick, to dump some canteloupe rinds that were stinking up Gin's place. Chickens love them."

"Why? They're disgusting."

"Chickens love everything," I explained shortly, wishing to adhere steadfastly to the subject at hand. "Do you have any idea what this means? The pick, I mean, not the canteloupe rinds."

"No."

"It's, it's like having Mom and Pop call me up from the Other Side and say, 'Hi, son, we thought we'd stop by and see how you fixed up your new place. Can we bring ice cream or anything?' It means there are miracles in the universe."

"I knew that already," Ondine said in a slightly supercilious voice.

"Well, I didn't. But when we take apart that earring and I have my pick again and my long and tireless quest is over at last, then I *will* believe it."

"What makes you think you're going to take apart this earring," Ondine demurred with stony obstinacy in her voice. "This is my favorite earring, and it took days for me to make it, not counting all the time I spent getting the materials together, and there's—"

"But it's *my* flatpick," I reminded her. "You made your earring out of something that belongs to me."

"I didn't know it was yours. It was a piece of rock or amber
or something I found on the ground."

"*Ohhh,* you're going to pull 'finders keepers' on me. That's
real ma*chur,*" I said, sounding at that moment very much like
a thirteen-year-old valley girl named Stacey.

Ondine's reaction was equally Staceyesque. "Great," she
said in an accusatory tone, "you're just like my brother who
used to take my jacket out of my room and then tell me he
found it outside. Then he'd say, 'So what are you going to do
about it, I'm bigger than you.' So I'll tell you what I did, I
waited till he was sleeping and when I knew he was sound
asleep I took a big ol' glassful of water and and threw it all over
him to cause him to have shock, then I ran like crazy to my
neighbor's to hide out, and I stayed there for days or else he'd
beat me up."

"If you don't give me my flatpick, I'm going to beat you up
myself," I threatened.

Ondine knew me well enough by this time to understand
I wasn't serious about my threat of physical abuse, so she felt
safe responding in kind: "Just try it," she bristled, "and I'll
nail you in the balls."

"You wouldn't."

"You're right, first I'll flatten your arch and *then* I'll nail
you in the balls."

This warning brought back to my ears the faint voice of Liz,
my erstwhile therapist who once said something about the secret to relationships being the ability to compromise and
make sacrifices. Now, I told myself resolutely, was as good a
time as any to test the Nails mettle. What could be a greater
sacrifice than the one thing in the world you value above all
others, and which you've sought with all the dogged persist-
ence of Sir Gawain seeking the grail? "It's yours," I said expan-

sively. "Keep the pick. I'm getting along fine with plastic anyway."

"That's OK, I didn't really want it," Ondine said. She tilted her head, removed a little grommet from the earring-post, and handed the whole baroque assemblage to me without ceremony. "I want you to make the best music," she said.

The next day I asked her to move in with me.

THE PLANET
THAT LIKES TO PLAY
HARDBALL

~♦~

That was back in April, in the spring following our Victorian summer, when I asked Ondine to move in. Actually, I didn't ask her, but did something much more romantic. I wrote her a poem on the eve of her birthday. To Ondine, this particular birthday — the twenty-ninth — is for all people a special occasion, a consequential passage identified by astrologers as "Saturn Return" because, as she explained, "It's when Saturn comes back to the place it was when you were born. It takes exactly twenty-nine years for it to go around the earth and get back around to where it started, so every twenty-nine years you have a chance to start over. It's kind of like taking your dresser drawers out and dumping them all over the floor and putting only the best articles of clothing back in the dresser and sometimes painfully letting go of the blue jeans that are too tight ex-etera. Saturn's the planet that likes to play hardball, meaning it brings the hardest lessons and yet the opportunity for the most freedom."

Ever since I was a kid, when I owned a Space Patrol jackknife with a picture of a quad-finned V-2 rocket puffing toward a jauntily tilted Saturn on one side of the knife, and a complete Morse Code listing on the other, I've always thought

246

Saturn was a pretty cool planet, with its rings and all. I could
consequently get behind Ondine's enthusiasm for Saturn's
coming back, in spite of my doubts about the planet's ability
to effect sweeping changes in her life or mine. To celebrate,
I took Ondine out to The Seal Rock, her favorite restaurant
because it has windows on the ocean and they serve a cream
of broccoli soup that's seasoned just the way she likes it, plus
there's a killer salad bar. After the meal, as we sipped chamo-
mile tea from stoneware cups, I sprang the poem on her:

> *THE FUTURE AS GLIMPSED*
> *THROUGH DUSTY RINGS*
> *AND PROLAPSED VALVES*
> *Yours is a condition of strapping girls:*
> *benign leaks of faith in the unfailing pulse*
> *of permanence. Your blood, blood of one*
> *who is nothing if not a universal donor,*
> *steals back into the heart, like shadows*
> *into the bedroom of a sleepless child.*
> *Girls' hearts should never buzz and click.*
> *Their only murmur should be the hum*
> *of dragonflies above a creekside boulder*
> *overhung with mugwort and live oak.*
> *The heart should whisper terms of love.*
> *So yours does, yet sometimes squalls*
> *for attention like the brood of children*
> *you've always kept at a distance, across*
> *the broad map of your youthful sorrow.*
> *Your doctors predict a normal life*
> *and I hope in all my atria they're right,*
> *that your valve causes no more harm*
> *than the rare hiccup in a heartbeat*
> *so predictable it bores death to sleep.*
> *I hope I distress you less—although,*
> *given our souls' constant churning*
> *toward integrity, any such quietude*
> *would likely scare us into coronaries.*

Still, I'll undertake to wage calmness
on the turbid circulation of our deep like,
with moons in ricefields, and mirrors,
and a squirt more truth than diplomacy,
for the risk and the richness of it all.
So on this birthday, as Saturn swings by
for its return round, tipping its rings
in a gentlemanly way as it passes,
a voice — not quite from the heart
but from a family place, somewhere
between my sternum and San Giovanni —
whispers this invocation as our gift:
I welcome you and your leaking valve
into this mansion of unlovely forms,
to restore its faded sheetrock with smiles;
to charge it with howls of endearment;
to swell it with the minty breath of god
and the quiet beauty of plain nonsense
now, and for as long as we both shall leak.

Is it any good? Would critics judge it a controlled expression of timeless and universal human experience which observes the unities of time and place and contains diction appropriate to its rhetorical ends? Doubtful, but then literary critics are thin and brittle horsetails in the remote, barren slough that is academe, and to quote Gin on the subject of horsetail ferns and Ondine on the subject of bookworms: "Fuck 'em." The irony is, for years I studied poetry and hated the process, and now here I was having poetry gush forth as a spontaneous, pleasurable release — which is what Ma must have been talking about when she advised me on her deathbed to pursue my own creative enchantment. Furthermore, the poem accomplished what it set out to do, namely get Ondine into my house. Whether *that's* good is the truly critical question, and the subject of my soul's ceaseless turning since the day Ondine moved her last stick of furniture (a rattan hamper, if I remember correctly) into my house.

Ever since that day, I've had this recurring nightmare: I'm sitting on the beach at Rincon with Ondine. We're watching the locals work over a windswell of moderate size, when a rogue twenty-footer comes out of nowhere, the lip of the wave looming above us, high as the palisade by Will Rogers beach and thick as the Redondo breakwater, and it hammers us, washes us up onto the steep, sandy fringe and then drags us out to sea where Ondine panics and, clinging to my leg, almost drags us both under. As a result, for the past two weeks I've woken up with this discomforting feeling that I have sand in my eye sockets, two lungsful of saltwater, extremities aching from the exertion of clawing through leagues of aerated foam and entangling kelp, and bisque for brains.

Stormy must have recognized my exhaustion, because yesterday evening, while we were unloading his pickup for the weekly Elbow Room gig, he asked me casually, "So, how's it going, Ritter Hans zu Wittenstein?" For some reason he had stopped calling me Elston Howard, and more strangely, he clicked the heels of his boots after he called me this latest stupid name.

"OK," I said wanly.

"You look kind of burnt."

"To tell you the truth, I haven't been sleeping all that well."

"Too much of a good thing?" he asked, making a suggestive gesture with his fingers but refraining from winking and nudging me.

"No, that never tired me out before. It's probably from all the furniture and stuff, you know, with Ondine moving in," I conjectured.

"*Ahhh,*" said Stormy with a knowing smile, "Wooer's remorse."

"Huh?"

He explained, "There's a thing in real estate called buyer's remorse, where people go around and look at lots of houses, finally decide on one, apply for a loan, get it approved, make an offer, get a counter, finally agree on a price, wait for escrow to close, and then when they finally get all their stuff moved in, they get all weird about it. They wonder if they made the right decision and start having nightmares about freeways running through their living room and their swimming pool overflowing raw sewage onto the patio."

"How do you know about buying houses?" I asked, not an inappropriate question, since Stormy and Junie are currently renting a soon-to-be-condemned two-story Victorian on the east side, decorated and furnished quaintly in early Haight highstyle, complete with overstuffed pillows on unswept hardwood floor, shiny baubles dangling from ceiling rafters, all manner of arcane high-fidelity equipment on lengths of scrap lumber supported by cinder blocks, musical instruments strewn all over, a couch with greasy arms and stuffing coming out the cushions in several places, a superabundance of mikestands, ski poles and shielded cable running everywhere, lightning-skull and *Blues for Allah* posters taped to walls and curling at the edges from moisture, a pink flamingo on its side, a disembodied mannequin leg, a plaster-of-Paris crucifix painted in day-glo colors and nailed to a bare wall joist, a derelict American flag thumbtacked to a door, one droopy philodendron in a plastic pot, and enough house dust, mildew, and incense and dope smoke in the air to keep my sinuses perpetually swollen.

"You didn't know I was a realtor?" asked Stormy.

"You?"

"Yeah. I got a license a few years back. I needed some extra money real bad and I thought it would be cool to drive people around and trip on houses for a living. Turned out to be a drag, 'cause a house is like the biggest purchase anybody ever makes and it pushes them over the edge, freaks them out bigtime. But I still take on a client once in a while," he said.

Shocked, I said, "I thought realtors all drove new Volvos and had blow-dried hair and use phrases like, 'Charming fixer-upper,' and, 'Park-like setting.' "

"No, man, you'd be surprised how many ex-freaks have bucks they want to plop down into a place, and the last thing they want to do is ride around with some trickle-down asshole talking variable mortgages and points."

"So you drive people around and talk about the blues?"

"Sometimes. Sometimes I just get 'em high and they do most of the talking. Mostly I think it's bullshit, though, and more often than not I end up trying to convince people not to own property — sure it's a bummer having landlords, I say, but you can always leave. You're free. With a house, you always have to work to make payments, and almost none of the money goes to equity. It's almost all interest, straight to the bank. Then there's all the maintenance, the new roof, painting every four or five years, paying the exterminator, the furnace goes out, all the gardening and lawn mowing. If they still want a house after my 'burden of ownership' rap, then I'm willing to take their three percent. Dope's what pays the bills, though. It's recession-proof."

"You're an amazing person," I observed.

"We're all amazing people," Stormy said with deep conviction. "What were we talking about?"

"Houses, I think."

"Ah yes, wooer's remorse," he said. "You've got a bad case of wooer's remorse. It's just like real estate, except with people instead of houses. You go after this woman, give her flowers, hang out with her weird friends, ingratiate yourself to her weird family, and then when you finally land her and move her in, you freak out and feel trapped and wonder if you did the right thing. Happens all the time with people our age."

"*Your* age, maybe," I said. "I never felt like this before. Did you feel it with Junie."

"Sure, I still feel it with Junie, whenever she gets pissed at me for missing a chord change or I start playing 'Piece of My Heart' when her voice is already blown."

"But you guys are tight. It seems like you have a lot in common."

"We do," he acknowledged. "It's true."

"See, that's the problem," I wailed. "Ondine and I have *nothing* in common. We like completely different things. She plays Kenny G records, but you and I know he's a billion-noted snotblower. She loves God, but I have compelling evidence that He's living on East Quinientos Street and hoarding a stash of Ludes. I like Italian food and she hates tomatoes. All she eats is organic broccoli and coffee ice cream. Everything else she thinks is disgusting. She watches daytime talk shows and I like the Lakers and Masterpiece Theater. She hates sports and thinks Shakespeare is 'just a bunch of thees and thous.' She loves to travel to exotic places and I refuse to go anywhere you can't get to in a day, by car. All her friends are chiropodists who believe we can heal the planet by meditating and levitating ourselves three inches off the ground, or else they're L.A. glam-queens with fake tits. All *my* friends are, well . . . like you."

"That bad, huh?"

"Doesn't get any worse. The only thing Ondine and I have in common is that we both hate to throw up. What good can come out of a union like that? We're too different."

"Different?" he said. "It sounds like you're from two different planets."

"I *know!*" I lamented.

"So let me get this straight: You have all these differences, and you love her anyway?"

"I think I do."

"How come?"

"That's the problem. There's no logical reason I can think of."

"*Greeeeeat!* As long as it makes no sense, everything'll be fine," Stormy said, and he laughed, "Haaahahahaa!" his teeth flashing in the sunshine.

"Great," I said, clinging to a mood of twilit misgiving.

But Stormy Petrel was never one to let himself be brought down by clanky reason or pouty fretfulness. He seemed to derive amusement from my vain, desperate attempts to find even a shred of logic in a proposition so inherently preposterous as love. Stormy laughed again and unreservedly, "*Haaa-hahahahaaaaaaa,* you're *perfect!*" and he laughed some more, until my resistance was worn down and I could do nothing but laugh along with that prodigious gush of maniacal abandon. Stormy might be right. If love is an illogical proposition, then what could be more perfect—more archetypally fitting, even—than a union of two polar foils who disagree about everything save the one irrefutable truth: that they are drawn together irresistibly, like a flowery memo-magnet and a refrigerator door? "Hahaaaha, *Greeat!*" I said in a voice frothy with lean, bareboned happiness[15] while my own dentition, laid bare by a beamy grin, may have contributed a few scintillas of sunlight at that moment to the tenuous, tilting positivity of the world.

---

[15]There, I can say it: Happiness!